Long Shot

ALSO BY MEL PARISH

Detective Rigby Novels

Silent Lies (prequel)
The Anniversary
Old Habits Die Hard
Under Suspicion
No Stone Unturned

Other
Ulterior Motives
Motive for Revenge

Trust No One

Long Shot

Detective Rigby Book 5

Mel Parish

ISBN: 9798858057185

Cover designer: Jonny Gillard

For Cerianne

Chapter 1

The roar of an engine disturbed the evening silence. Some idiot too eager to reach their destination to pay heed to the snow-slicked roads and the sparsely lit side streets. Gail Cooper edged closer to the ridge of shoveled snow along the roadside. Two more blocks and she'd be home. Five more minutes to enjoy just being Gail rather than Mommy. Although hopefully by now her two were fast asleep and she could enjoy another glass of wine, snuggled up to her husband Martin while she gave him the lowdown of her sister's girls-only Christmas party.

She glanced over her shoulder at the approaching vehicle, grateful she'd taken Martin's advice to wear her light-colored coat for her walk in the dark. Fat flakes pelted her face, blurring her vision. She debated stopping to let the car pass, then heard the squeal of tires followed by a loud thud as pain filled her body and she flew up in the air.

Chapter 2

Detective Paul Rigby turned onto Pinewood Avenue, a quiet residential street ablaze with pulsating red and blue lights. He pulled up behind an ambulance, his heart sinking at the sight of the wide-open doors and empty interior. There'd been ample time for the injured party to be whisked off to hospital. The emergency vehicle's continued presence signaled that beyond the crime scene tape strung from mailbox to mailbox across the road a dead body awaited him.

He cursed out loud while there was no one to hear him. His second shift back on the job after fracturing several ribs in the course of another investigation, less than two weeks until Christmas—his first as a father—and now a homicide to deal with. And to think, he could have extended his leave until after the holidays. The chief had even suggested it. His girlfriend Becca had advised it. But no, he'd ignored them both. Pretended he was fighting fit. Ha! What a joke, it still hurt to walk. All to get back to the job he loved. Except when it involved dead bodies.

He eased out of the car, glad there were no witnesses to his awkward movements, and pulled his jacket collar up against the frigid night air. The cold and snow had not kept the onlookers away. Local residents, he assumed, stood in a huddle by the tape, their voices low and urgent. Did they know the victim? Was it one of their neighbors? No doubt he'd find out soon enough. And whether any of them could shed a light on who was responsible for the hit-and-run.

The chatter subsided as he approached the tape. The officer

on the other side recognized him and raised it slightly for him to duck under, then stood bewildered as Rigby instead detoured onto the grass and around the mailbox. Snow soaked into his shoes, a small price to pay to avoid the pain and possible embarrassment of the alternative.

He nodded at Docherty, the first officer on the scene, who stood with two paramedics next to the body. The victim lay sprawled backward over a mound of snow, her head at an awkward angle, her eyes wide open. Blood pooled around the back of her head, seeped into the collar of her off-white coat and turquoise scarf. Rigby guessed she was in her late twenties, early thirties. He swallowed hard. One minute there, the next gone. Life was so fragile.

He glanced over at the paramedics.

"She was already gone when we got here," one of them said. "Probably instantaneous. Let's hope so, anyway, for her sake."

"Got any witnesses?" he asked Docherty.

Docherty gestured at the nearest house. "Owner says he heard what sounded like a car skid and then a loud thud. He looked out of the window and saw a vehicle disappear off in that direction." He pointed to the right. "He put his outside lights on to see if he could work out what the car had hit and that's when he saw the body. He called it in."

"Where is he?"

"Back inside. Pretty shaken up. I told him someone would come in to take a statement."

Rigby glanced at the small crowd. "This lot?"

"Neighbors. Came out when they heard the noise or the sirens, but none of them say they saw the actual accident or the car." Docherty gestured at the body. "They want to know who it is. They're worried it could be a neighbor, someone out walking their dog, maybe."

"Seen any dogs running around loose?"

"Not while I've been here."

"I think if there'd been a dog, it would have been either injured or it would have stayed with its owner." Rigby thought of his own pup at home. "And made a lot of noise. It might have run off when you arrived but you'd have seen it." He shuffled his feet to keep warm. "Though why anyone would be out walking in this weather if they didn't have to is beyond me."

"Maybe they weren't going far and thought it would be safer to walk rather than drive given the conditions."

How tragic would that be? A decision meant to keep someone safe turning deadly. The odds of being hit by a car would be miniscule compared to those of slipping on the icy road.

"Maybe she'd been drinking, didn't want to get behind the wheel."

Rigby glanced at the body. "And most likely the person who hit her didn't have such consideration or why didn't they stop and call it in?" He cursed silently. "For all they knew she could have been injured not dead. They were willing to leave her there in the cold?" He grimaced. "Do we have any ID?"

Docherty shook his head. "There's no sign of a purse. Haven't had a chance to check her pockets yet. We didn't get here much before you and I wanted to seal off the area before anyone trampled on possible evidence. Fortunately for us, it's been a while since the road was plowed. We might be able to get some tire impressions from the snow. Is Gina coming out?"

Rigby nodded. Saw the relief on Docherty's face. Gina Rogers was their part-time forensic expert. Until she'd moved to Lewisville, they'd had to collect forensic evidence themselves, work they were trained for but not to Gina's level of expertise. It was painstaking, time-consuming work and, on a snowy night, work that had to be done before a fresh layer of snow obliterated the evidence.

Rigby noticed the camera in Docherty's hand. "Get a few photos of the body before I check for ID."

"Already done."

Rigby smiled. That's what he liked about Docherty, an officer who could be relied on to be thorough. He pulled on latex gloves and crouched down beside the woman, stifling a gasp as his ribs protested the move.

"Still hurting?" Docherty asked.

"It's nothing." Rigby glanced over his shoulder. "Why don't you finish up with the photos?" Hopefully that would keep Docherty from noticing what it cost him to straighten back up. "And you two," he said to the paramedics, "We'll take it from here. There's nothing more for you to do. Thanks."

"Becca okay?" the older of the two men asked.

"Yes. Fine. Great." A lie but he doubted Becca would want them to know how exhausted she was. He put his hand in one of the woman's coat pockets. The paramedics got the message. The conversation was over. This wasn't the place or time for a conversation about their colleague's wellbeing. He sensed rather than heard them move away.

The pocket was empty, as was the other one. It didn't make sense. She had to have something on her—keys, ID, a phone. He pulled his phone out, used it as a flashlight to scan the area around the woman. Nothing.

Damn, were they going to have to wait until they got a call about a missing woman to determine who she was? And what if she lived alone, no one waiting for her to arrive home that evening?

He partially unzipped her coat, checked for an inner pocket. Nothing. He zipped the coat back up, wanting to protect her from the snow. Not that it would bother her any more. They needed to get a tarp over the body, protect it from the elements until they could move it. Just because she was dead didn't mean she didn't deserve to be treated with dignity.

He eased upright bracing for pain but experienced only a slight twinge. He scanned the area again. The woman must have been carrying something, but the snow around about lay undisturbed.

A car door slammed nearby. Rigby looked over. Was it too much to hope it was the culprit returning to the scene in a fit of remorse? It happened. The initial panic and shock on impact replaced by a sense of overwhelming guilt at fleeing. But as the driver headed for the trunk of their car, Rigby realized it was only Gina.

She pulled a protective suit over her already bulky outerwear and then hauled a large canvas bag from the car. Rigby smiled as instead of ducking under the tape she followed in his footsteps around the mailbox and across the grass.

"Heard on the way over it was a fatality not an injury." She dropped the bag at Rigby's feet. "Figured we'd need a cover." She glanced over at the body and then at the tire tracks on the road.

"How the hell did this happen?"

Rigby knew what she meant. A quiet residential road. A lone person walking on the left side of the road facing oncoming traffic. A single car on the other side happens to skid out of control. What were the odds they'd collide?

"I haven't been able to find any ID," he said, trying not to wince as he helped Gina erect the cover. "Do you know anyone who goes out without at least a set of keys?" Not that a set of keys alone would be much help in the identification process.

"Assuming she was carrying something, depending on the size, it could have traveled a lot further than she did after she was struck by the car."

Rigby switched on his phone flashlight again.

Gina scoffed. "What do you hope to find with that?"

She rummaged in her bag and tossed a heavy-duty flashlight toward him. "It's a spare, but don't forget to give it back."

Rigby shone the powerful light along the ridge of snow in the direction the woman had been walking. No sign of any bag. He swung the light out into the middle of the road, walking slowly forward until he was well past the point an object could have landed.

He swung around, scanned the entrance of the driveway of the house next door. Two garbage cans had been rolled to the roadside, presumably ready for the next morning's pick-up. Why couldn't the car have hit them instead of the woman? Scattered garbage rather than leaving a dead body.

A sparkle of silver at the base of one of the cans caught his eye.

He moved in closer.

A small sequined purse lay wedged against one of the wheels. It was surprisingly heavy for its size and stuffed so full he had difficulty opening the zipper. Two partially gift-wrapped bars of soap had been rammed inside but to Rigby's relief they hid a phone, a driver's license and a set of keys.

The photo on the license matched the woman in the snow. Gail Cooper. Thirty years old. And based on the address, he barely needed to get in his car to do the notification. He closed his eyes at the thought of the task ahead.

A house not an apartment. Who would he find there? A husband? Kids? Parents? Did it matter? Whoever they were, he was going to break their hearts. Two weeks before Christmas.

Chapter 3

Rigby stared at the house, reluctant to get out of the car. White icicle lights decorated the front of the small green colonial. Giant red and white candy canes lined either side of the footpath to the front door, which was almost hidden behind a huge Christmas wreath. Wooden cut-outs of snowmen, deer and Santa dotted the grass and, through one of the front windows, he could see the glow of a lit tree. It was a house ready for Christmas, a home ready for Christmas. A family home judging by the small sleds propped against the side of the porch.

He swallowed hard. Glanced at Docherty. "Ready?" As if they could ever be ready for what they were about to do. He certainly didn't feel ready. His first notification as a father, his emotions were too close to the surface. Should he let Docherty handle it? But that wouldn't be fair. And they weren't there to notify her family just that she'd died, but also how she died and that there'd be a criminal investigation and he would lead it.

He took a deep breath, instantly regretting it, and got out of the car.

"You sure you should be back at work?" Docherty asked.

Damn, was it that obvious he was still in pain?

"I'm okay," he snapped.

Docherty raised his hands in surrender. "Okay. Okay."

"Sorry." He couldn't take his frustration over his perceived weakness out on others. He forced a smile. "Long as I don't have to chase after anyone, I'm good."

At Docherty's dubious expression he added, "Good job I've got you to do the running." He broke off. "Though I doubt anyone's going to be running tonight."

They headed toward the house, up three steps onto the porch. A line of snow boots stood under a wooden bench to the left of the front door. Four pairs, two so small they could only belong to toddlers.

Damn, his worst fears were right.

Docherty pressed the bell. Rigby prayed they didn't wake the kids. Their father would need time to process what he was about to hear. Crying kids would make it so much more difficult.

The door opened. The smile on the lanky, bespectacled man's face disappeared as his gaze settled on Docherty's uniform.

Rigby held up his ID. "Mr. Cooper?" At the man's bewildered nod he added, "Detective Rigby. And this is Officer Docherty. I'm afraid we have some bad news. Can we come in?"

Mr. Cooper stared at them as if he didn't understand. Then he glanced at his watch. "My wife should be home soon."

"Can we come in?" Rigby repeated softly. He'd rather not have to stand on the doorstep and tell Mr. Cooper his wife would never be coming home.

Mr. Cooper stepped aside to let them pass and ushered them into the room with the tree. A room where he'd obviously been enjoying a quiet night in. A log fire burned in the grate, a documentary played out silently on the TV, and a glass of beer and a bowl of chips sat on a side table next to an overstuffed armchair.

The color in his face drained as Rigby explained what had happened, his expression flitting rapidly from confusion to disbelief and finally to anguish. He glanced up at the ceiling, his Adam's apple bobbing furiously either in an attempt to keep his emotions in or get some words out, maybe both.

He slumped down on the sofa, his tear-filled eyes pleading with Rigby to tell him this was all a mistake—his wife was going to walk through the door any minute. Rigby hated this part. Felt so useless in the face of such grief. There was nothing he could do to alleviate the pain.

"Where is she?"

Rigby hesitated. "She'll be taken to the morgue." No point in telling Martin Cooper his wife's body was probably still lying in the snow, waiting for Gina to get as much evidence as possible before they moved it. The last thing they needed was a distraught husband rushing to the scene when he found out how close to home the accident had happened. And Martin would be better off without the image of his wife's body on the side of the road seared into his memory.

"Can I see her?"

"In the morning. If you wish."

"What do I do now?" Martin glanced upwards again. As hard as these notifications were, Rigby could only imagine what it would be like to have to explain to children that a parent had died so suddenly, so senselessly.

"How old are your children?"

"Almost two and four." Martin blew out hard. "How am I supposed to tell them? Get them to understand they're never going to see their mommy again?" His voice cracked.

Rigby wanted to tell him it was okay to cry, that he needn't put on a stoic face for the police.

"I'd wait until morning. Give yourself a chance to process what's happened first. Is there anyone you could call to come over?"

"It's so late."

"Under the circumstances, I don't think they'd mind. And the rest of the family are going to have to be told. Your wife's parents. Siblings."

Martin sank his face into his hands. "Hannah. How am I going to tell her? That's where Gail was tonight." He dragged his fingers from his face.

"Who's Hannah."

"Her sister. Her elder sister. She has two. She was having a Christmas get-together at her house. Just for the moms. There's a group of them. Friends. They all have young kids. Gail was so looking forward to it. A night off, so to speak. That's why she was walking. Hannah's place is only about twenty minutes' walk from here. It meant she could drink without worrying about having to drive home."

He broke off, the irony hitting him full force. "If only she'd driven. This would never have happened."

If only.

Chapter 4

The onlookers had disappeared by the time Rigby and Docherty returned to the scene, driven back indoors by the bitter cold and the realization there was nothing for them to see. A coroner's van stood in the spot where the ambulance had been. The medical examiner turned from his conversation with the officer at the tape as Rigby approached.

They gaped at each other in surprise.

His doctor smiled. "What are you doing back at work so soon? I heard you cracked a few ribs not so long ago."

Rigby scowled. "More to the point, what are you doing here? Where's Dr. Ferrango?"

"Came to his senses and decided cruising the Caribbean had a lot more going for it than another winter in Lewisville."

"He retired?" Why hadn't anyone mentioned it? Dr. Ferrango had been the medical examiner long before Rigby had become a cop, possibly even before he was born.

"He was pushing seventy," Dr. Bingham said. "And he's been having health issues. I think he decided enough was enough. Getting called out at all hours in all weather. Who can blame him?"

Rigby doubted the job in Lewisville was that demanding. Or no more demanding than being a doctor in the first place. "So you applied for the position?"

"More like approached and asked if I was interested."

Of all the doctors in town, they had to ask his family doctor, someone who'd known him since he was a kid. Knew his parents, his sisters, his childhood fear of needles—which he still had but was much better at hiding nowadays—and which bones he'd broken. There'd been a few. Except Dr. Bingham shouldn't have known about the ribs because all the treatment had been at the hospital. He'd intended to mention it at the next annual physical but that wasn't for some time. Which meant one of his parents must have told him. Probably his father.

"Oh, and by the way, I hear congratulations are in order."

"Thanks." Rigby waited to see if there was anything else the doctor had heard about him secondhand.

The doctor eyed him as if he could see the fractured ribs through the layers of clothes. It had taken some persuading to get the hospital doctor to sign him off as fit to return to duty. He suspected Dr. Bingham would have made him wait so he'd left him out of the loop, or so he thought. Damn his parents. Though really, what did he expect, spending his life in a small town?

The slam of car doors distracted his attention. He glanced back. Groaned so loudly a look of concern flashed onto the doctor's face.

Josh Brook, crime reporter for the Lewisville Chronicle, hurried toward him, a photographer in tow. The guy seemed to always be the first to turn up to crime scenes and he was no friend.

Rigby turned to Docherty and gestured at Josh. "Deal with him. I'm going to speak to the homeowner. But no names. Give Martin time to notify the rest of the family." Without giving Docherty a chance to protest he headed up the path, almost slipping in his haste to avoid Josh.

A motion-detecting light came on as he approached the front door of the ranch style house. What chance there'd also be a security camera that had recorded footage of the accident? Unfortunately for him, the light was more likely for the convenience of the owners returning in the dark than to deter intruders. Crime wasn't a huge concern in Lewisville so few saw the need to spend money on security. But maybe for once, luck would be on his side.

A burly middle-aged man answered the door and ushered him in before he had a chance to introduce himself. A blast of heat engulfed him. The only place that hot in Rigby's home was the boiler room and yet the guy wore a bulky sweater over a shirt and showed no signs of sweating.

The living room offered no relief. As he sat opposite Colin Farmer in the minimally furnished room he was tempted to take off his jacket. But that would be unprofessional, not least because his shoulder-holstered firearm would be on display. He needed Mr. Farmer to be calm and relaxed, or as calm and relaxed as someone could be after seeing a dead body on their lawn.

"You told Officer Docherty that you heard a noise? Went to the window?"

Colin gestured at the television. "I was watching the news when I heard the noise. Like the squeal of tires. A car skidding, maybe. Then a walloping noise. I thought a car must have hit the garbage cans by the driveway. So I got up to look. The driver didn't stop though. By the time I got to the window the vehicle was almost out of sight. I only caught a glimpse of the taillights.

Rigby grimaced. So much for the hope they'd get a good description of the vehicle.

"I knew the car had hit something. I thought it might have been my garbage can, so I put the outside light on to see whether I needed to go out and pick it up before, you know, wildlife got at it. They make such a mess. Especially the crows." He rubbed nervously at his forehead then clasped his hands between his legs, maybe to stop them shaking. "Then... then I saw it. The body. Lying on the snow. Not moving. I called an ambulance. Then... then I went outside to see if there was anything I could do. The dispatcher told me to stay on the line until the ambulance arrived, tell her what I saw, but I knew... I knew as soon as I saw the open eyes that she was dead. It was just a blank stare, you know, there was no life behind there." He exhaled hard. "She didn't look very old." He gulped. "She must have been walking, which I guess means she's from around here, but it's not anyone I recognize."

Rigby walked over to the window. Colin followed him. The canopy Gina had erected was directly in front of the house. He watched as Dr. Bingham and his assistant zipped up the body bag, gently lifted it onto a stretcher, and made their way back to the van.

"Do you know who it is?" Colin asked.

Rigby sighed. "Yes. I can't release her name, but she's a wife, a mother." He hesitated. "A daughter, a sibling, a friend."

"A mother? Jeez, the kid can't be much more than a baby. She looks so young."

Rigby sighed again. "Kids. There's more than one."

"Oh, jeez." Colin sank into silence.

Docherty stood in front of the photographer presumably to stop him snapping pictures of the body bag being carried to the van. Why anyone would want such photos was beyond Rigby. Published, all they'd do was add to the anguish of Gail's loved ones. It was a sight they didn't need to see.

Rigby smiled as the reporter gesticulated wildly and then stormed back to his car, the photographer following. Josh obviously had a hit-and-run headline, but no details to spice it up. For those he'd have to wait until the information was made available to all the media. Still, knowing Josh Brook, he'd find a way to craft it into a front-page story. And to hell with anyone he might hurt in the process.

"What's she doing?" Colin pointed at Gina kneeling in the road.

"Taking tire impressions."

"That will help you find the car?"

"No, not find it. But when we do, it could provide additional proof it was the vehicle that hit her." No need to mention how much luck they were going to need to find the vehicle. No eye witnesses. No traffic cameras. "Do you have a security camera?"

"No."

They'd have to hope some of the neighbors did. Cameras that had recorded the passing vehicle before or after the hit. But even then, the quality of the image and the fact it was dark at the time, snow adding to the poor visibility, might mean all they could garner would be the approximate size of the vehicle and whether it was light or dark colored. Not much to go on at all.

"I think it was a light-colored sedan," Colin said.

"What?" Rigby swung around to face Colin.

"The vehicle. If I had to guess, I'd say it was a sedan. The taillights, they looked like the taillights of a sedan, not a SUV or a truck." Colin hesitated. "I'm sure they were."

"I thought you barely saw the vehicle?"

"I did. I mean, I didn't see it, not really, just the taillights but they're different on a sedan than on a SUV, aren't they?"

"Thanks." Rigby tried to hide his disappointment. Assuming Colin was right, the search parameters for the vehicle had been reduced but not by much. There had to be thousands of sedans in Lewisville County alone. And if the car belonged to a visitor rather than a resident, tracking it down could be impossible. Their best hope would be that the car had sustained some damage, needed repair, and turned up in a local body shop.

"Have you lived here long?" Rigby asked. "Do you know your neighbors?"

"Only to say good morning to. My wife, she's the one who knew everybody, being at home with the kids all day." Colin sighed. "But she's not here anymore."

"I'm sorry." Rigby didn't know what else to say.

Colin scoffed. "Oh, she's not dead. She took off. Decided I wasn't exciting enough for her once the kids had grown. Twenty-five years. I thought we were happy. And suddenly she announces she wants half of everything and she's gone."

Which would explain the sparsely furnished living room. She must have taken half of the furniture too.

"Didn't see it coming at all," Colin added.

Rigby found that hard to believe. There had to be some signs of discontent. More likely Colin had chosen to ignore them, taken his wife for granted, or refused to acknowledge his behavior had played any part in his wife's decision. But he wasn't there to investigate the cause of Colin's marriage breakdown and he doubted Colin would be able to provide any other useful information, so it was time to go.

He handed Colin his card. "Thanks for your help. If you think of anything else, let me know." He headed for the door.

"I hope you get them, Detective." Colin shook his head. "How could anyone do that? Hit someone and just drive away?"

Rigby left without replying. The job had taught him that sometimes there was no answer.

Chapter 5

Rigby arrived home to find Becca propped up in bed, feeding Lotte. She gave him a resigned smile as he leaned over and kissed her on the forehead and then stared smitten at his daughter.

"Maybe this will be the night when she sleeps for more than two hours."

He could hear the tiredness in her voice. He wished there was more he could do to help. It seemed no sooner had Becca finished feeding Lotte than it was time for the next feed. He hadn't realized how often babies fed in the first few weeks. There was a lot he was learning about babies. Like how even though all they did was feed and sleep they could take up every minute of every hour if you let them. And it was hard not to, which was why he'd wanted to go back to work. To try and regain some semblance of normality after the chaos Lotte had brought into their lives. And for as long as Becca was breastfeeding, he thought it only right that he be the one to keep the rest of their lives on track. Except the fractured ribs had made that difficult.

Luckily, his mother had risen to the occasion. She'd called in every few days, bringing home-cooked meals and other goodies for the pantry, whizzing around with a duster or the vacuum, even providing a far more sympathetic ear to Becca's turbulent emotions in adjusting to being a mother than he could.

He wasn't sure what they'd have done without her. And she'd done it without seeming to intrude. The previous week, Becca had jokingly suggested they should ask his mother to move in with them. At least, he thought it was a joke. But it had made him realize he needed to go back to work. Pull his weight, even if it was a little painful.

"Quiet evening?" Becca asked.

"I wish." Rigby told her about the hit-and-run. He'd prefer not to, but she'd hear about it on the news the next morning. A young mother killed so close to Christmas. The local media would be all over it. And the police would be in the spotlight until they found the driver. Rather, he would be in the spotlight. Dammit, if he hadn't gone back to work it would have been one of his colleagues' problem. Maybe Harper. Or Turner or Gaines. None of them had a similar history with the press as he did.

Tears welled in Becca's eyes. "How sad. I know it shouldn't make any difference. But so close to Christmas. It just seems that much worse." She hugged Lotte a little tighter. "But can there be anything worse than losing your partner? Or your kids losing their mother?"

Rigby tried to imagine what Martin Cooper was feeling. He couldn't, even though he'd been a victim of tragedy himself several years earlier. But there hadn't been children to deal with. He'd been able to fall into the abyss of grief without thought for anyone else. Martin Cooper wouldn't have that option.

After leaving Colin Farmer, he and Docherty had called at some of the nearby homes where there were signs the occupants were still awake. For most it was only the sound of police sirens that had alerted them to something being amiss in their neighborhood. It was a rare occurrence. Some were visibly shaken by the accident happening almost on their doorstep, most expressed horror that the driver didn't stop, but all had more questions for Rigby than answers. And no one had a security camera.

"Bet it was some kid," one man had said. "They drive far too fast along this street. It's like the speed limit doesn't apply to them. And in these conditions, it's all too easy to lose control, especially if you're an inexperienced driver."

And that might explain why they hadn't stopped. A young driver terrified by what they had done, panic pushing them on rather than making them stop, self-preservation their initial instinct. But in the ensuing hours, with guilt preying on their minds, would they realize they had to do the right thing and turn themselves in? Especially when the story hit the news.

Or would the news headlines, with the probable outrage over the driver's failure to stop, make it even more difficult for them to come forward? Having to face both what they'd done and the backlash from friends and neighbors for fleeing the scene. A lot for anyone to deal with let alone a teen.

Whoever the driver, likely there was another family in Lewisville, in the neighborhood, whose lives were about to be ripped apart by the events of the evening, parents or children who'd suffer the consequences of one moment of recklessness. And one bad choice.

Chapter 6

Rigby returned to the scene of the hit-and-run early the next morning. Becca had protested. Pointed out that there were others who could canvas the neighborhood and find out whether anyone had a camera which might have picked up the suspect car either before or after the accident. Thanks to Colin Farmer they had the advantage of knowing the time frame they were looking at and in what direction the vehicle was traveling, but they didn't know where the vehicle had come from or where it went. Had it traveled straight along Pinewood Avenue? Or had it turned onto it from one of the many cross streets?

Logic suggested that the driver, like Gail, was probably heading home. There was little other reason to be in the area at that time of night. And Pinewood Avenue was the main thoroughfare in the neighborhood so it would be reasonable to assume the car had traveled the several blocks along the road from the highway before the driver lost control. Where the car had gone afterward was more of a guess. Even if the driver had intended to continue on along the road, the sense of panic following the accident might have made them turn off earlier than planned to avoid being seen.

He'd called into the station house, requested a patrol officer to assist him, but was told he'd have to wait at least an hour before someone could get to him, possibly longer. The department was already short-staffed and two officers had called in sick, Collins the duty sergeant told him.

Rigby didn't want to wait. Soon some of the residents would

be leaving for work. He wanted to catch them before they left otherwise it would be evening before he could speak to them. All he needed was one neighbor with a security camera—two would be even better—and he'd have something to work on.

He started with the houses closest to the scene, the ones that had been dark the night before. The first one he tried there was no answer, which was too bad because it was in a prime position to have caught the accident if there was a camera. He made a mental note to call back later.

An elderly woman answered the next door he tried. She scrunched her face up as he spoke, obviously straining to hear or understand. She peered at his badge, shook her head and mumbled what sounded like, "I don't want anything today," and promptly shut the door on him. He wondered what she thought he was selling.

Not an auspicious start. He pulled out his phone and called Harper, one of his colleagues.

"You busy?" he asked.

"No. I'm sitting here twiddling my thumbs."

Rigby sighed loudly down the phone. "I meant busy busy."

"What do you need?"

He told her.

Harper groaned. "Door to door? Really?"

"Hey, listen, if I wasn't back at work, this one could have landed on your desk anyway."

"I'm supposed to be grateful?"

"No gratitude needed. Just get over and help me out." He hesitated. "Please?"

"What?"

"Please. I'll owe you."

Her sigh was louder than his. "You sure will."

He grinned. Gave her directions. Ended the call before she could change her mind. He liked Harper. Not only because she was too new an addition to the department to know his history—sure she'd probably heard the stories, there were plenty of them, but she judged him on his current behavior rather than on his past—but she was smart, dedicated and easy to get along with. He suspected she had her own baggage. There had to be a reason why she'd moved from Albany to small-town Lewisville, but so far he hadn't pried. If she wanted to tell him, she would.

He moved on to the next house. This time a young guy in a suit and tie answered the door. "Damn sirens woke the baby," he said as Rigby introduced himself.

"There was a hit-and-run, Sir. A fatal hit-and-run."

"Oh." The guy grimaced. "We didn't realize. We were too busy trying to get the baby back to sleep. He doesn't much seem to like it. Sleep that is." He gave a tired smile. "Not at night anyway." He shook his head. "Sorry. You were saying?"

Rigby sympathized. He would have sympathized a lot more if the guy had installed a security camera, but he hadn't and he didn't know anyone on the street who had. It was a safe neighborhood, friendly, people watched out for one another.

Though apparently not when they were dealing with wailing babies. And it turned out he didn't know any of his neighbors well except for the family three doors down who also had a baby and they definitely didn't have security cameras. Although maybe Rigby should check anyway.

Rigby thanked the guy and left before he said something he shouldn't. He stood at the bottom of the driveway and stared down the street.

So many more houses to go.

Chapter 7

Rigby had covered another six houses before Harper arrived, all with the same result. Zilch. And to make matters worse, it had started to snow again. Not a light dusting but a blizzard-like intensity, plastering his hair against his scalp and threatening to breach his supposedly waterproof jacket even in the short walks between front doors.

No one invited him in. Not even to step across the threshold and enjoy a moment's warmth in the hallway while they talked. He couldn't blame them. A total stranger with a badge—he'd be wary in that situation too. But it would have been nice if just one of them had taken pity on him. And to think he could have been snuggled up in bed with Becca. And Lotte. And this would be someone else's problem.

He shivered as he walked over to Harper's car. She laughed as he brushed snow off his coat and eased inside.

"Feeling sorry for yourself?"

"Does it show?" Just wait until she'd trudged up a few driveways. She wouldn't be laughing then.

"Collins said he'd had a call about a strange man knocking on doors in the neighborhood."

Rigby almost choked. "Somebody called the police on me?"

Harper eyed him over. "Not sure I'd open the door to you either." She smiled, the twinkle in her eyes giving her away. "And no. Not yet anyway."

He relaxed into the seat. Enjoyed the blast of warm air. "Why do I do this job?" he said, more to himself than Harper.

"Martin Cooper."

Martin Cooper. Who even now might be trying to explain to his little ones why Mommy wasn't there to get them up, make them breakfast. How she would never be there again. And to do it in a reassuring way, as if he had the situation under control, even as his own heart was breaking.

Finding the hit-and-run driver wouldn't bring Gail back. It wouldn't ease the heartache, but it would let Martin know that they cared. That he deserved justice. Unfortunately, giving him that justice could prove easier said than done. They needed more than the probability that it was a sedan they should be looking for.

Harper handed him a takeout cup. "Thought you might appreciate a coffee."

"You're a life-saver." He enjoyed the warmth of the cup against his cold fingers before taking a sip. He groaned quietly at the pleasure of the hot liquid snaking down his throat.

"Gloves, Rigby. Have you ever thought of wearing gloves when it's like this?"

He didn't like gloves. Found them cumbersome. It was far easier to stick his hands in his pockets. And he couldn't lose his pockets. But it didn't look too professional turning up on someone's doorstep with his hands in his pockets. Which was why his hands were cold.

Harper rolled her eyes when he didn't respond. "Men!" He noticed her gloves fit like a second skin. She stared despondently out the windscreen. "Couldn't have picked a worse day for it."

"You didn't have to come."

She sighed. "And yet here I am." She smiled again. "To think I could be sitting in the office warm and dry, doing my paperwork." The smile slipped. "Not much of a choice when there's some bastard out there willing to leave a young mother dying in the snow on the street."

"Doctor said it was probably instantaneous."

She glared at him. "And that makes a difference? A total disregard for another's life?"

"Of course not." And she knew him well enough by now to

know that. Something about the case had hit a nerve. Maybe because of Gail's age—she was only a little younger than Harper. Or the random manner in which she'd died. It was enough to give anyone pause for thought.

"Where have you covered so far?"

He told her.

"I'll start on the other side of the street." She pulled her woolen hat down over her ears. "At least one thing's in our favor."

"What's that?"

"School's been canceled. Means there'll be more folk at home."

Rigby glanced at the snow swirling against the windscreen. That was supposed to cheer him up?

Her loud sigh told him she knew it wouldn't. But Harper was one of those people who always seemed to look on the bright side. Though he noticed her shiver before she even opened the car door.

"Might as well get on with it. I'll leave you to defrost."

He watched her cross in front of the car, walk up the nearest driveway, her shoulders hunched and her head down to protect her face from the elements. As soon as she stepped onto the porch, she straightened up, brushed snow from her shoulders, and knocked on the door. It opened almost immediately but he couldn't see who answered. Harper raised her hand, showing her badge no doubt, and then stepped inside. The door closed.

Rigby stared at it. The first call and they let her in? How did she manage that? Was it because she was a woman? She looked snug and warm in her long navy padded coat which reached to the top of her sensible snow boots. Not at all in need of protection from the elements, while he…

He glanced in the rearview mirror. Ugh. The dark circles under his eyes combined with the drowned rat effect gave him a sinister look. He'd think twice before inviting such a character inside, even if they did show a detective's badge. Or there was a raging storm. It was the stuff of movies—an escaped convict, the murderous kind, about to unleash terror on the unsuspecting household. He looked the part without the help of any make-up.

He drained his coffee. Braced himself to get back out there

regardless.

The door opened. Harper came out, turning to speak to the still hidden occupant. She was all smiles. She'd either got some useful information or a date. No, that was mean thinking. He'd never known Harper to be anything other than all about the job. And he shouldn't begrudge her warmth. Unlike him, she didn't have to be there. He'd called her because he knew she'd help, unlike say, his colleague Gaines who'd take one look at the weather and find something more urgent he had to do.

He smiled as Harper hurried back toward the car. Yes! She must have struck lucky or she'd have moved on to the next house.

She opened the door, bringing a cold draft with her as she got in.

"Not much, but I've got you something," she said, pulling out her phone.

"Ring?"

She nodded. "Mr. Jenkins sent me a copy of the file. He wasn't home when the accident happened so he hadn't heard about it. He works night shifts. Said that's why he installed the camera." She fiddled with her phone. "Don't blink."

She held her phone out, the screen showing an image of the empty street. A light-colored car suddenly flashed across the screen so quick he understood her comment.

The timing was right. The direction of travel was right. And the vehicle was going too fast. The driver must have lost control seconds later, veered across the road with no time for them or Gail to avoid the collision. Rigby shuddered as he pictured the sequence of events in his mind. Gail must have heard the car. Had she turned and seen the vehicle plow toward her? The tire tracks confirmed the vehicle had veered sharply. Judging from the speed on the footage, Gail wouldn't have stood a chance of getting out the way.

"Why would they have been going so fast?"

"Late for curfew?" Harper said.

"At ten-thirteen? Seems early for someone old enough to drive."

"School night? Maybe it was a learner driver, not supposed to be on the road on their own after dark."

"Oh, no. Please, not some young kid." A future wrecked before it could begin.

"If it was, there could be some parents somewhere hearing about the accident this morning, knowing their kid was out here at the time, in the neighborhood."

"Or the parents had no idea what their kid was doing. Too busy living their lives to pay attention, especially to a teen deemed old enough to look after themselves."

"Were your parents like that?" Harper asked.

"No way." Rigby laughed at the thought. "If anything they leaned the other way. Or so I used to think at the time. They wanted to know where I was going, who with and when I'd be home. It used to drive me crazy."

"Because they cared."

"Yeah, but I didn't see it that way then. I had this one friend, I don't think his parents ever knew where he was. Sometimes he'd stay over at my place and he'd always tell my mom that he'd told his parents he was staying the night, but he never did." Rigby scoffed. "I used to feel guilty because I knew he was lying to my parents." He shrugged. "But what was I going to do? Rat him out?"

"Where's your friend now?"

Rigby shrugged again. "No idea. He left school, left town and I've never seen him since. He probably went to the city."

"He just disappeared?" Harper frowned. "Weren't you curious as to where he'd gone?"

"It was no great mystery to solve. Nobody was surprised when he left." He laughed. "He knew I wanted to be a cop so I figured I'd be the last person he'd tell where he was going."

Harper looked askance. "I'm still in touch with my school friends despite becoming a cop." With emphasis, she added, "Male and female friends."

"But you left home. I mean your hometown." Was this his chance to find out a little of Harper's back story?

"A lot of people do." Harper sighed. "Let's hope our driver hasn't. Maybe we should check for any missing person reports. In case the kid couldn't face going home."

"Assuming it was a kid," Rigby said, disappointed that

Harper had once again got him to reveal more about himself without giving anything back in return. "Can you send the footage to Turner. Ask him what he can do with it? Other than confirming it was a light-colored sedan, I'm not sure what else it gives us. But if there's anything there to be found, Turner will find it."

Turner was the department's computer expert. His ability to dig up digital evidence left Rigby in awe. But no matter how many identifying marks he might be able to come up with on the car, this footage was unlikely to give them the most useful evidence, the license plate. What they needed was footage from a camera with a wider angle so they could get a good view of the front or back of the car rather than the side.

He raked his fingers through his hair, hoping to make it look a little more groomed.

"Forget it. It's not going to work." Harper reached into the back of the car. Tossed a black knitted hat onto his lap. "Take this."

Rigby hated hats. And he doubted a black beanie would make him look any more approachable. But it might add a modicum of warmth. Reluctantly, he pulled it on.

Chapter 8

Rigby watched the footage a second time, then a third. He could sense the impatience of Mr. Lowry who'd been reluctant to let him see the recording in the first place. It made Rigby wonder what Lowry had been up to. Whatever it was, it hadn't been recorded.

But then neither had the car. He checked the timing again. It had to be right because there was Gail Cooper, strolling past Lowry's house minutes before dispatch logged the call from Colin Farmer about the accident.

Rigby swallowed hard. He was watching what would be the last minutes of Gail Cooper's life. Two more blocks and she'd be lying broken in the snow. He could be imagining it, wanting to believe her last minutes on earth had been happy ones, but she looked as if she was enjoying the walk despite the weather. Or maybe because of the weather. An unhurried, unencumbered stroll in the snow, past the brightly decorated yards, Christmas on the horizon and a loving family waiting for her return. All supposition, of course, but she definitely wasn't huddled and hurrying.

Mr. Lowry cleared his throat. "Doesn't matter how many times you watch it. It's not going to change."

Rigby swallowed back a retort. Where Mr. Lowry saw an empty scene, he saw a potential clue. Since Gail Cooper had disappeared out of camera range there'd been no movement on the street. No cars. Not until the first emergency vehicle flashed by, Docherty responding to the call. Which meant the car that had hit Gail must have come from a side street between Lowry's house and the accident site. Which in turn meant they were wasting their time canvassing any more houses on this block.

"I need a copy of this video."

Mr. Lowry's jaw dropped open. "You're not taking my phone."

Rigby rolled his eyes. "Not your phone. Just a copy of this file."

Mr. Lowry looked blank. "How do I do that?"

Rigby hesitated. He didn't actually know. There had to be a share button or something. But he didn't want to waste time figuring it out. He called Turner. Interrupted the other cop's ribbing about his lack of tech knowhow and asked him to please just walk him through what he should do. Turner made it seem embarrassingly easy. The ribbing was probably deserved and no doubt he'd be in for more of it when he got back to the station house.

He thanked Mr. Lowry who still seemed confused by his level of interest in the footage, but was also casting annoyed glances at the pool of water Rigby had left on his wooden floor. The guy obviously didn't believe in doormats but at least he'd had the decency to invite him in out of the cold.

He caught up with Harper as she emerged from a house across the street. Her expression said it all. She'd had no more luck than him. It was a fruitless search. When he told her what he'd learned she glanced down the block at all the houses she'd visited and hadn't needed to.

"Too bad your guy didn't live nearer the corner." She sighed. "Now I guess we'll have to start on the cross streets."

"There's only two of them between here and the accident site."

"But we've no idea whether the car turned right or left onto Pinewood Avenue or whether it had come straight down the side street or turned onto it from another side road."

From that perspective, it did look hopeless. But what else could they do? Or rather, could he do? He had to remember this wasn't Harper's problem. And he couldn't expect her to stay out all day. She had her own cases to deal with.

"Let's go back to the office. See if Turner's gleaned anything useful from the first link I sent him." Unlikely, because Turner would have called if he had, but at this point any excuse to get out of the miserable weather would do. Besides, Harper was right. If the car hadn't come straight from the highway, the search area had increased exponentially.

And the snow was forecast to continue all day.

Chapter 9

Turner grinned at the sight of Rigby. "Didn't take you long. What four, five weeks?" He winked at Harper. "The joy of changing diapers worn off already?"

"Good to see you again too." Rigby crossed to his desk, stripped off his sodden jacket and hat, and tossed the latter to Harper. "Thanks."

He slipped his feet out of his shoes. His socks were soaked through. Boots. Boots would have been the obvious choice if he'd stopped long enough to think about it rather than grabbing the nearest footwear to hand in his haste to get out the house before Becca and Lotte woke up. His plan hadn't succeeded. Since Lotte's birth Becca woke at the slightest sound. She'd followed him from the bedroom to the bathroom and then to the kitchen, haranguing him, making him feel like a heel for wanting to go to work hours before his shift started. For going back to work before he needed to.

He'd almost given in. Everything she said made perfect sense and she knew the chief would back her to the hilt. But then the thought of Gail Cooper lying in the snow, the little kids who were now motherless, and the look on Martin Cooper's face when he heard the news made his sore ribs and lack of sleep fade into insignificance. He couldn't hand it over to Harper or Turner. Couldn't let Becca's concerns for his health sway him from doing what he needed to do.

He'd have to make it up to Becca later somehow. He glanced over at Turner. With seven kids, Turner should be the expert on navigating fatherhood while being a detective. But it was too early to ask for advice. Weren't the first few weeks always the hardest?

Turner would probably laugh and say what did he expect? And if he thought it was tough now, just wait until Lotte was a teenager. Rigby reckoned if Turner lost any sleep nowadays it would be down to his teenage daughter, not the younger kids.

Damn, that was a depressing thought. He shook his head. Definitely time to focus on the job. "Got anything for me?" he asked instead.

"Other than it was an extremely fast-moving vehicle?"

Rigby grimaced. "Nothing? Even frozen?" He padded over to Turner's desk. There had to be something. One small clue not obvious on the small screen of a phone, but blatantly clear once enlarged. That's all he wanted. Was it too much to ask?

Turner shook his head. "Rough estimate, I'd say the car was doing fifty."

"On that street? In those conditions?" No wonder the driver lost control.

"Gina should be able to give a more accurate figure but based on the amount of street we can see and the time lapse between the car appearing and disappearing from view, yes, I'd say at least fifty, possibly more. Watch."

Turner hit play. He fast-forwarded until a figure appeared on the right of the screen. He let it play out at normal speed as they watched Gail pass by and then disappear from sight. Less than a minute later a vehicle whizzed by on the other side of the road, a blur visible for a mere fraction of the time it had taken Gail to cover the distance.

Turner went back to the vehicle's first appearance and played it again at the slowest speed possible. Even so, the vehicle was still a blur, impossible to spot any identifying features. Then Turner pulled up a still shot he'd captured.

It told them nothing Rigby didn't already know. "What happens if you enlarge it?"

Turner obliged. The photo became even fuzzier.

"Isn't there's something you can do to make the image clearer?"

Turner didn't bother answering.

Rigby perched gingerly on the corner of Turner's desk. All that effort and they had nothing to show for it. Except to learn they'd been looking in the wrong place. But even if they went house to house on the cross streets and were lucky enough to find another camera, if the car was still traveling so fast, were they going to get any better images of it?

"By the way," Turner said, "the chief said he wanted to see you when you showed up."

"Now you tell me." Rigby stood up.

Turner shrugged. "You asked about the footage. I figured you'd want to know so you could give him a full update."

There wasn't anything to update. Which probably meant he was going to get a lecture on unnecessary overtime. Could the morning get any worse? He headed for the door.

"Rigby."

He turned back. Turner had a huge grin on his face.

"You probably should put your shoes back on."

Chapter 10

The door to the chief's office was open but Rigby still knocked. No point in getting off on the wrong foot before he even opened his mouth.

"Sit," Jim Pearson said without looking up from the document he was studying. The frown on his forehead confirmed Rigby's suspicion that he hadn't been called in for a warm welcome back to the workforce.

He sat. Though he'd rather have stood so Pearson couldn't bear witness to his attempt to conceal his pain. Not much escaped Pearson even when he appeared to be otherwise distracted. It was an unnerving trait; one Rigby had fallen foul of several times. He decided to let Pearson speak first. Set the tone for their conversation.

Finally, Pearson picked up a pen and signed whatever he'd been reading while he asked, "What are you doing here?"

The question caught Rigby off guard. Damn, was this Turner's idea of a joke? "You asked to see me."

Pearson exhaled impatiently. "You know that's not what I mean."

So his first instincts were right. This was about overtime.

"I'm following up on last night's hit-and-run."

"You're not on duty until three."

"If it's the overtime you're worried about—"

"It's not the overtime." Pearson paused then added sharply, "It's the small matter of you not being cleared for active duty."

Rigby stared dumbfounded at the chief. Realized Pearson

was serious. He found his voice. "The call came in last night. Was I supposed to ignore it?"

"Docherty could have handled it perfectly well. And then this morning one of the others could have taken it over."

"But I was here at my desk."

"Which is where you were supposed to be. It's why it's called desk duty. You were the one so desperate to come back to work."

"You agreed to it."

"To desk duty. Not so you could traipse around the streets in a blizzard when you can barely walk."

"That's bullshit. I—" Rigby took a deep breath before continuing. "I'm fine."

Pearson snorted. He tossed his pen down on the desk, sending it spinning toward Rigby and over the edge onto the floor. "Grab it for me, will you?"

Rigby scowled. Damn Pearson and his rules. Yes, there were certain movements that were still painful. But there was nothing wrong with his mind. And how much physical action was this case going to need? How much did any case involve? Most of their work was interviewing and phone calls and reviewing evidence. Hell, it wasn't as if he was on patrol. That would be different. He'd understand that. But he wasn't on patrol. He was a detective and more than anything right now he wanted to find the bastard who'd cut short Gail Cooper's life. He needed this case, needed something to get him back on track. Why did Pearson think he'd been so desperate to come back to work?

He made no effort to pick up the pen. It would only prove Pearson's point. He could pretend all he wanted that he was okay but his range of pain-free motion was still severely limited. And the inability to be active compounded the sense of helplessness Lotte's birth had engendered. Becca treated him like an invalid when it should be him tending to her needs. This wasn't the way he'd imagined the first few weeks of fatherhood, being a hindrance rather than a help. And to make matters worse, he couldn't pound out his frustrations on a long hard run.

Pearson got up and retrieved the pen. Instead of returning to his seat, he leaned against the desk and eyed Rigby resignedly. "I also have yet to see anything from Nancy Tuccino."

Rigby grimaced. That would be because he'd yet to visit the department psychologist.

"It was an order, Rigby. Not a request."

"I just haven't had time. With the baby and all."

"You've had four weeks."

Rigby shrugged. "There's nothing I need to talk to her about anyway."

Pearson raised his eyebrows. "You had a gun held to your head. Your own gun. I think that should be plenty to start with."

What good would talking about it do? He'd lived through it. He couldn't talk the memory away. The feel of the metal pressed against his forehead, the stomach-turning fear, the rapid gun shots— they visited him most nights in his dreams. Why would he want to rehash them again in the daytime? He had more important things to think about now. Lotte. Becca. They were what mattered.

"I can't sit around at home all day. It's not fair to Becca. All Lotte does at the moment is sleep, cry, and feed. And even if I was totally fit, for as long as Becca's breastfeeding, there's not much I can do to help. I feel like a spare wheel. Worse." He raked his fingers through his hair. "When I'm at home she wants to look after me too. She looks exhausted. Sounds exhausted. I told her when Lotte sleeps she should sleep but if I'm there she won't do it. Least not during the day. Says there's too much else to do, but when I offer to help, she says no."

Pearson smiled. "It's an adjustment. Having a baby. For both of you."

"I think she's mad at me for missing the birth."

"It was hardly your fault."

"I promised her I'd be there." He hesitated. "I wanted to be there. She shouldn't have had to worry about me while she was trying to bring our daughter into the world. It should have been a happy experience for her."

"I'm not sure too many women would describe the actual birth process as a happy experience."

"Yeah, but most of them aren't worrying whether the father's still going to be alive or not by the time the baby's born."

"She had no idea how serious it was. Not until after."

"She's not stupid. She tried to call me. Got Dean instead. She must have known something was seriously wrong."

"Have you talked about it?"

"Not really. She doesn't want to talk about it." Seeing Pearson's hard stare he added, "So that makes two of us."

Pearson straightened up. "That settles it. I want you out of here until Nancy Tuccino clears you to return."

"What? What about my shift tonight?"

"We've managed the last few weeks without you. I'm sure we can manage a little longer."

"But the hit-and-run?"

"I'm sure it won't be the first hit-and-run Harper's dealt with."

Rigby's jaw dropped. Harper?

"You have a problem with that?" Pearson's thin smile was a signal not to answer. "By the sound of it, she's already up to speed on the case."

Rigby eased himself up from the chair not bothering to hide his discomfort and headed for the door.

"My suggestion," Pearson called after him. "When Lotte sleeps, both you and Becca try to sleep. You look as if you need it."

Rigby left without responding.

As if his problems would be solved that easily.

Chapter 11

Jim Pearson let out a huge sigh as Rigby left the office. He hoped he'd made the right decision. Rigby wouldn't think so, that was for sure, but the department had gone through so much in the last year—his own accident, Detective Kendrick's death and then the incident involving Rigby—he couldn't let his desire to help Rigby put them at risk of yet another front-page story.

Rigby was a good cop. No one could doubt his dedication, but since the death of his first girlfriend it had been a struggle to keep him on the straight and narrow. Trouble seemed to follow him. Especially in the early days, there'd been numerous occasions when it would have been easier to get rid of him. Any other detective, he would have done so, but he'd seen the potential in Rigby from his start in patrol. He'd acted as a mentor when Rigby first became a detective, often partnering with him on more serious investigations. They worked well as a team. And then Katy died.

And Rigby unraveled. Saw the future he had planned disintegrate. Blamed himself despite being the one betrayed. Pearson knew if there was to be any hope of Rigby getting through the pain it would be through work. If he took away his job completely, Rigby would have nothing, be nothing, and he couldn't bear to see that happen. He didn't have a son, but Rigby had become almost a proxy, and maybe that was his problem.

If he'd known the angst it was going to cause him, would he have been so supportive? Probably not. But once he'd set out on the path to rehabilitate Rigby it had been difficult to give up, admit defeat, even if it had required some underhand tactics on his part. Luckily they had worked. Eventually.

And then Rigby had met Becca. And for a brief time he had hoped Rigby was back on track, or at least heading that way, but then he'd had a near death experience at the very time his daughter was being born. It was enough to screw with anyone's mind but given all Rigby had already gone through, why did it have to be him?

Chapter 12

Rigby flipped through the pages of a parenting magazine, skimming articles on how to deal with problems that surely awaited him as Lotte grew to adulthood interspersed with ads touting the bliss of family life available on purchase of a particular product.

He tossed the magazine back on the table and glanced around Nancy Tuccino's waiting room. It had been given a coat of paint since his last visit, had a more welcoming feel to it, but did nothing to combat his sense of dread. It felt akin to sitting outside the principal's office. Except in this instance it would be him doing the talking, revealing his own fears and flaws rather than an authority figure pointing out the errors of his ways.

Pearson's ultimatum had prodded him into action. Instead of going home and sleeping, he'd cast aside the temptation, told Harper and Turner he'd be back later, and gone out to his car to call the psychologist. The snow had continued unabated while he'd been in the office, coating the car in a blanket of white. Perfect. The kind of day that made people want to stay home and cancel appointments at the last minute, especially those they hadn't been looking forward to in the first place.

Luck was on his side. Nancy Tuccino had not one but two canceled appointments. If Rigby could get there within the hour she could see him immediately. He was there within fifteen minutes, would have been quicker if he hadn't first had to clear the snow from the car. If his plan worked he could be back at his desk by three.

The door to the inner office opened. Rigby pulled out his

phone, pretended to be absorbed while surreptitiously eyeing the departing person. A woman. Thankfully, no one he recognized. She swept out of the waiting room without a glance in his direction, her expression furious. Rigby sympathized. Facing up to one's demons was never easy. And that could easily be him in an hour's time.

Nancy Tuccino appeared at her office door, all smiles, seemingly unfazed by whatever had made her previous client so angry.

"Detective Rigby, so good to see you again."

Was it?

She beckoned him into her office, waited until he'd settled into one of the four high-backed armchairs that dominated the room, and asked, "What brings you here?"

As if she didn't know. Pearson would have chased her up for her outstanding report on Rigby's fitness to return to work after a traumatic experience only to learn she'd yet to see him. He could only imagine the nature of the conversation thereafter. Which put him at a disadvantage. So feigning innocence was the best place to start.

"The chief wants you to sign off on my mental fitness to return to work." Hopefully she didn't know he already had gone back.

She smiled again. Was it a genuine smile or an "I know your game" smile? He couldn't tell.

"I hear congratulations are in order."

He saw his chance. He pulled out his phone, brought up his photos, and showed her the screen. Then he scrolled to the next photo and the next. He had masses of them already. Rather this than talk about himself. But after the third photo Dr. Tuccino switched her gaze from the screen to his face, an unmistakable sign that she wanted to move on. He put his phone away.

"She's beautiful. What's her name?"

"Lotte."

"Nice name. And how are you and Becca finding parenthood?"

"Wonderful."

At the slight quizzical rise in Dr. Tuccino's eyebrows, he

added, "I mean, more sleep would be nice, but..." He shrugged. Winced. "It's what we expected."

"And is it only Lotte that disturbs your sleep?"

Damn, he'd walked right into that. Should he tell her how grateful he was when Lotte woke him from his nightmares? The huge relief to hear a baby's cry rather than a gunshot as he relived the sense of helplessness over and over again in his dreams. How he wanted to be the one to cradle Lotte back to sleep, partly because he knew how close he'd come to missing out on being there for her, but also because awake he could keep the nightmares at bay. But it was Becca that Lotte needed. He was merely a bystander to the feeding ritual. And while he tried to stay awake to keep Becca company exhaustion would often win out, pulling him back to his unwanted dreams. And in those rare instances of dreamless sleep, Lotte's cries would wake him from that too. He couldn't win. And what could Dr. Tuccino do about it?

"Rigby?"

Damn, he'd paused too long. What would she read into that?

"Yes, of course it's the baby. What else would it be?"

Dr. Tuccino merely nodded. "I believe you missed her birth?"

Rigby almost laughed. She knew damn well he'd missed the birth because if Pearson hadn't told her then she'd have read about it in the news. The press had lapped it up—a feel good story to wrap up the reporting of a horrible crime.

"You want me to talk about what happened?"

"Isn't that why you're here?"

He did laugh then. "No, I'm here because the chief insisted I see you."

"Because the regulations require it. You'd been through a traumatic ordeal."

"And I survived it. Intact. Well, save for a few sore ribs. They haven't helped either. With the sleeping. Especially at the beginning. The pain would wake me every time I moved. So new baby, sore ribs, that equals exhaustion. I don't see how talking is going to solve that."

A glimmer of anger flickered in the doctor's eyes. "You're

not here because you're exhausted. You're right. It's to be expected. And it will pass." She hesitated. "Unless there's something else, underlying, that you're repressing, denying." She paused again. When he didn't speak she continued. "What you went through that day must have been horrific. And I'm saying that based only on what I've heard on the news. And we know that's only the surface story. An arrest gone wrong. A hostage situation. An unnecessary death."

"He chose to die!" Rigby gulped, regretted the outburst. Did the doctor think she was helping, laying it out so blatantly? Damn right it was an unnecessary death, as his would have been if he hadn't made it out alive. "But I gave him the means to do it."

"Because he used your gun?"

"There were no other guns in the apartment. I don't think he'd held a gun before let alone fired one." Rigby shuddered. "I didn't think he intended to kill me. He had nothing to gain from it despite what he said, but I could see it happening accidentally, which is why I did what I did. I had no idea he'd turn the gun on himself."

"How could you?"

"He should never have had my gun."

Nancy frowned. "But it's not as if you gave it to him. He took it off you, right?"

"Of course I didn't give it to him!" He broke off, swallowed back his anger. Taking his frustrations out on the doctor would serve no purpose. He needed her on his side. "I shouldn't have let them take it."

"Could you have stopped them? The press reports said you were overpowered."

Rigby didn't respond. Bad enough to lose his gun but for the whole damn world to know about it was beyond embarrassing. If he ever found out who leaked that aspect of the story, he'd make them pay. The reports made him sound incompetent. Only he knew how blindsided he'd been by the attack. Once he'd entered the home he'd never stood a chance, but he'd acted instinctively on seeing his quarry try to escape out the back. He should never have crossed the threshold but how was he to know there'd be someone waiting for him with a baseball bat? A man built like a line-back.

"I should never have barged in." He hesitated. "And it was

all for nothing. Even as they were taking my gun, my colleagues had already made the arrest. Turns out one of them can run like the wind and scale high obstacles. Thank God she didn't follow me inside."

Nancy frowned again. "But surely if she had, she would have been able to respond to the attack on you. However big the guy was, he couldn't take you both out at the same time."

The doctor had a point, but he'd made the call. And he couldn't blame Harper for his actions. The whole fiasco was a result of his decisions. And he accepted that and would have to live with it. The doctor had helped him after his first girlfriend had died. Helped him see he couldn't hold himself responsible for the choices Katy had made, but he couldn't see how she could help with this. Other than to clear him to go back to the job so he was too busy to let the guilt that someone had used his gun to kill himself play over and over in his mind. Should he tell her that was what haunted his thoughts during the day? Let her assume that was also the stuff of his nightmares?

"It was my mistake. No one else's. I take responsibility and, yes, at the moment it plays on my mind. But that's because I don't have other cases to distract me. It's been four weeks. If it wasn't for the ribs I'd have been back on the job almost immediately. Would have been able to start putting it all behind me. Instead I've been sitting around with Becca treating me like an invalid when, if anything, it's me who should be looking after her."

"She had a baby. She isn't sick or injured."

"She still deserves to be looked after. What about her traumatic experience? Giving birth worried about me. It's not how it should have been. I promised her I'd be there for her. Just one more time I've let her down."

"Is that what she's said?"

"Becca?" Rigby spluttered. "No. She's too nice. But I see it in her expression sometimes when she thinks I'm not looking. In the way she insists she can manage even though she looks exhausted."

"Is she breastfeeding?"

Rigby nodded.

"Well that's something only she can do."

Rigby looked away, out the window at the rooftops of the

buildings opposite. The white rooftops. There'd been no letup in the snow. His car would need clearing off again. His driveway would need shoveling. But he wouldn't even be able to do that. And knowing Becca, the moment Lotte went down to sleep, she'd be out there. Doing what he couldn't.

He glanced back at the doctor. Did she realize how much power she had over his life right now? Had she already decided his immediate future?

As usual she didn't say anything. Waited for him to fill the silence. Much like he did when he was trying to get a suspect to confess. The need to fill the silence could be overwhelming, especially when guilt or fear was involved.

Finally, he gave in. "I feel so damn useless." He exhaled loudly, looked everywhere but at the doctor. "I need to be back at work. Yes, physically I'm not a hundred percent fit. Yet. But mentally, I'm fine. And I'll be even better if I've got something to think about other than hashing over what happened, what I did wrong, what I should have done."

Dr. Tuccino sat impassive.

"I need to be back at work."

Still no response.

"Please." He'd beg if he had to. "And I know Becca would be eternally grateful to you."

That lie got him a reaction. Almost a smile, quickly replaced by a penetrating glare. "So tell me more about this "hashing" you do. And why you feel it's necessary."

Damn.

Chapter 13

Rigby must have said something right. Dr. Tuccino cleared him on the proviso he continued to see her for several more sessions. He didn't want to but it was a small price to pay. And maybe she would be able to help him sort out his feelings. That could only benefit Becca. The doctor had hinted maybe Becca could join him at one of the sessions. He wasn't too sure about that but pretended it was a good idea. He'd say whatever she needed to hear to persuade her she could call the chief and tell him there was no reason Rigby couldn't be back at work. And to do it before three that afternoon.

To his surprise she agreed. He'd have loved to hear her conversation with the chief but she obviously had no intention of doing it while he was still in her office. No doubt he'd be able to gauge Pearson's opinion on the matter when he got back to the office.

On the way back he stopped in at home to tell Becca he'd been to see the doctor. She'd be pleased. It might go some way to make up for him going out first thing. But Cocoa was the only one pleased to see him. Becca and Lotte were fast asleep.

He stood by the bassinet, watched the gentle rise and fall of Lotte's chest. Found himself syncing his breath to match hers. A sense of calm and wonder flowed through him. So tiny. So beautiful. His daughter.

He glanced over at Becca. She hadn't stirred when he'd walked into the room. Possibly a first since the birth. He'd planned to change into some warmer clothes but didn't want to risk disturbing her. She looked so peaceful. And she needed to sleep.

He crept out of the room, eased the door shut to keep Cocoa from getting in, and went to grab a sandwich. He found a pot of lentil soup on the stovetop. His mother's lentil soup. She must have called over earlier, despite the weather. He'd told her she shouldn't drive in bad weather, not unless it was an emergency and providing them with meals was hardly that, but she didn't listen. She could be as stubborn as he was, probably where he got the trait from in the first place. So what did he expect?

He wolfed down a bowl of soup and some crusty bread, another of his mother's offerings. Just what he needed on a winter's day. He poked through the laundry basket and found a pair of thick dry socks. He couldn't tell whether they were waiting to go into the wash or had just come out but they were better than those he had on.

Cocoa got all excited as he pulled on his heavy boots and padded jacket. He hated to disappoint the pup but he didn't have time for a walk. He scribbled a note for Becca, distracted the dog with a treat, and dashed out the door before Cocoa could follow.

Several inches of snow covered their driveway. In the short time he'd been home another thin layer had coated his car. His ribs ached at the mere thought of having to sweep it off again so he made do with using the wipers to clear the windows. As he drove down the street he noticed a teenager clearing the driveway of a neighbor's house. He pulled to the side of the road, attracted the kid's attention and asked him if he wanted to earn some money. The kid struck a hard bargain. He ended up paying twice what he'd expected but if it saved Becca from doing the work, it would be well worth it. He sent her a text to let her know not to worry if she saw a strange kid shoveling the snow then drove off feeling good.

The detective bureau was empty, as was Pearson's office. A quick chat with Collins, the desk sergeant, confirmed that Turner had left for the day, Harper had gone back to continue the door-to-door, and he had no idea where the chief was. "But he did say you wouldn't be in this evening."

"Change of plans."

Collins eyed him suspiciously. "Does the chief know this

change of plans?"

"Of course. You think I'd be here otherwise?" Rigby flashed a grin.

Collins didn't need to reply. His expression said it all.

"If he comes back, tell him I've gone out to relieve Harper. I guess she was going to cover for me, but there's no need now."

Collins sighed. "On your head be it."

Rigby didn't like the sound of that. What had Pearson told the others about his sudden departure? Had Nancy Tuccino managed to get hold of the chief to let him know her verdict? Maybe not. In which case, best to make himself scarce before Pearson returned and slapped him with any more restrictions on what he could and couldn't do.

He dashed out to his car as fast as his ribs would allow. As he drove out of the parking lot he saw the chief's car approach from the opposite direction. He acknowledged him with a quick wave as he passed then let out a huge sigh of relief. That was close.

Would the chief expect him to turn back? Probably. Was he going to? No. All it would do was waste time. And the chief would understand.

He spotted Harper's car on the side street nearest the accident site. Judging from the amount of snow on her car roof, she'd been there for some time. He pulled in behind it and waited until he saw her emerge from a driveway a considerable distance down the road.

He got out the car. Called her name. She didn't hear. She turned away from him, heading for the next driveway. He trudged down the road and caught up with her as she came away from the house.

"What are you doing here?" She made no effort to hide her surprise.

He feigned ignorance. "Starting my shift."

"I thought—" She shook her head. "Pearson told me you wouldn't be back for a while. I thought he meant a few days not a few hours." She shook her head again. "He told me to take over the case."

"He did?"

Harper made a face. Nodded.

Damn, Pearson. That annoyed him. Though really, what did he expect Pearson to do? Put the case on hold until he returned? Pearson had no way of knowing it would be so quick. Though given who he was dealing with, he might have guessed.

Rigby smiled. "I'm back now." And he wanted his case back too.

"Okay."

She said it so casually, Rigby half expected her to rush off to her car and leave, pleased to be relieved of the tedium of the door-to-door.

"So far," she continued, "I've done nine houses on this side of the street. Four no answers and five no cameras." She grimaced. "It's not going well."

Which could be why she was happy to be rid of it.

"I've got a guy, Shore, working on the next street down."

"Brad Shore?"

"Yes. Why? Do you know him?"

"Sort of." Katy's brother, though this wasn't the time or place to go into the history.

"Haven't heard anything from him so I assume he's had no more luck than me." Harper shivered. Stamped her feet. "Shall we get on with it then?"

"You're sticking around?"

She shrugged. "It'll be quicker with three than two. Not that I'm particularly hopeful we're going to get anything useful out of it. But to be honest, the thought the driver's going to get away with this? No. Not if I can help it." She grimaced. "And what else do we have to work with? The car came from somewhere."

"Maybe we'd have more luck trying to track where it went afterward." He frowned. "Have you heard from Gina?"

"I gave her a call. After Pearson told me the case was mine. She's got some good tire impressions from where the car swerved across the road, but there'd obviously been other traffic along the road beforehand and it was impossible to get anything definite from the tracks before or after the swerve, especially as it kept snowing. She said if it had been on one of these quieter side streets we might have a better chance of determining the car's route."

Rigby surveyed the street in the fading light, the twinkle of the lit decorations against the snowy landscape creating a winter wonderland effect, a fake sense of cheer. He doubted Martin Cooper would be turning on his Christmas lights that day. And then he'd have to go and tell him there'd be no justice for his wife's death.

"I think we should focus on the houses up to the next junction. No way can we cover the whole street. And then get some boards out, asking for information. Someone might have seen or heard the car and not made the connection."

"It's in hand," Harper said.

"What do you mean?"

"I asked Collins to arrange it before I came out. They'll be in place before first light tomorrow."

Rigby stammered out a thanks, not sure whether he was pleased or annoyed. Harper was one step ahead of him again. He wasn't used to that except when it came to Pearson. But this wasn't a competition. And on this case he sensed he was going to need all the help he could get.

Harper's phone buzzed. She answered brusquely. Her eyes brightened as she listened. "We're on our way." She cut the call. Smiled at Rigby. "Shore. Finally, we might have something."

Chapter 14

Rigby pulled up outside a dilapidated house, two properties up from the junction of Pinewood Avenue. The front door opened and Brad Shore waved them in. If he was surprised to see Rigby he didn't show it. He introduced them to the homeowner, an elderly lady who gave Harper a dubious glance when Brad said she was the detective in charge. Rigby didn't correct him.

Mrs. Henderson asked them to wipe their feet and then invited them into the kitchen. The appliances looked as old as she was but the room was spotlessly clean. A golden retriever trotted over to check them out but with one word from Mrs. Henderson it returned to its bed by a side door.

"Can you tell the detectives what you told me?" Brad said.

Mrs. Henderson crossed to the window and pointed to Rigby's car. "There was a car parked in almost the same spot last night but facing the junction. I'd never seen it before. I didn't think it was one of the neighbors. It must have been there for about an hour. And at one point there was definitely someone sitting in it."

Rigby wondered how good Mrs. Henderson's sight was. She wasn't wearing glasses and in the dark it would be hard to tell from this distance whether someone was in the driver's seat. "What time was this?"

"It would have been... about nine o'clock. I was filling the kettle at the sink here. I like to have a cup of chamomile tea and a cookie before I go to bed." She smiled. "My little bedtime treat. And I happened to look out and I noticed the car." She gestured at Brad.

"As I said to the officer, it probably caught my attention because there's not usually cars parked there. There's no need to park on the road. And this time of year, it only makes it difficult for the snow plows."

"And there was definitely someone sitting in it?"

Mrs. Henderson made to speak then hesitated, her forehead furrowing in concentration. "Well, I can't say I definitely saw someone sitting inside then, but when I came back to wash my cup and plate, the car was still there, only this time there was a light inside."

"The interior light was on?"

Mrs. Henderson grimaced. "I think it was more like the light from a phone or one of those other devices everyone uses."

"And what time would that be?"

"I'd just finished watching my program so I'd say about nine-fifty, nine-fifty-five?"

Colin Farmer's call about the accident had been ten-thirteen so the car's presence at that time could be significant. Though why would the driver be sitting outside Mrs. Henderson's house? He must have been visiting a neighbor. Had Brad spoken to the people on the corner yet?

"Do you know what kind of car it was?"

Mrs. Henderson laughed. "Small and white. Or maybe beige. I don't know anything about cars. I left that to my husband, God rest his soul. But as I told the officer, I did take a photo."

"Of the car?" Rigby glanced at Harper who looked as incredulous as he felt. "Why did you do that?"

"I thought it was odd. The car being out there all that time. I thought it might have been a burglar waiting until all the lights went out. You hear such horrible stories nowadays. Not that Goldie would let anyone get in here."

At the sound of her name, Goldie trotted over to her mistress.

"But I thought if something did happen overnight then it might be useful." She laughed again. "Small and white's not going to be much help, is it?" She smiled broadly at each of them in turn.

"Can we see the photo?" Harper said.

"Of course, I was just going to get it when you turned up." She disappeared out the room. The dog followed her.

Harper smiled, raised her eyebrows. "At least we'll be able to tell whether it's the same car as the one on the video footage. Though why would it be parked outside?" She turned to Shore. "Have you been next door yet?"

Brad shook his head. "There was no one home. But I have been to the two houses opposite and neither of them mentioned having a visitor yesterday evening."

"Unless they didn't want to admit they knew someone who'd driven off at about the right time of the accident," Rigby said. "That would be a tough call to make, especially if it was family."

"What? And ignore the fact their visitor might have killed someone?" Harper looked horrified.

"No. But try and persuade them to turn themselves in rather than be responsible for dropping them in it." He sighed. "Anyway, it's all speculation because why would a visitor be sitting outside in a car? That is, if Mrs. Henderson is right."

"I most certainly am." Mrs. Henderson shot him an imperious glare then turned to Harper and handed her a small digital camera. "Here. Look. It's not a bad photo even though I say so myself."

Harper studied the photo. Her eyes sparkled. She passed the camera to Rigby. A light-colored sedan, remarkably like the one they were looking for, the interior in darkness except for a small glow on the driver's side. A phone screen, if he wasn't mistaken. But it was the angle of the photo that made him smile.

"Where did you take this from" he asked.

"The guest room on the other side of the hallway. I didn't want to take it through the window, it makes them all blurry, and I didn't want to risk the person seeing me, so I went in there, didn't turn the light on, and opened the window a crack so I could get the photo. I did wonder whether he'd notice the flash. Maybe that's what made him drive off. Because a few minutes later the car had gone."

Mrs. Henderson's face fell. "You don't think that could have been what made him speed off and hit that poor woman, do you?"

"The timing's not right," Rigby lied. The woman had handed

them the best piece of evidence yet, he didn't want her taking any blame for her actions. He looked again at the photo, taken at an angle from the rear of the car rather than from the side. Capturing that all important piece of information, the license plate. Too small to read on the photo, but he didn't need Turner to solve that problem.

Chapter 15

Back at the station house Rigby pulled up a copy of the photo on his computer. Harper and Shore peered over his shoulder as he zoomed in on the image, trying to hit the exact spot where the numbers were neither too small nor too blurry. It wasn't easy, especially with the audience. They were all hyped up, sensing they were about to crack the case, making his fingers clumsy. Even before he could make out the numbers, he recognized the orange logo in the middle of the plate. His spirits sank. It was an out-of-state registration. Florida. Their suspect could have fled home, could be on the I-95 heading south at that very moment with hundreds of options on route to stop off and repair any damage caused by the accident.

Or it might not even be the right car. Though what were the chances of two almost identical cars in the same quiet residential area at the same time on an inclement snowy evening? No. It had to be the vehicle they were looking for.

"Could be a rental," Harper said. "Wouldn't mean the driver's not local."

"Is a burglar going to rent a car?" Shore straightened up and glanced at the white board next to Harper's desk, his action bringing it to Rigby's attention for the first time.

Harper must have started it as soon as Pearson assigned her the case. There was a headshot of Gail from her driving license, alive and smiling. Another of her dead in the snow. That was it. Rigby wondered why she'd bothered. He only used a whiteboard when a case required a team investigation. This was unlikely to rise to that level. Still, they each had their own way of working. Maybe this was Harper's.

He took a screenshot of the enlarged license plate, hit print and then also ran off a copy of the original photo. Might as well add them to Harper's board.

Rigby drummed his fingers on his desk. A burglar might rent a car. They made good getaway cars. Give a false ID to the rental company and the chances of being tracked down were slim unless you were captured on the rental office's cameras. But use a disguise and a fake ID and identification would almost be impossible. But to go to those lengths would suggest a crime with a substantial pay-off, hard to conceive as likely in the Pinewood Avenue neighborhood.

"The relatively short distance between Mrs. Henderson's house and the accident site would suggest that if this was the vehicle it must have taken off at some speed to lose control so quickly."

"He sees the flash of Mrs. Henderson's camera. Realizes he's been made. What choice does he have?" Shore said.

Rigby shook his head. "If her timings are correct, there's too much time between her taking the photo and the accident."

"Could be a getaway driver. Had to wait for his pals to get in the car," Harper suggested.

A possibility. Except there'd been no reports of burglaries in the area the previous night. It just didn't make sense.

Shore's radio squawked. "I'd better get back on patrol. Good luck with the hunt."

"Yeah. Thanks," Rigby said absentmindedly. What was he missing?

He plugged the registration number into the national database. Held his breath. The moment of truth. The response would either give them their driver or lead them off on another tangent if it turned out to be a rental.

"Yes!" He punched the air. "Dale Jessup. Orlando, Florida. Twenty-six years old." He turned to Harper who had returned to her desk. "Field trip?"

Harper laughed. "You're kidding?"

Rigby sighed. "Course I am. Wonders of technology. Get most of the answers we need without leaving our desk. Takes half the fun out of it." He imagined Pearson's response if he told him he wanted to go to Florida. "Even though it means I have to wait for someone in Orlando to check this out for us. And it's hardly likely to be a priority for them."

She nodded. "It would be easier if it was someone local."

"Too true. I wouldn't be sitting here now. I'd be out ruining their plans for the evening."

"Why would someone from Florida be sitting outside Mrs. Henderson's house?"

"I guess we'll find out if I ever get to talk to them."

"It seems weird though." She hesitated. "Unless it's someone who's relocated and they haven't got around to changing their registration."

Rigby frowned. "Relocated from Florida to Lewisville? Who does that? It's more likely to be the other way around." He groaned. Raked his fingers through his hair. "Let's hope not, or how the hell we going to find them if the address in Orlando turns out to be a dead end?"

Harper grinned. "Wishing you hadn't come back to work?" She put her coat on. "I don't think there's anything more I can do here tonight." She glanced at her watch. "Might just make it back in time for book club."

"Book club? You go to book club?"

"Don't sound so surprised. The library here has a really good book club. Not that I'd expect you to know that."

Rigby did know. His mother had been a member for years. She'd already met Gina Rogers through the meetings. Did she know Harper too? Damn, that was the downside of small towns. He'd prefer his mother wasn't socializing with his colleagues. The potential for embarrassment was enormous. Though maybe now his mom finally had a grandchild, she'd have less time for books.

"Isn't the library closed? Snow day?"

Harper headed for the door. "Wonders of technology, Rigby. You said it yourself. Tonight's meeting is online. Good luck with Orlando."

Online. That had to be better than in-person. Less scope for personal chat, though he'd heard some book clubs were more about the gossip than the book. The book was an excuse. Surely the library club wouldn't be like that. Though Gina seemed to know more about his family than she should, which was bad enough but he didn't have to see Gina every day. Unlike Harper.

He opened his browser. Searched for the number of the Orlando Police Department. No use worrying about things he couldn't control. Hopefully, tracking down the driver was something he could.

Chapter 16

The duty sergeant in Orlando told Rigby they'd send an officer around to the address on the license, but he couldn't be sure when that would happen. They were busy enough with their own concerns. Besides, didn't he realize there were a lot of people with Florida plates who didn't actively live in Florida all year around? If the plates were spotted in New York, chances were he'd have more luck contacting the owner than they did.

By the time Rigby put the phone down he was ready to explode. Yes, he knew it was a long shot, but the address was the only lead they had. He ordered a BOLO for the car but he suspected that by now the car would be either well-hidden or well away from Lewisville.

Now what could he do? Until he heard back from Orlando, they were stuck. He reopened the file with the photo of the car. Why was the driver sitting there? Mrs. Henderson had a right to be suspicious, but he'd double-checked and there definitely hadn't been any reports of other incidents in the area the previous evening.

He opened up a map, zoomed in on the Pinewood Avenue area. It was all residential. If it was a getaway car he couldn't see what the driver would be waiting for.

Was he lost? That could explain why he was looking at a device. But it wouldn't take as long as Mrs. Henderson had said he'd been there to work out where he should be. And he couldn't have broken down or run out of gas because the car had disappeared too quickly after the photo had been taken for a recovery truck to arrive and deal with the problem.

He drummed his fingers on the desk. What, what, what could the driver have been waiting for? And what made him take off in such a hurry? Had he noticed the flash, reported it to another party, and been told to get the hell out of there? Gail must have crossed the road minutes earlier. Had the driver seen her? Or had he been too focused on his phone?

Mrs. Henderson's comment about the snow plow came back to him. From November to April local laws banned overnight parking on the street. An out-of-town visitor might not be aware of the rule, might have failed to see the signs prohibiting it. Had a snow plow come down the street, forcing the driver to move? But then where was the snow plow when the accident happened? It would still have been close by. The driver would surely have stopped, gone to see if he could help. Wouldn't ignore an accident like that.

He drummed his fingers faster. What was the driver waiting for? Or who was he waiting for? As far as they could tell the streets were quiet. No one they'd spoken to had walked their dogs or arrived home around ten o'clock. The only recorded activity had been Gail's walk and the speeding car.

He stopped drumming his fingers. Frowned. Looked closer at the photo. Not at the car but at the junction in the background.

Gail had crossed the road. Within minutes the car that had been there for almost an hour had gone and Gail was dead. It was a crazy thought but could they be looking at this all wrong?

They assumed the driver had lost control, but maybe he had perfect control.

Could Gail be who he'd been waiting for?

Chapter 17

Pearson heard Rigby out without interruption. The suggestion that what they'd thought was a fatal hit-and-run was potentially premeditated murder was outrageous. If it hadn't been for the birth of Lotte, he would have assumed Rigby was angling for a trip to Florida, but Rigby wouldn't want to be away from his daughter overnight. Not at this early stage. Would he?

"What possible reason could there be for someone wanting Gail Cooper dead?"

Rigby shrugged. "Who knows? We know very little about her. Maybe she's been leading a double life."

"A married woman with two young kids? In Lewisville? What kind of double life might that be?"

Rigby shrugged again. Settled back in his chair. A sign he had threads to untangle. Wanted to bounce his ideas off the one person who understood how his mind worked, however outlandish the ideas.

Pearson smiled. It had been a while since they'd had one of these conversations. Not since his accident. His smile faded. The whole department had gone through a lot since then, especially Rigby. Nancy Tuccino told him she had some concerns but thought Rigby would be better off at work than forced to sit out for longer. He'd guessed as much but it wasn't Nancy who'd have to deal with the fallout if they were wrong. The buck stopped firmly with him.

He had no legal grounds to stop Rigby working. He'd been signed off both physically and mentally. How he'd managed that only

Rigby knew, though Pearson could guess. He hadn't been exactly honest about either his physical condition or the nightmares that still plagued him in his own quest to return to work. If his wife Molly had her way he'd still be at home, but he needed to keep busy. The job was his life. After his family, of course. But his family couldn't fill his days, especially now his two oldest were off at college and the youngest was heading there next fall.

As an empty-nester what was he supposed to do? Sit home and watch TV? He had no hobbies. Given the demands of the job, all his spare time had been devoted to his family. And that was fine. He had no regrets, but his enforced lay-off had shown him that if he was ever going to retire he needed to find something to occupy his mind other than crosswords.

"I assume you've already started digging into her background?"

"Not much to find online. Usual social media stuff. All private accounts so I couldn't get past the basics. She didn't crop up in any other searches. Doesn't have a record, not even a parking ticket. Though this is all under her married name. Her maiden name might tell a different story."

"And how do you plan to find that out?"

"Her husband must know."

Pearson sighed. "And when he asks why it's relevant?"

"If she's been murdered, he deserves to know."

"And if she hasn't you're only going to add more pain and anguish to his grief." Pearson hesitated. Stared at Rigby until he knew he had his full attention. "You follow up on this idea. But until you have evidence that proves it's more than an idea, this doesn't leave the department. I don't want to read about it in the papers or hear that Mr. Cooper has heard a whiff of it. Understand?"

"How am I supposed to find out more about Gail if I can't tell her husband why I need to know her background?"

"I'm sure you'll think of something."

For a moment, Rigby looked as if he were about to protest. Then he shrugged and stood up. "Okay. I'll also have to see what I can dig up on Dale Jessup."

Pearson eyed him suspiciously. "If that's a suggestion you

should go to Florida, the answer's no."

Rigby grinned. "The thought never crossed my mind."

Chapter 18

Rigby spotted Gail's sister's house as soon as he turned onto the street. It was the only one without the twinkle of Christmas lights and where the inflatable decorations remained deflated. Chinks of light at the draped windows were the only signs anyone was home.

What a difference twenty-four hours could make. He imagined the yard lit up and welcoming as the guests arrived the previous evening. The laughter, the chatter, the hugs and goodwill, no clue their night would end in sorrow.

He picked his way up the unplowed path to the front door trying to avoid the deepest snow. Judging from the footprints those who had arrived before were still inside.

"Rigby?"

He recognized the tall, well-built man who answered his knock. John Chapman had been the captain of the high school football team when Rigby was a sophomore. Everyone at school knew who he was. Rigby had no such claim to fame so was taken aback that John recognized him. The smile of recognition died when Rigby showed John his badge.

"Come in." John stepped back to allow Rigby to enter. "Do you mind taking your boots off? Hannah, she's very particular and she's upset enough as it is."

Rigby hesitated. Normally, he'd make do with a hearty thump of his feet on the doormat. But he was only there for some background information. Why risk antagonizing the one person who could help him the most?

He added his boots to the line of footwear by the door and followed John down the hallway into an empty family room.

John motioned for him to take a seat. "I'll fetch Hannah. I guess that's who you want to talk to? Her parents are also here but as you can imagine they're devastated."

"I'll need to speak to them too. After Hannah."

"Why?" John raised his hands in protest. "They're upset enough as it is. They're not going to be able to tell you anything Hannah can't. We were told it was a hit-and-run. How could they have any information to help you find the driver?" John's voice cracked. "The bastard. Who does that? Hits someone and drives off." He broke off. "Will you find him?"

"Or her."

John scoffed as if the idea it could have been a woman was untenable. "I offered to drive her home. But she refused." He swallowed hard. "Said she'd enjoy the walk in the snow on her own. Didn't get much chance to do it nowadays." He hesitated. "I should have insisted."

Nothing Rigby said would change John's mind. John had offered. She'd refused. At least that was some consolation. If he was going to feel guilty about not insisting, how much more guilt would he feel if he'd never offered at all?

"You were at the party?" Rigby asked, more to deflect John's thoughts than out of curiosity.

"No way!" John looked at Rigby as if he was crazy. "There were ten women, all determined to enjoy a few childless—and men-free—hours. I was relegated upstairs, out of sight, to keep an eye on the kids. I almost had to go down a couple of times and ask them to keep the noise down. For the kids, you know. Judging by the amount of laughter they were sure enjoying themselves, but I guess Hannah had it under control because it would quickly quiet down again."

Rigby smiled to cover the unease that crept over him. Could one of the women be the driver they were looking for? "You think they were getting drunk?"

"One or two of them, most definitely, according to Hannah and Gail. Gail was the last to leave. She stayed to help Hannah clear up."

"How were they all getting home?" He had visions of drunken women piling into their cars on a snowy evening. "The other women?"

"The neighbors walked. The others got a ride from a friend who was pregnant and not drinking."

Rigby relaxed a little. If Gail left after the others it was unlikely the woman driving was anywhere near where the accident happened at the time. Still, he'd have to double-check.

"Was there anyone at the party called Jessup?"

John frowned. "Jessup? Why do you ask?" When he realized he wasn't going to get an answer, he continued. "I don't know. You'd have to ask Hannah. It's not a name I've heard but then I don't know all the women's names. Most of them are friends she sees when I'm at work. At the park, playgroup, whatever. She's got more friends now than she ever had before the kids." He shut up, grinned apologetically. "Sorry. I'm rambling. It's just—" He sighed. "I can't believe it. She was just here and…" He headed for the door. "I'll get Hannah."

"No need," a voice said.

The resemblance was obvious, but unlike Gail, Hannah's blonde hair was cropped short and her figure more curvaceous. She gazed at Rigby through red-rimmed eyes but he got the impression she wasn't really seeing him.

"Have you caught him?" Her voice came out hoarse, devoid of emotion, as if she already knew the answer.

"Not yet." Rigby bit back the temptation to say "but we will." Promises like that were best kept unspoken. Sometimes no matter how hard they tried such a promise couldn't be fulfilled.

"So how can I help you?"

Rigby took a deep breath. "Just a little background information about Gail."

Hannah frowned. "How will that help find who killed Gail?"

Rigby grimaced. Idiot. He should have said they were merely seeking confirmation of Gail's last movements. Got Hannah talking then he could have slipped in some questions about Gail's maiden name, etcetera. "What time did she leave? Do you remember exactly?"

Hannah glanced at her husband and shook her head. "The others started leaving about nine-thirty. Gail, she…" Hannah blinked hard. "She insisted on helping to clear the glasses and plates. I told her there was no need, it wouldn't take me long. But I think she wanted a post-party chat."

Rigby perked up. "About anything in particular?"

Hannah gave him a strange look. Maybe he should have tampered down the excitement in his voice but he was so desperate to get anything that might back up his theory that they weren't dealing with an accident.

"The usual post-party gossip. A couple of our friends had surprise announcements. We talked about them." She paused, obviously sensing Rigby's curiosity. "Nothing you need to know."

Ouch. But no point in antagonizing her. "So you were saying she left at?"

Hannah glanced at her husband again. "Ten. Maybe a few minutes before."

John nodded.

Hannah looked back at Rigby, tears in her eyes. "If only she hadn't stayed to help. She wouldn't have been where she was when the car went out of control." She spun away as the tears came unimpeded. "I'm sorry," she mumbled, wiping ineffectively at them.

John embraced her in a tight hug. "You mustn't think like that. If only won't bring Gail back."

Words John would be wise to heed given he'd used the same phrase to Rigby earlier. "If only" was always too late a lament, however true it might be.

But in this case, whereas if John had insisted on driving Gail home she would probably still be alive, Rigby's gut instinct suggested that whatever time Gail had left to walk home, death awaited.

Chapter 19

Gail was a loving wife, mother, daughter, sister, friend to all—her family's grief erasing her flaws and there must have been some, nobody was perfect—but Rigby let them talk, hoping that in the sad reminiscences he'd pick up on something to work with, an innocent offhand comment that would give him a lead. But they gave him nothing to work with except for Gail's maiden name. He hadn't had to ask. The introduction of Gail's parents solved that problem.

Jack and Maisie Heaton reminded him of his parents, which made it so much more difficult to witness their grief. How would they react if they knew what he was thinking—that someone might have a reason to want Gail dead? It was preposterous, the stuff of TV shows, a result of a rabid imagination caused by sleepless nights. It had to be. He didn't want to bring any more sorrow to this family.

Unless of course, if members of the family were also involved. He watched their expressions as they talked. Saw no indication of deceit in their behavior, just pain and anguish and the need to comfort each other. He suspected they were already a tight-knit family. God knows they'd need to be to get through this ordeal. Then he remembered a comment Martin had made.

He turned to Hannah. "Your other sister, she wasn't at the party?"

Hannah shook her head. "Izzy... She doesn't have kids. She's not part of the moms' group." A wry smile played on her lips. "And no matter how much we try, the conversations always seem to end up being about kids. Not much fun if you don't have your own."

Rigby understood that. Pre Becca's pregnancy, babies and kids were topics he generally avoided, save for the obligatory congratulations whenever a colleague, usually Turner, added to their family. Now apart from work, even when he should be thinking about work, Lotte was upmost on his mind.

"She's been told about Gail?"

"Of course!"

Okay, it sounded a stupid question but he had no idea where Izzy was. For all he knew they might not have been able to contact her yet. It happened.

"She's over there now." At Rigby's puzzled reaction she added, "At the house. To help Martin with the kids. They know her well. And with no family of her own to worry about she can help take the pressure off Martin."

"What about Martin's family? Won't they be able to help?"

"Martin's an only child. And he was a late baby. His parents are older than Mom and Dad and not in the best health. They are there, they went straight over when they heard, but I doubt they'll be able to offer much practical help. If anything, it'll be another thing for Martin to worry about. Gail helped out with his parents, running errands and the like. She was…" Hannah broke off. Took a moment to compose herself. "She was good like that, always had time for them even when her hands were full with the babies."

Rigby took her quick guilty glance at her husband to mean she wasn't as obliging with her in-laws. But how many people were? The saying you didn't get to choose your family was almost as true for your in-laws. They came as part of the package deal of marriage. Or in his case, co-habiting. Becca's mother might not legally be his mother-in-law but she might as well be. And making her a grandmother hadn't raised him in her estimation at all, merely linked them forever through blood. A depressing thought.

He pulled his thoughts back to the case. If his theory was right about Gail being targeted, she'd obviously had secrets she hadn't shared with her family. Unless they were lying. But he didn't think so. He saw nothing to suggest that in their expressions or mannerisms, and he sensed his presence was compounding their grief.

He stood to leave.

John ushered him out. Made to open the front door and hesitated. "They're not exaggerating, you know. Gail really was a special person. She'd do anything for anybody. And always with a smile. I'd be surprised if you find anyone who has a bad word to say about her."

The comment caught Rigby off guard. He thought he'd been circumspect. Why did John think he was looking for anything negative about Gail?

Pearson's warning came to mind.

"Nobody's perfect," he said as he let himself out.

Chapter 20

Tempted as he was to pay Martin Cooper another visit, Rigby decided to put it off until morning. After the first full day without their mother, who knew what state the kids would be in? And if Martin was having problems getting them to bed he wouldn't welcome any interruptions.

Instead he drove back to the station house. The detective bureau was empty, one of the benefits of being on the evening shift. He could give full attention to his cases undisturbed. Assuming there were no more call-outs.

First he phoned Becca. She didn't pick up. He frowned. It was way too early for her to have gone to bed. Not a good sign. Nor was the absence of any messages from her. It wasn't his fault she was asleep when he'd gone home. She surely wouldn't have wanted him to wake her. Damn, this was so difficult. He felt useless when he was home and guilty when he was at work because being on the job was like a refuge from the chaos Lotte had introduced into their life. A refuge he had, but Becca didn't.

At the beep, he apologized for having to work all day and told her he loved her. It wasn't much but what else could he do?

Go home?

He could tell Davis, the duty sergeant, to call him if anything came in he needed to deal with in the next three hours. He'd already put in more hours than a shift. There was nothing that couldn't wait until the next day. And by leaving early that evening maybe Becca wouldn't be too upset if he had to go out again in the morning to pay Martin Cooper a visit.

He looked down at the case file on his desk. Nothing that couldn't wait. Go home. It was the right decision. Though first, he should update the file with notes on his visit to Hannah's home. It didn't take long. The only new information of possible interest was Gail's maiden name. Something to work on the next day. He closed the file. Although it wouldn't hurt to have a quick look now.

He entered her maiden name in the search engine. It was more common than he'd imagined. He scrolled through the first few pages. None of the entries related to a younger Gail Cooper.

He added Lewisville to the name in the search box. Hit enter. The first entry was an old report from the Lewisville Chronicle. Gail Heaton was among a group of seniors from Lewisville High School who'd raised money to help build a school in a small African village. Rigby had never heard of it so he looked it up too. Kenya. Interesting, but hardly relevant. Still, he clicked on the news article.

A group photo headed the article. Four girls, two boys, all beaming smiles. Youthful and full of optimism. One of the boys had draped his right arm around Gail's shoulders, but it was one of the other girls in the photo who drew his attention—his sister Louise.

Louise knew Gail? Or at least did when they were at school together. He shouldn't be surprised. Lewisville only had one public high school so with the exception of those who'd been sent to private school, any locals of a similar age would have been at school together. What surprised him was that he didn't run into more of his fellow classmates on the job.

Was Louise still in touch with Gail? Or rather had she been in touch? And did she know Gail had died? He would surely have heard from her if she'd heard the news, but Louise refused to get sucked in to online news, even broadcast news. She bought the Sunday New York Times, said it gave her all the news she needed, so she could easily have missed the story.

He called her phone. Got her voicemail. He hung up. It wasn't the kind of news to leave as a message. He looked back at the photos. The guy with his arm around Gail looked vaguely familiar too. He scanned the names in the caption. Whistled his surprise. The Martin Cooper he'd met the previous evening bore little resemblance to the slightly chubby, long-haired eighteen-year-old. What a difference ten years or more could make.

Martin had told him he'd been married for six years. Judging from the photo, the relationship went back a lot further than that. Had Gail been Martin's first love? How much harder would that make it to bear the loss?

There were a couple of other mentions of Gail in the search results but nothing that would help in the investigation. If Gail had a secret life, she'd kept it offline.

He sank back in his chair. Was he on a wild goose chase? Did he really believe that a small-town mom would have a secret life that could get her killed? He drummed his fingers on his desk. He should stick with what he did know. The car owner, Dale Jessup—he was the key. Find him and hopefully they'd have all the answers they needed.

His desk phone rang. He sighed. What now? He groaned as Davis explained. Another near-fatal drug overdose, the second in two months.

He glanced at his watch. So much for going home early.

Chapter 21

It was midday before he made it back to the Coopers' home. His ribs ached from a night on the sofa. If you could call four hours a night. Unfortunately, Becca and Lotte were both awake when he'd arrived home shortly after two. And his excuse of having to deal with a youngster's overdose at Lewisville Youth Center's Christmas Party did little to mitigate Becca's anger, frustration and tiredness. She spewed it all out, barely giving him a chance to get a word in, and then retreated to the bedroom with Lotte and slammed the door. It was so out of character he decided it was best to give her some space. Especially when he wasn't in the greatest of moods himself. Hence the sofa.

He tried to make it up to her in the morning by being conciliatory. She even offered her own apology. Explained that she found it hard being alone all day with the baby. Her emphasis on "all day" made him feel even more guilty. He was going to have to try harder to avoid being the absentee dad who put work before family and he was determined to start that day by not going in until three, no matter how much he'd like to start earlier.

But luck was on his side. Becca had a lunch appointment with the girls from her childbirth class. He offered to look after Lotte so she could enjoy her lunch in peace but apparently Lotte and all the other babies were the point of the event to start with. The thought of several squalling babies in one room didn't sound much fun but then what did he know?

What it did do was give him an unexpected two-hour

window to visit Martin Cooper. And Becca would be none the wiser.

Martin Cooper looked as if he hadn't slept since Rigby last saw him. Or showered. Or shaved. He stared blankly at Rigby until Rigby asked if he could come in, and then stepped silently aside to let him do so.

The sound of childish chatter came from the kitchen. A female voice encouraged someone to eat their avocado rather than throw it on the floor. The despondent sigh that followed suggested the advice had been ignored.

Martin motioned for Rigby to go into the same room as on his last visit. A cartoon played out soundlessly on the TV. An elderly man dozed in a chair by the unlit fire and a white-haired lady knelt on the floor picking up scattered building blocks in a desultory manner and tossing them into a colorful bucket.

Martin's parents, he presumed.

The woman stopped her task as Rigby entered. Eased herself up from her knees with a grimace. "Easy getting down," she said. "Not so easy getting back up." She gave him a smile which belied both her physical and emotional pain. She held out her hand. "Detective Rigby, right?"

She smiled again at his surprise. "As soon as Martin mentioned your name, I recognized it. You're the one who was involved in that awful hostage situation while your wife was giving birth."

Rigby didn't bother correcting her. Wife, partner, it didn't matter. The thrust of the story was true. He shook her hand. "I'm sorry for your loss."

"Yes, well…" She sighed. Looked at her son then her still sleeping husband. "I'm not sure it's sunk in yet."

A loud clatter followed by "I want my mommy!" drowned out Rigby's attempt to empathize.

"Oh, dear." Mrs. Cooper glanced toward the door. "I'd better go and see if I can help. It's so difficult. How to explain?" She hesitated. "I'm not sure you can. Only time will heal."

"Thanks, Mom," Martin said through gritted teeth. As his mother left the room he added, "I don't want time to heal. I want her back." His face creased with grief. "The kids need her. I can't do this on my own."

Rigby struggled to respond. "You will. You have to. You have no choice." Damn, listen to him, trotting out platitudes. What? He was a psychologist now? It sounded like something Nancy Tuccino might have said to him when he was dealing with his girlfriend Katy's death. Though then there weren't kids to consider. He glanced at Martin's tear-filled eyes. And no true love either as it turned out, at least not on Katy's part.

"I'm sorry. I didn't mean to be blunt." He took Martin's slight shrug as acceptance of his apology.

"Do you have some news? Is that why you're here?"

"We're making some progress, but I'm afraid at this point I can't go into details."

Martin looked nonplussed. "But it's my wife you're talking about."

"I know. And I know you're eager for answers."

"So why are you here? If you can't tell me anything?"

"I was hoping you could tell me a little more about Gail. What was she like? What did she like to do?"

Martin's eyes narrowed, his lips curling up to a furious scowl. "What has that to do with her death?"

"Nothing." Rigby hesitated. Pearson's warning came to mind. Damn, he couldn't tell Martin why he wanted to know, but if he didn't he was unlikely to get any answers.

"Martin, is there any—" A mousy-haired young woman appeared in the doorway. "Oh, sorry." She smiled at Rigby. "Hi."

"Izzy, this is Detective Rigby. He's here about... He's the one leading the..." Martin turned his head away. Put a hand over his mouth.

Izzy rushed to embrace him. "Hey. It's okay," she said. "It's okay."

The guy had just lost his wife. It was hardly okay. But what were the right words in a situation like this? And Izzy's seemed to offer some solace to Martin as he wept quietly into her shoulder.

Rigby glanced around the room, not wanting to intrude on such a personal moment. Damn, he should never have come. Maybe he should leave. But even if Martin was in no state to talk, this was a chance to hear what Izzy had to say.

He noticed a photo propped on the mantelpiece that he was sure hadn't been there the first evening. Martin had one arm around Gail, the other around a little girl. A sleeping baby, not much more than a newborn, lay in Gail's arms and the three of them were looking down at it with huge smiles.

It was hard to look at and it wasn't even his family. He didn't know how Martin could bear to see it so prominently displayed. He hadn't been able to look at photos of Katy for months after her death. But maybe that was the difference between love and betrayal.

He cleared his throat.

Martin pulled out of the embrace. Ran his hands over his face and blinked rapidly before giving Rigby an embarrassed glance. "Sorry."

"Nothing to be sorry about."

"You okay?" Izzy reached out to wipe a rogue tear from Martin's face.

He batted her hand away.

Rigby saw the hurt in Izzy's eyes. She'd only wanted to help. He also saw a way to get out of the awkward situation. "Actually, Izzy, I was hoping to speak to you."

Izzy froze like a rabbit in headlights. "How can I help?"

"I spoke to your parents, yesterday. And Hannah. They told me you were here, helping Martin."

"Oh, right." Her expression relaxed into a smile. "I knew he'd need some help with the little ones." She bit her bottom lip. "And it's the least I could do for my sister."

"You were close."

"Absolutely." She broke off. Seemed to consider her next words. "Until she got married we used to do everything together. And even then I still used to see her once or twice a week. We used to have a family dinner together every Sunday night." She glanced at Martin for confirmation.

Martin's nod suggested it was something he'd tolerated rather than encouraged.

"The whole family? Your parents too?" Dinner every week with his family? Rigby couldn't think of anything worse. And he loved his family.

"No! Just the three of us." She laughed. "Though sometimes there were four when Gail tried to set me up with one of her or Martin's friends."

"You're not married?"

Izzy pouted. "Unlike Gail, I never managed to snag Mr. Right. Yet."

"And Hannah."

"What?"

"Hannah, she's married too."

"Yeah, but—" Izzy grimaced. "I think she only married him because he asked. She had three long-term boyfriends before John. None of them came to anything despite her expectations. I'd say more Mr. Available than Mr. Right."

Rigby stared nonplussed. Too much information. True, his fault for mentioning Hannah, but if Izzy was prepared to reveal her opinions on one sister to a relative stranger, what might she say about the other?

With a side glance at Martin, he asked, "Is there somewhere we could talk in private?"

Another high-pitched shriek emanated from the kitchen. Izzy turned to leave. Martin made it to the door first. "I'll deal with it," he said, a hint of relief in his voice. "You stay and talk to the detective."

Rigby glanced at the old man. He was still sleeping. Or was he pretending and listening to every word?

"Don't worry about him." Izzy settled down on the sofa. "He hasn't got his hearing aids in. Won't wear them. Says the kids are too noisy. Most of the time, we have to communicate by mime." She rolled her eyes.

Izzy struck him as the kind of person who found fault with everyone. Maybe that was why she was still unmarried. It wasn't a Mr. Right she was looking for, but a Mr. Perfect. Though she had to know the latter didn't exist. Still, he wasn't there to discuss her foibles. It was Gail he was interested in.

"Did Gail get along with Martin's parents?" He knew the answer but hoped it might spark some unexpected revelation.

"Gail got along with everyone."

Damn, was that all he was going to get? He kept quiet, hoping his silence would encourage Izzy to keep talking.

"Everyone loved Gail."

He resisted the temptation to roll his eyes. It was like a broken record. Did everyone love Gail only because she was dead? Was it a "don't talk ill of the dead" attitude? If he'd been asking these questions while she was alive would he have got far different answers? If his suspicions were right, there was at least one person out there who didn't love Gail. Not by any stretch of the imagination. Someone who wanted her dead. And where there was one, there were most likely others.

"She sounds like a saint," he said, trying to provoke a reaction.

Izzy scraped at the red polish on one of her fingernails, a wistful look spreading across her face.

"Nobody's a saint, Detective. You of all people should know that." She stared at him until she had his full attention. "But some people are luckier in life than others. Gail was one of them. Life turned out exactly as she wanted. Always did. She was pretty. She was bright. And she was popular. She never had to worry about what people thought of her or about being bullied. She married her high school sweetheart, had two beautiful kids, her own home." She hesitated, chewed on her bottom lip. "It's easy to be nice when you've got everything you want."

Rigby couldn't agree. He knew real bastards who had everything they could possibly want. And people who scraped by from day to day, often dealing with unimaginable tragedy, who put the first group to shame. Being nice had nothing to do with what life gave you and everything to do with the kind of person you were inside.

And how could Izzy possibly talk about her own sister being lucky when her life had been cut short at such a young age?

Chapter 22

Rigby didn't know what to make of Izzy. She claimed to have been close to her sister but unlike her parents and Hannah she showed no visible signs of being overly upset at Gail's demise. Though maybe that was because reality hadn't fully sunk in yet. And it had allowed her to soften the practical blow for Martin by taking over all the immediate household matters including child care.

As soon as she heard the news from her parents, she'd rushed over to Martin's house even though it was the middle of the night. She chided Rigby for leaving Martin alone after breaking the news of the accident. Said he should have ignored Martin's claims that he would be okay, should have known Martin was in too much distress to know what was best. She almost made Rigby feel guilty, but Martin was a victim not a criminal. They couldn't force him to do anything.

She'd found Martin in a frozen stupor, deaf to the sound of the baby's cries. She could only imagine how long Susie might have been left to cry if she'd waited until morning to turn up. But she knew how devastated Martin would be. How helpless without Gail to run the home. How much he would need support.

She gestured with her hands. What else was she supposed to do? She had to help. She'd met his parents before, knew they'd be no use. And Hannah had her own family to consider. And her parents, well..." She shook her head.

Rigby was tempted to remind her that her parents had lost a daughter, had their own grief to deal with, but Izzy rattled on with barely a pause.

Grief made people react in the most peculiar of ways.

"Besides, I'm Susie's godmother." A broad grin lit up Izzy's face. "It's my duty to help in these circumstances."

True, but there was no need to be so cavalier about it.

He glanced at his watch. He'd have to leave soon to get back before Becca. It had been a waste of time really. He hadn't learned anything new. All it had done was reinforce his view that there was no such thing as the perfect family. They might look normal from the outside but look closer and there'd always be some dysfunction. And secrets the family wanted to keep but that during investigations he needed to know.

He stood up to signal he'd heard enough. Izzy stood too, still talking. Something about how she'd called work and told them she needed time off and she didn't know how long. And if they didn't like it they could fire her. Family before work. That's what mattered.

A nice sentiment. Except for the little matter of having a roof over your family's head and food on the table.

Rigby stuck his head into the kitchen to tell Martin he was leaving. The avocado war appeared to be over and it was clear who the victor was. Mrs. Cooper wiped spots of avocado off the floor. Suzie sat in a high chair, her chubby cheeks smeared with green mush, as she banged on the tray with her sticky hands, defying Martin's attempts to clean her up. The older girl giggled as if it were all for her amusement.

As Rigby got into his car, he added avocado to the list of food to be banned from his kitchen for the next few years.

Chapter 23

Harper was still at her desk when Rigby arrived for his shift. He told her about the interview with Izzy, curious to get her opinion. She shrugged and said maybe it was Izzy's way of dealing with grief, keeping so busy she didn't have time to think about it. Maybe if he'd seen her when she first heard the news, he'd have seen a very different reaction.

Then he told her about his theory that the driver had been waiting for Gail. He waited for her to tell him he was crazy. He actually wanted her to tell him he was crazy. Instead he saw by her expression that she was giving it full consideration.

"But why?" she said eventually.

"You tell me." Rigby sighed. Leaned against his desk. "All I've heard is how wonderful Gail was. Loved by all. She even helped build a school in Kenya while she was a senior in high school."

"Maybe that's your connection. Maybe she got involved with something she shouldn't have while she was there."

"What?" Rigby rolled his eyes and shook his head. "No, she wasn't in Kenya. She just helped raise the money."

Harper glared at him. "Don't look at me like that. You said build. Sometimes volunteers go out and help actually build those schools or wells or whatever."

"I don't think this involved getting her hands dirty."

"Are you sure?"

Rigby hesitated. Was he? Or had he just assumed it had only been the fundraising. Then he remembered. "Louise. She was in the photo too. No way did she go to Africa." He smiled. As big-hearted as his sister was, she drew the line at physical labor.

Harper frowned. "Who's Louise?"

"My sister. She was in the photo with Gail and her husband—"

"Gail was married while she was still in school?"

"No!" Rigby rolled his eyes again. Saw the glimmer in Harper's eyes. She was being deliberately pedantic. He took a deep breath and told her about the article from the beginning.

"I'd remember if Louise went to Africa." He hesitated. "No one in my family has been outside the States."

"Doesn't mean Gail didn't go."

"Her family didn't say anything about her going to Africa."

"Why would they if it was such a long time ago? Did they mention the fundraising?"

Harper had a point. He hadn't seen the article about the fundraising until after he'd spoken to Gail's parents. To them it was probably just one of many activities Gail had been involved in at school. They would never consider that something so many years ago could have such tragic results now. Too bad he hadn't mentioned it to Izzy. He might have if she'd let him get a word in edgewise. Or Martin.

"Martin," they both said at the same time. Rigby nodded at Harper to speak first.

"You said he was in the photo. Maybe he's the one with the secret background, involved in something nefarious. Pissed the wrong people off and this was a final warning to him to toe the line." Harper wrinkled her nose. "Or maybe I read too many thrillers?"

It did sound like the plot of a movie. And especially far-fetched for a place like Lewisville. But Harper had voiced exactly where his thoughts were leading. And they, rather, he had barely touched on Martin's history except as it related to his marriage. Could Martin's grief be two-fold? Had he lost the love of his life but also been indirectly responsible for her death? Leaving his kids motherless and possibly in danger if he told the police the truth?

He sighed. It had to be far-fetched. But whether it was or not, he was going to have to look more closely at Martin Cooper.

Harper stood up and grabbed her bag. "Wish me luck. I'm off to look at a rental, a studio apartment above a garage. Not ideally what I'm after but it would be better than the B & B."

Rigby smiled. He was glad all that business was behind him. "Hope it works out for you." He straightened up. "Wish me luck. I have to go and update the chief."

Chapter 24

Pearson listened to Rigby's update without comment. It was a welcome break from the matter that had been upmost on his mind until Rigby arrived. A matter of both great pride and a cause for despair.

His youngest daughter Emily had called almost beside herself with excitement. She'd received a letter of early acceptance from her dream college. Even her counselor had thought it was a reach given her grades, but they'd let her apply anyway. For the price of an application fee, better to let the college crush her dreams rather than her parents or teachers. But somehow she'd beaten the odds. And she'd even got a scholarship.

A very small scholarship compared to the cost. The college was out of state and way more expensive than any of the other colleges she'd applied to even before extras like travel costs had been factored in. And the travel costs were not inconsequential. He assumed Emily would want to come home from California for the vacations.

He and Molly had put money aside to help with the girls' college fees but with three daughters the pot wasn't huge. They were sharing it equally between the girls but luckily both Sarah and Annie had chosen in-state colleges and while they still had needed to take out loans, they were nothing compared to what Emily would need. He hated to think of his daughter being saddled with such debt and, in his eyes, so unnecessarily. If she'd been accepted into a university in California, he was sure she'd have acceptances from New York.

He was going to have to have a serious conversation with her and he was dreading the prospect. Interrogating a criminal was child's play compared to shattering his daughter's dreams. Would she hate him forever?

He realized Rigby had stopped talking and was waiting to hear his views. All his daughters had been involved in fundraising activities for causes both locally and abroad. None of it had required them to leave the country. He doubted Kenya had anything to do with Gail Cooper being a victim in a hit-and-run. But as usual, Rigby was leaving no stone unturned. If they never found the driver, nobody could say they hadn't tried.

"No word back from Florida yet?"

Rigby shook his head.

"Want me to make a call? Pull some strings?"

Rigby grinned. "What strings are they?"

"Hey, who do you think you're talking to?" He tried to look insulted but found himself grinning too. Rigby was right. He had no strings. He was a small-town police chief. They were a big city department. Rigby's request probably lay at the bottom of a huge pile of similar requests. He couldn't blame them. They had to prioritize their workload. A small-town hit-and-run was not going to be a priority, regardless of whether it was a detective or chief of police asking.

"Have you looked up the guy on social media?" He could tell by Rigby's expression that he hadn't.

"Not sure what good that would do. We need to interview Jessup about where he was on the night of the accident, not review his background."

"But there might be something to give us a clue as to whether he does live in Florida. You said the officer down there warned you the Florida address might turn out to be a dead end. The guy was young, right? Maybe that was his home address and he's at college somewhere or vice-versa."

"He's twenty-six. He should be out of college by now."

"Grad school? Or moved away for a job? Hasn't got around to changing his address?"

Rigby groaned. "That's what Harper suggested."

Pearson flashed a smile. "Great minds think alike."

Rigby rolled his eyes.

"Worth a look, don't you think? In case Orlando takes a long time to get back to us. Assuming they ever do. Think of the time wasted if the address is a dead end."

Rigby stood up, looking less than enthusiastic. "Knowing my luck there'll probably be hundreds of Dale Jessups on social media."

"You've got his age, you know he presumably lived in Florida at some point, you've even got his photo from the driver's license. You should be able to narrow it down."

"Assuming this particular Jessup is even on social media."

"At twenty-six? I thought everyone was on social media in their twenties."

Rigby sighed.

Pearson decided to shut up. Rigby already knew his opinions on social media. No need to display the full extent of his ignorance.

He waited for Rigby to leave. It was almost time to go home. Go home and face his daughter. Ruin her life, as she would no doubt say. How long before she would speak to him again? Little Emily. The baby of the family. But always so feisty. So determined to be different from her sisters. Was that why she wanted to go so far away to college?

"You okay?" Rigby asked.

"Yes. Fine." Pearson gestured at the papers on his desk. "Just. Busy."

"Aren't we all?" Rigby said, obviously not convinced by his answer. "You seem unusually distracted."

Pearson was about to brush Rigby off but hesitated. He'd spent countless hours trying to give Rigby advice, most of which Rigby had ignored but some of which had stuck. He usually stayed clear of discussing any of his personal issues with him. He was after all the boss. But Rigby knew what was going on in the girls' lives and, being younger, might be able to come up with some silver lining to soften the blow for Emily. He told him about the acceptance letter.

A huge smile lit up Rigby's face. "Congratulations! You must be so pleased."

Pearson told him why he wasn't.

A wary grimace replaced the smile. "You're going to tell her she can't go?"

"What choice do I have? There's no way we could afford it."

"It would sure put the retirement plans on hold."

"What?" Pearson frowned. "What retirement plans?"

"You mentioned a couple of times since your accident... that maybe it was time to retire."

Pearson struggled to keep a straight face. "No doubt I did. And no doubt out of frustration. Possibly due to the antics of a certain individual." He stared Rigby in the eyes.

Rigby held the stare, his mouth forming unspoken words. Eventually he gave up, switching his gaze to out of the window.

"Rigby, I'm not even fifty yet. I've got three daughters, soon all to be in college. Not to mention several years left on the mortgage. Besides, why would I retire? I love my job." He paused, waited for Rigby to look back. "Most of the time."

He saw a hint of a smile in Rigby's eyes.

Interesting. Rigby had taken his threats of resigning seriously. And the smile suggested he hadn't been too happy at the idea. Not surprising given Rigby would be hard pushed to find another boss willing to put up with him. There'd been many times when he'd doubted the wisdom of trying to keep the guy in the department. But now Rigby was settled. He had a steadying influence in Becca, a house of his own, and now a baby. At least on the work front things should be looking up.

"What about student loans?" Rigby asked.

He sighed. "I don't want her saddled with huge debt. What if she meets someone at college? Gets married, wants to have kids? And she's got this huge debt to pay off."

"That's a decision for her to make."

"Is it?" Pearson scoffed. "You reckon an eighteen-year-old can make that kind of decision? And she's not even eighteen yet, not until the fall."

"She's going to hate you for it."

"Thanks. That really helps."

"Unless you can explain the situation in a way that makes it her decision."

"How the hell do I do that?"

Rigby shrugged. "Lay it all out on paper for her. Show her what it's going to cost her compared to if she goes elsewhere. Tell her what you're prepared to help with so she knows exactly what's up to her. It might scare her off the idea."

Pearson sighed. "But I hate to disappoint her. Sarah and Annie went to their first-choice colleges." Pearson bounced his pen on the desk. "We should never have let her apply. Should have told her then it was out of the question financially. Then we wouldn't have had this problem."

"Too late to think that now."

"Yeah." Pearson sighed again. "Hindsight's a fine thing. As it is we'd already decided to rent out our apartment again. Can't say I'm thrilled with the idea, not after last time, but at least this time we can do it at the full market rate."

"Good luck with that."

Pearson smiled. Rigby had been the last tenant. And it hadn't ended well. But the rent had bolstered the college fund which was why they were considering doing it again. "Molly says she's already got someone going to look at it today. We only put the advertisement up this morning."

For some reason Rigby seemed to find his comment amusing.

"What?"

Rigby shrugged. "Nothing." He strolled nonchalantly out of the office.

Pearson frowned. Nothing?

No, definitely something. He sighed. No doubt he'd find out what soon enough.

Chapter 25

Pearson was right. Dale Jessup was a graduate student at the University of Florida. His name appeared several times in Rigby's search results as the author of papers, the titles of which meant little to him, and in references to various conferences. It was definitely the right guy. The photo attached to his profile was almost identical to his driver's license.

By the time Rigby finished the search, he knew Dale had also been on the university soccer team as an undergrad, actively involved in at least two environmental organizations, and a keen skier. What he didn't know was where the hell the guy was.

He sat back in his chair and drummed his fingers on the desk. The guy had a bright future ahead by all accounts. Was that why he hadn't stopped after the accident? Had he seen his future disintegrate in an instant? Seen a possible prison sentence because he was drunk or on drugs or somehow negligent? Had he made the split-second decision to stamp on the gas and flee rather than hit the brake and face up to what he'd done?

Moments. That's all it took to change lives, usually for the worse.

But no, this couldn't have been a momentary decision. Not if they believed Dale had been waiting for Gail to go by. In which case there had to be a link between the two. Otherwise why would Dale be sitting outside the Henderson house for so long?

He slumped forward, elbows on his desk and raked his fingers through his hair. He was going around in circles. The internet wasn't going to give him any answers. He needed to find Dale Jessup, bring him in for questioning.

Pearson stuck his head into the office, said he was leaving for the day. Rigby gave him a quick rundown of what he'd learned.

"He has to have some connection to Lewisville. It's not the kind of place you just happen to find yourself in. And if it really was deliberate—" Pearson's tone said he doubted it—"then he'd have to know Gail from somewhere. And by the sound of it, she hasn't been outside the state."

"They could have connected online. Maybe they're both part of some—" Rigby exhaled hard. Damn, he really was grabbing at straws. He'd already checked Gail's online presence and found little to work with.

"Some what? Some international crime ring? What? Drugs? Human trafficking? I think you're over thinking this. If it was an online connection isn't it more likely a romantic one? We all know how easily they can go wrong."

"If Gail is online, it's under a false name. And if it was for romantic reasons as you put it, her husband's hardly likely to know about it, is he? So that's another dead end."

"So you're left with Jessup. Find him, Rigby. You have to find him."

Luckily, Pearson disappeared from view before Rigby could reply.

Chapter 26

Find him. Easy enough for Pearson to say. What did the chief think he'd been doing? And they had found him. They had an address but without being able to go and knock on the damn door himself it was all but useless.

He slumped back in his chair. Stared at the photos on the whiteboard. Gail and Dale, was there a connection? What about the car? Was there anything about the car they were missing? The alert to the body shops requesting to be notified if any light-colored sedans were brought in with damage to the front of the vehicle had produced only one response. They hadn't had to check it out—it was already in their records. Patrol had responded to the accident. The car in question had slid into the rear of another vehicle waiting at a red light. No, the car they were looking for was either locked out of sight by now or across state lines. The only way they were going to find the car was to find Dale Jessup.

Coffee. He needed coffee. The pot was empty. Typical. No consideration for the guy on the evening shift. He looked at his watch. What the hell. It was near enough to dinner time. He put another pot on to brew—he had a feeling he'd need it later—then he bundled up and told Davis he was taking an early dinner.

The diner was busy but he found an empty seat at the counter. The waitress gave him a warm smile and took his order immediately. It was one of the perks of being a cop. The diner was across the road from the station house and the staff knew the cops often didn't have long to linger. The coffee was hot and plentiful, his cup refilled without him having to ask as he devoured a burger and fries and then a piece of peach pie. The latter was a delaying tactic. The thought of the empty office and continuing the pointless search provided little impetus to get back to the job.

As he signaled for the check, his phone rang. The desk duty sergeant's number showed on his screen. He answered it with a curt, "I'm on my way back now," and hung up before Davis could speak. He left cash on the counter, hoped it was enough to cover his bill, grabbed his coat and left. Whatever it was Davis thought important enough to call, he didn't want to have the conversation in a crowded diner.

Davis gave him a strange look as he skidded to a halt in front of the reception desk. "What's the emergency? I just wanted to let you know an officer from Orlando was trying to contact you. Collins told me you were waiting on them."

"You have his number?" Rigby asked impatiently. At last. Now maybe he'd be able to move forward on the case.

"Of course." Davis scowled as he handed him a piece of paper. "Don't need to be told how to do my job."

"Wouldn't dream of it." Rigby waved the paper. "Thanks."

"Not good news," Officer Dudley said when Rigby finally got through to him. "Dale Jessup shares the address with two other students. They said he hadn't been there since the beginning of the month. Apparently he's spending a semester traveling around the country doing research. All they know is that he was spending Christmas with his folks in North Carolina, then after that, no clue where he was headed."

"I don't suppose you got an address for the parents?"

"No. Nor a phone number or email address." Officer Dudley sighed. "I guess kids nowadays think if anything happens to them their emergency contacts are on their phone. But without their phones, what are we supposed to do?"

"What about his phone number? Did you get that?"

Officer Dudley reeled it off. Gave him an email address too.

At least it was something to work with. Especially if they could track the phone. It could lead them straight to Jessup.

"I also contacted the university," the officer continued. "They usually require the students to provide emergency contact details. But the parents' address is listed as Bedford, New York, and the number is a New York number. His roommates said he was from New York so I guess he never got around to changing the record after his parents moved. Two or three years back, they thought it was."

Rigby took those details down too. At this point he'd take whatever he could get. And if it came to it, he'd drive to Bedford and knock on doors until he found someone who knew the forwarding address or number of the parents. If Dale had grown up in Bedford his parents must still have friends there. Dale might even have old school friends there that he was still in touch with.

"Sorry I couldn't be of more help," Officer Dudley said.

Dudley had done a lot more than Rigby could hope for given it wasn't his department's case. Many officers would have given up after hearing Dale had gone out of town.

Rigby stared at the information he'd written down. How to proceed? Up until now, Dale Jessup had no idea the police were onto him. He might well believe he'd got away with his crime. An attempt to contact him by phone or email would alert him that the police were looking for him. Give him time to either flee or create a cover story. But there was always the possibility one of Dale's roommates had already told him of Dudley's visit and while the roommate wouldn't know why the police wanted to speak to him—Dudley hadn't disclosed the reason—Dale would know immediately.

The question would be whether Dale was savvy enough to know the police could trace him through his phone and either turn off the tracking or ditch the phone altogether. He could only hope if Dale watched TV his viewing leaned more toward nature documentaries than crime shows.

Rigby called Turner, talking him through what he'd learned. As the department's technology expert Turner would handle the tracking element of the investigation, but first they'd need a search warrant for the phone and that was Rigby's immediate task.

Chapter 27

The next morning Rigby paced between the desks as Turner worked his magic, praying that this one lead wouldn't turn out to be a dud. It couldn't be. He'd promised Becca they were close to an arrest, that he couldn't wait until his official shift but the case would be over soon and he'd be back to regular shifts and around more to help out.

Becca hadn't actually agreed, but neither had she said no. She'd merely picked up Lotte, went back into the bedroom and closed the door. Though it was more of a slam.

He wondered if Turner was having similar family issues as the guy sat stony-faced in front of his monitor, tapping furiously at the keyboard. At least Turner was officially on duty so that couldn't be his problem.

"Sit down." Turner's yell stopped him in his tracks. He was about to protest but thought better of it.

He sat down. Checked his phone for offers of forgiveness. Zilch. He rummaged through his paperwork looking for something to distract himself with. Nothing appealed. This one case, that's what mattered. Maybe it was because it involved a young mother, or because of the little kids now motherless so close to Christmas. Or maybe it was because it was the first case since he'd stared death in the face that he just wanted, needed to get answers for the Cooper family. Justice.

Becca could understand that. Should understand it. Would. Surely?

He stood up. "Coffee anyone?" His offer was met by silence.

Not even a grunt from Gaines. He tipped out the remains of his first cup of the day and poured a fresh one then scanned the bulletin board for any new notices. He smiled as his eyes came to rest on the photo of Lotte attached to her birth announcement.

His daughter! He was a father! This time last year he would have laughed if someone had predicted this in his future.

"You're going to be a happy man, Rigby," Turner said.

Rigby rushed over and peered over Turner's shoulder. Dale Jessup wasn't halfway across the country, not according to his phone. He was two miles from the station house, a mile from the accident site.

Rigby punched a fist in the air as Pearson walked into the office. "Got him."

Pearson looked at the screen and then glanced at his watch. "I say, let's go and get him."

Rigby hesitated. Thought he'd misheard. "You want to come?"

"Why not? Been a while since I took an active part in an investigation. Can't have my skills getting rusty." He smiled at Rigby. "It saves pulling someone off patrol. Keeps Collins happy."

Rigby frowned. Since when did Pearson have to worry about keeping Collins happy? Pearson asked, Collins jumped willingly. Unlike if Rigby asked. Then it was as if Collins was doing him a huge favor.

So what was Pearson up to? Was he afraid that without his calming influence they'd have a repeat of the last time Rigby had gone to arrest someone in a private home? No way. He'd learned his lesson. And his still sore ribs were a constant reminder of the consequences of a hasty decision.

"Lucky you," Turner said as the chief went to get his coat. "Looks like you're back in his good books if he wants to partner with you again."

Rigby scowled. He doubted it. But what could he do? He loaded the address onto his phone, pulled on his coat and headed out the door.

Pearson was already in his car when Rigby got to the lot so there was no discussion over who would drive. Pearson had always been a more cautious driver than Rigby but since his accident he'd become even more so. Although it was a bright sunny day and the roads were clear of snow, the journey took twice as long as it should.

Their destination was a ranch-style house with a two-car garage, in need of a paint job. To Rigby's disappointment there was no light-colored sedan in the driveway, only several inches of hard-packed snow. The path to the front door was an icy slope showing no signs that anyone had been in or out in the last few days.

Had Dale holed up here since the accident? Or was the house merely empty? And were they going to break their necks trying to reach the front door? A fall right now was all he needed. Why did the house have to be set so far back off the road?

They made it to the front door, out of breath but unscathed. "Should be easier going back," Pearson said between pants.

"I hope the effort was worth it." Rigby rubbed his ribs, stopping abruptly as Pearson gave him a concerned look.

He rang the bell, keeping his finger on it longer than necessary. The door was flung open by a furious-looking white-haired young man.

"What the hell?" he said in a whispered yell. "Did you have to make such a racket? Grandpa's on his deathbed—" He broke off at the realization he had no idea who the two men on his doorstep were.

"Dale Jessup?" Rigby asked. It was either him or his twin.

Dale nodded. "Who are you?"

Rigby held up his badge. "Detective Rigby." He gestured at Pearson. "This is Chief Pearson."

Dale looked momentarily dumbstruck and then fear filled his eyes. "What do you want? Has something happened?"

"May we come in?" Pearson stepped forward to let Dale know it wasn't really a question.

Dale ushered them inside and into a large eat-in-kitchen. He didn't offer them a seat, merely stopped as soon as they were in the room and asked again, "What's happened?"

Rigby watched Dale's expression as Pearson confirmed that Dale was the owner of the car they were looking for. All he saw was confusion.

"Why are you interested in my car?" Dale asked.

"Where were you on Tuesday evening?" Pearson said.

"Tuesday? What?" Dale shook his head nervously. "I... I was here. I... I've been here since Saturday." Another head shake. "What do you want to know about my car for?"

Pearson ignored the second question. "By here, you mean Lewisville?"

"Yes. In Lewisville! Will you please tell me what's going on? I've got a dying grandfather in the other room. I'm expecting my parents to arrive later today. Can you just get to the point?"

Damn, if Dale was telling the truth he was having one bad day. But it was about to get worse.

"So where were you between nine and eleven on Tuesday night?"

"I told you. I was here. I've been here since Saturday. Barely left the house, except to do some grocery shopping."

"Is there anyone else here?"

"Only Grandpa."

Rigby grimaced. A dying grandpa made for a dubious alibi. That time of night, the old man was probably asleep, wouldn't know if Dale slipped out for an hour or two. "Where's your car?"

"Where do you think?" Dale sounded exasperated. "In the garage."

Rigby thought of the snowed-in driveway. But it had only started snowing heavily late on Tuesday. Time enough for Dale to get his car out and back again and for the snow to cover his tracks. "Where was it on Tuesday night?"

Dale glanced at Pearson as if to ask if Rigby was an idiot? "Just answer the question," Pearson said.

"In the garage! Where else would it be?"

If it was an act, it was a good one.

Pearson gestured at the table. "Mind if we sit?" He sat without waiting for an answer. Rigby followed his lead and eventually Dale did too, taking a seat on the opposite side of the table.

"You say you were here and your car was in the garage on Tuesday evening?" Rigby took a paper from his jacket pocket, unfolded it and slid it across the table to Dale. "So how do you explain this?"

Dale studied the photo of the car. Puzzled, he glanced up at Rigby.

"It's your registration number, yes?"

Dale looked back down. "When was this taken?"

"Tuesday evening, shortly before ten p.m."

"No. That can't be right. I did not go out on Tuesday night." He broke off. Slapped the table top. "Tuesday morning. I went to the grocery store. Maybe the timing on the camera or whatever picked this up is off. It would have been about ten in the morning. You can check. A nurse comes in each morning so Tuesday, while they were here, I decided I'd better stock up on groceries given the weather forecast."

Rigby glared at him. Did Dale think they were stupid? "It's dark in the photo. That's not ten in the morning."

"Oh, right. Sorry." Dale suddenly looked toward the kitchen door and started to rise from his seat.

"Sit down." Pearson left no room for disagreement and Dale would surely not be stupid enough to try to make a run for it, but Rigby readied himself just in case. Hoped his ribs wouldn't let him down.

"I... I thought I heard my grandpa calling."

"I didn't hear anything." Pearson glanced at Rigby. "Did you?"

"No."

"Please let me go check. He's very sick."

Pearson sighed. He gestured at Rigby. "Go. Keep an eye on him."

Dale laughed nervously. "What do you think I'm going to do?" He paused. "You haven't even told me why you're so interested in my damn car. Why you're here at all."

"We have reason to believe the car in the photo was involved in a hit-and-run on Tuesday night," Pearson said.

Dale's face blanched.

"A fatal hit-and-run," Rigby added.

Dale stared open-mouthed at them. Then he gulped. "A fatal hit-and-run?"

"The woman died in the street. Left to die in the snow." Rigby studied Dale. The horrified expression could be genuine. Maybe Dale had persuaded himself whoever he hit was only injured not dead to ease his conscience. Still a crime, as was leaving the scene, but easier to live with.

Dale gulped again. "You're talking about the woman who was killed? I heard it on the news. On the radio." He gave another nervous laugh. "You can't possibly think I had anything to do with it."

Pearson held up the photo. "Then tell us what your car was doing on Lilac Road on Tuesday night."

"Dale!" They all heard the feeble cry.

Dale shot out of the door, leaving Rigby to scramble after him just in time to see him disappear into a room on the other side of the hallway.

The room was dark save for the glow of a bedside table lamp. Rigby stood in the doorway and watched as Dale tenderly raised his grandfather's head and shoulders and propped a pillow behind him before holding out a cup so the old man could drink through a straw.

Rigby had to look away. He'd seen plenty of horrible sights on the job, had even become hardened to most, but not to the sick and dying. The sight of the old man, frail and almost colorless, terrified him. Presumably once hale and hearty, he'd been reduced by the ravages of illness to this. A shell of his former self, the battle for life all but over and nothing to be done except wait for the release of death, leaving loved ones to watch and grieve. It was a cruel way to die.

"Shouldn't he be in hospital?" he asked as Dale wiped away the drool of water on the old man's chin.

"He wants to die in his own bed. Surrounded by people he loves, not strangers. After all he's done for the family it's the least we can do for him." Dale's words were imbued with so much love Rigby had to blink several times.

"Who's that?" the old man said. "Is it Billy?"

"No, Grandpa. It's just a friend." Dale cast a pleading look at Rigby.

A friend. Hardly. But if that was the way Dale wanted to play it while they were in this room, so be it. Why burden the old guy further?

"I think I'll rest now." The old man sighed as if exhausted. "Be sure to wake me when Billy comes."

Dale silently removed the extra pillow and gently lowered his grandpa's head down, kissing him on the forehead before he straightened up. He stood there for several minutes, only turning away when Rigby cleared his throat.

"Who's Billy?" Rigby asked as they headed back to the kitchen.

"His younger brother."

"They sound close. I hope he gets here before your grandpa passes."

"Billy died sixty years ago. He was only ten. Knocked down in the road when he ran after a ball. Dead on impact apparently. Grandpa never forgave himself. He was the one who kicked the ball. He's talked about Billy a lot in the last few days." Dale hesitated. "You believe in ghosts, Detective?"

Rigby shook his head.

"Me neither. But sometimes he talks as if Billy is there in the room. Has conversations with him." He smiled wistfully and shrugged. "Or at least I hear his side of the conversation and it sure does sound as if he's getting replies."

"It's probably all in his imagination. When you're sick like that, who knows what tricks the mind plays?"

"Yesterday he told me Billy wanted a lemonade. The day before it was chocolate."

"Did you get it?"

"He's dying. I'd do anything to humor him."

"Anything?"

Dale scoffed as he sat back down at the table. "Anything legal. And last I heard fetching lemonade and chocolate for invisible people was not illegal."

"Did Billy drink the lemonade?"

Dale scowled at Rigby. "What do you think, Detective?"

Chapter 28

Pearson asked Dale when he'd last used his car. Dale rolled his eyes. Answered without hesitation. "I told you. I went out for groceries on Tuesday morning. I haven't been out since."

"So the car's been in the garage the whole time?"

"How often do I have to tell you? Yes."

Pearson smiled. "So we can go and have a look at it?"

Dale leaped up again. "Sure. Follow me."

Rigby noted Dale's eagerness. Was this the moment Dale was going to discover his car had been stolen? Conveniently snatched from under his nose before the hit-and-run? It was a popular excuse among those who'd committed crimes. Why they thought it would work was a mystery to Rigby. Yes, stolen cars were often used to commit crimes, but someone only realizing their car had been stolen after the police turned up days later raised red flags galore.

Dale led them down to the garage, flipped on the lights to reveal two cars, a blue SUV and a white sedan. The sedan was the same color, make and model as the one in the screenshot. Complete with the Florida license plate.

Rigby smiled at Pearson. "Looks like we've found our car."

Dale scoffed. "But it can't be. It's been here the whole time. I'm telling you. I haven't left the house since Tuesday morning. I—" Dale's forehead creased in concentration. "No. Wait. I took Grandpa's car on Tuesday. His has four-wheel-drive. And mine was running low on gas." He shook his head. "I haven't used my car since

I arrived. On Saturday."

Rigby only half listened to Dale's excuses. He wandered around the car scanning for signs of damage. There had to have been some. A body didn't bounce off the front of a car without leaving some tell-tale signs. But the car looked immaculate. Too immaculate. The weather had been lousy for days, there should have been some road dirt, slush marks. The car appeared to have been cleaned recently. If that didn't scream cover up, what did?

"Anybody else have access to your garage?" Pearson asked.

Rigby knew what Pearson was thinking. They might have the vehicle but they couldn't prove Dale was the person behind the wheel.

"No. Except for Grandpa, of course. And it's been a while since he last drove a car."

"Let's get Gina over to have a look at the car," Pearson said. "She can decide whether we need to tow it for further examination."

"What? You can't...I mean, I have to..." Dale glanced back and forth between them in disbelief. "This is ridiculous. This is—"

"A woman is dead." Pearson cut him off. "And we have evidence to believe this car was the cause of her death."

"It's not possible." Dale paced back and forth, raking his fingers through his hair. "This can't be happening. First Grandpa. Now this." He looked hopelessly at Pearson. "What am I supposed to do?"

Confess, ideally. Save them all a lot of trouble. But Rigby doubted that would happen. Dale seemed set on sticking to his story, no matter how unbelievable it sounded and, as of yet, they didn't have enough to arrest him.

He called Gina. Told her what they needed.

She said she'd have to drop the kids off at school first, but then would come right over. Rigby wondered what other plans for the morning she might have to cancel. She had the flexibility of only being part-time but never knowing when she might be called out had to be a pain.

Then he called Collins. Asked him to send an officer out, primarily to make sure Dale didn't touch the car again before Gina arrived, but also to make sure Dale didn't run. He wanted to canvas the neighbors, see if one of them had a security camera that might have picked up any comings or goings from the grandfather's house. Failing that, whether any of them might have seen Dale on Tuesday.

Pearson glanced at his watch. "I have to get back. Meeting with the mayor."

Rigby eyed Pearson suspiciously. "Really?"

"Yes. Really," Pearson said in a tone that brooked no argument though his thin smile said he knew exactly what Rigby was thinking.

Rigby gave in. If the chief didn't want to do door-to-door, it was his prerogative. He couldn't blame him. But if it came to a choice between meeting the mayor and knocking on doors, he'd knock on any number of doors.

"We came in your car, remember? How am I supposed to get back?"

Pearson shrugged. "I'm sure you'll think of something."

"I could give you a ride," Dale said. "When the nurse gets here."

Rigby glared at him. "Your car isn't going anywhere, not until we say so."

"I meant in Grandpa's," Dale said sullenly, "Unless you want to examine that one too."

"That won't be necessary, thank you." Pearson pre-empted Rigby's response. "But we would like to speak to your nurse when they arrive."

Dale frowned. "Is that really necessary? People are going to start talking, you asking all these questions."

"It's how we work," Pearson said. "We keep asking questions until we get the answers we need."

"You're not from around here, right?" Rigby said. "Why should you be worried? These people aren't your neighbors." The only thing Dale had to worry about was a neighbor contradicting his story.

"My mom's family has lived here for generations. Some of them still do." He gestured at the house. "This place will be passed on to one of them. It's them I'm concerned about."

"We'll be discreet," Pearson said.

"Yeah. Right."

Dale didn't sound convinced. But he also didn't sound guilty either.

Chapter 29

Pearson took off, leaving Rigby to wait for whoever Collins was sending over. Rigby made small talk as he and Dale sat in the kitchen, trying to learn as much about the guy as he could.

Dale had grown up in Westchester County. He only knew of Lewisville from visits to his grandparents so Rigby couldn't draw any immediate connections between him and Gail. He claimed not to know Gail or her family. His mother might, he told Rigby, given she'd grown up in Lewisville, possibly in school at the same time as Gail's parents.

Dale fidgeted as he spoke. He rolled and unrolled the edge of a napkin on the table then rearranged the condiments before returning to the napkin. Rigby wanted to tell him to stop but doubted it would have much effect. He'd be fidgeting if he were in Dale's place, guilty or innocent. And the odds of Dale being innocent were incredibly slim.

The car in the screenshot was Dale's. The police had to prove Dale was behind the wheel. Dale had to prove someone else could have been driving, presumably without his knowledge otherwise why wouldn't he already have admitted someone had borrowed his car? Unless he didn't dare because he was somehow mixed up in whatever was going on.

A car door slammed. Dale got to his feet. "That's probably my parents."

More likely the replacement officer or Gina, but Rigby merely followed Dale to the front door.

"Damn, son. Couldn't you have at least cleared the path?" A tall, overweight man inched his way toward them, trying to keep the equally plump woman who was clinging to his side upright. "You knew we were coming."

"Not this early." Dale made no attempt to help them. "I was going to do it, but then I had visitors." He turned and glared at Rigby.

Rigby cringed but not at the comment. The woman's legs suddenly shot out from under her, threatening to topple the couple though somehow the man prevented it. The woman laughed but the man looked anything but amused. "Damn, why does anyone want to live in such a godforsaken place?"

Rigby took an instant dislike to the guy. The mother, she seemed okay, though given she'd grown up in Lewisville she should have had more sense than to wear high-heeled boots in such conditions.

The couple finally made it, huffing and puffing, to the doorstep. Dale stepped aside to let them in and then introduced Rigby. Mrs. Jessup smiled. Mr. Jessup didn't.

"You know why we're here, Detective?" Mr. Jessup didn't give Rigby a chance to answer. "My wife's father is dying."

"And I'm sorry to intrude at such a time," Rigby said. "But a young woman is dead and our investigation led here."

"Bullshit. Dale wouldn't hurt a fly." Mr. Jessup said.

"We have evidence it was Dale's car that hit the woman."

Mrs. Jessup gasped.

Her husband sneered. "What evidence?"

Rigby let Dale tell his father—maybe Dale would slip up in the telling. He noticed a look of disgust pass from father to son.

"Dale would never leave the scene of an accident. We've taught him better than that."

"In the heat of the moment sometimes we forget what we've been taught," Rigby countered. There were certainly times when he had.

Mr. Jessup glared at his son. "Did you?"

"No!"

The glare switched to Rigby. "My son doesn't lie, Detective."

How many times had he heard a variation of that from

parents? They always thought they knew their kids better than they actually did. And in this case he detected an animosity between Dale and his father. He'd wager there was a lot that Jessup senior didn't know about his son.

Luckily he was saved from having to respond by the sound of the doorbell. He followed Dale out to the front door, relieved to see both Gina and Brad Shore had arrived at the same time.

"You could have warned me, Rigby." Gina glanced back over her shoulder. "I'd have brought my crampons."

Dale laughed.

"You won't be laughing if someone falls and hurts themselves," Shore said. "And then sues you."

"I think that's the least of my concerns." Dale wandered back toward the kitchen.

Shore looked questioningly at Rigby.

Rigby filled in the details. Told them both what he wanted.

"Have you touched the car?" Gina asked.

Rigby pretended to be insulted. "Of course not."

"Just checking." Gina smiled. "Sometimes in the heat of the moment, it's easy to forget."

Brad Shore laughed. "And things are often heated when Rigby's around."

Rigby glared at him. Told him where to go.

"Boys!" Gina headed for the garage. She pointed at Shore. "You, make sure no one else comes in here."

"Yes, Ma'am." Brad gave a mock salute. Then he smiled at Rigby. "Just realized I haven't said congratulations. You and Becca must be delighted. How's the little one?"

Rigby hesitated. If things had turned out different, Brad would have been his brother-in-law. Would have been an uncle to any babies Rigby and Katy had. Instead, Brad's family had been decimated by Katy's death and yet he never held it against Rigby, unlike his father and brothers. It couldn't be easy for Brad to stand there and wish him well.

He smiled. "She's beautiful. Loud, exhausting, but beautiful."

Chapter 30

Rigby trudged to each of the neighbors' houses hoping to catch them before they left for work. Luckily they had been more conscientious about clearing their driveways and paths so after slipping and sliding down Dale's path it wasn't such a struggle to get to the other front doors.

He called at the houses either side of the grandpa's home and the three directly across. They were the ones he figured were most likely to have seen any comings or goings. To his surprise he found someone home at every house, but only the neighbor directly opposite claimed to have seen any movement. That was the arrival of the nurse, and the neighbor couldn't say for certain whether that was Tuesday or Wednesday. The days tended to roll into each other, the lady said. Her memory wasn't what it used to be.

She'd lived opposite Dale's grandfather, Fred, for over fifty years. Their kids had grown up together. Of course, they were all scattered now and Fred had been lonely since his wife died, as she had been since her husband passed, so they'd often stop for a chat when they saw each other in the street. It was such a shame he was sick. He was a lovely man and his children didn't visit as often as they should, but the grandson, Dale, he was such a nice boy. Came to visit regularly, even though he lived a long way away now. Florida, she thought. Or was it California? Always smiled and said hello in passing. Though with the weather so bad, who wanted to go outdoors? She guessed the nurse had no choice but to come but apart from the snowplow that was probably the only vehicle she'd seen all week. Except for that morning, of course.

She glanced over Rigby's shoulder at the row of cars as she took a breath. She'd thought Fred must have died when she saw the police car turn up but given he was so sick, she couldn't understand why they were involved. Had there been a burglary? Was that why he wanted to know if she'd seen anyone?

As she paused for breath again, Rigby saw his chance to get a word in. He ignored her question, thanked her for her time, and took off before she could depress him further with the loneliness of old age. In his haste he missed the patch of black ice on the road and landed painfully on his butt.

Fortunately the woman had already gone inside and there was no one else around to witness the fall. Gingerly, he eased up onto his feet. He grimaced at the twinge in his right ankle. But it was only a twinge. It could have been worse. Damn weather.

He limped across to Shore's car. He'd planned to go back to the garage, see what Gina had found, if anything, but no way was he going up the icy path again. Not with a limp. But thanks to Pearson, he didn't have any transport.

He leaned back against the patrol car. Took out his phone to call Gina to find out how much longer she was going to be.

A dark green SUV pulled up behind Gina's car.

More family?

A short stocky guy got out. He glanced curiously at Rigby, the patrol car, and then up at the house.

"Has something happened?" He hoisted a messenger bag onto his shoulder and clenched the front of his padded jacket closed over his scrubs.

"You're the nurse?" Rigby straightened up.

"Yeah." The guy's eyes narrowed. "Who are you?"

Rigby introduced himself.

"Has he... has he died?" The guy looked visibly shaken. "Nobody told me. Why... Why are you guys here?"

"No, nothing for you to be concerned about. We're here on a completely different matter."

"I'd better get inside then." The guy turned toward the house.

"No. Wait. I did have some questions for you."

The guy froze, then turned back, obviously reluctant. Rigby studied him. Most people would display some curiosity as to what the other matter could be. This guy didn't seem at all interested. Then again, he was about to tend to a dying man. Maybe that was enough to cope with for one day.

"What's your name?"

"Scott Yates."

Rigby frowned. The name sounded familiar.

"You were here on Tuesday?"

The question seemed to startle Scott. "I come most days."

"And is Dale always here when you come?"

"Yes. At least, he has been since Sunday. I think he arrived Saturday after I left." Scott hesitated. "What's this about?"

"I can't discuss details of our investigation at this point." The less Scott knew, the more honest his answers were likely to be. Or that was Rigby's hope. "So on Tuesday, Dale was here at the house with you."

"Yeah. As I said, been here every day. Barely leaves his grandpa's side. Too bad more people aren't as devoted as he is."

"As far as you know he never goes out?"

Scott shook his head. "Said he won't leave him on his own. Even sleeps on the floor in his room in case he wakes in the night. I got the impression he was looking forward to his folks arriving though. Today, I think. Take some of the pressure off." Scott scuffed at a small snow pile with his right foot. "It must be lonely being in that big house alone with just his grandpa."

Rigby wouldn't have described the house as big but guessed it was all relative to what you were used to.

"Oh wait." Scott stood still. Cocked his head. "Dale did go out for groceries while I was here. Said the fridge was getting bare. Asked if I minded staying until he got back." He scoffed. "I told him to take his time. I didn't have anywhere I needed to be until that afternoon. I figured he could do with the break." He laughed. "He left and came back so quickly I'm surprised he had time to get any groceries."

Rigby nodded. So one part of Dale's story had an alibi. Not

that it proved where he was on Tuesday evening. "Do you know what he was driving?"

Scott frowned. "Is he in some kind of trouble? Because I'm telling you, he wasn't gone long enough to get up to anything."

"No. No, he's not in trouble." Yet.

"I know he was looking for his grandpa's keys. Said he'd rather use the four-wheel-drive." He laughed again. "But also he mentioned he'd spent a fortune having his car cleaned before he drove to Lewisville. I think he didn't want to get it dirty. All the slush you know from the snow on Sunday."

Rigby cursed silently. That could explain why the car was so clean. In which case Gina's efforts would be for nothing. Or maybe it was all part of a well-thought-out plan. All set up so that's exactly what the police would think. Create an unwitting alibi and why should anyone doubt it?

Dale might think he was being clever and had covered every angle, but there was always something overlooked. Often it could be the tiniest, stupidest thing that would crack a case.

And Rigby was determined to find it.

Chapter 31

Gina sounded as frustrated as Rigby felt. She'd found nothing to indicate the car had been in an accident or had recently been repaired. In fact, she said, just the opposite. The car was pristine— as if it had just come out of the showroom.

Rigby wondered how that was possible but Gina laughed his comment off and pointed out that some people did take great care of their cars. She didn't need to be told he wasn't one of them, her tone of voice said as much. Then she got all serious and said she'd have to do a tire tread comparison to prove once and for all if they were looking at the right car.

Assuming Dale hadn't changed his tires since Tuesday.

Pearson rolled his eyes when Rigby tried that theory out on him. "That's a hell of a reach, especially when there's no apparent damage to the car."

"I have no idea how that's possible unless he had help, but it has to be the right car." Rigby paced up and down in front of Pearson's desk. "It's the right make and model and the right license plate. Even the right color. How can it not be the right car?"

"Hold on. We don't even know for sure the car in the photo is the vehicle that hit Gail."

That stopped Rigby in his tracks. He glared at Pearson. What? No. He refused to believe the car was a red herring. And that he'd fallen for it.

"But we do know the car in the photo is the same one as in Dale's garage. And he's denying he took it out on Tuesday night and why would he do that if he was innocent?" Rigby resumed pacing.

"Sit down," Pearson said. "You're making me nervous."

Rigby snorted. As if. But he sat anyway.

"Maybe Dale thought if he admitted he was out that evening, he'd be dragged into the investigation. When you first asked him about it, he didn't know you had the photo."

"But once he knew we had the photo, why wouldn't he admit he'd been out? Why continue to insist he hadn't when the evidence was right there in front of him?"

Pearson shrugged. "Maybe he thought if he changed his story it would make him look guilty. He'd obviously heard about the accident on the news. Must have realized he'd been in the area. He could have been terrified we'd arrest him on the spot. Then what would have happened to his sick grandpa?"

Rugby stared at Pearson, trying to get his mind around the chief's logic.

"But he still kept denying it even after his parents turned up."

Pearson sighed as if it was obvious. "If we arrested him he wouldn't be there when his grandfather died. He'd be sitting in a cell or the interview room. I'm guessing he was very close to the old man. It would make sense he'd want to be there at the end."

Rigby wasn't sure he'd want to watch anyone die. It was bad enough seeing dead people, but to be there at the moment their last breath left their body was something he hoped he never had to face. His job was tough, but nurses, doctors, EMTs—he didn't know how they coped. He'd seen the effect having someone die in the back of her ambulance had had on Becca and yet she was still determined to return to the job after her maternity leave. He'd never try to stop her but he couldn't help hoping she'd change her mind.

"You think after his grandfather dies, he'll admit it?"

"He might." Pearson hesitated. "But barring a full confession we still can't prove it was his car that hit Gail. Or even that he was driving."

"Colin Farmer saw a light-colored sedan speed away."

"But he didn't get the license plate and he didn't see the driver."

"But if Gina can match the tire treads."

"Then we have the car."
Rigby cursed silently.
But they'd still need a confession to close the case.

Chapter 32

Rigby decided to go home for lunch. See if he could make amends with Becca. But she wasn't there. Neither was Cocoa. He stood in the hallway and listened to the silence. He'd forgotten what it was like to come home to an empty house. First Becca had moved in, then Cocoa and now Lotte. And what had been normal had become unusual.

Where had Becca gone? She hadn't said anything about plans to go out and while the weather was better than it had been, it was hardly conducive for going out for a walk or a drive. Not with a baby in tow.

He checked the kitchen for a note, the wall calendar for a forgotten appointment. Nothing. She must have assumed she'd be back before he returned.

He checked his phone. He hadn't missed any messages. Guilt niggled at his conscience. Lotte wasn't even two months old and he was already failing as a father. Not that Lotte would know, but Becca must. Must be wondering what she'd let herself in for.

The thought unnerved him. He hurried into the bedroom. Everything looked as it should, but still he opened Becca's closet door with trepidation. The relief at how normal the contents looked surprised him. Becca wouldn't leave him. Not without telling him first. But deep down the fear was always there. It had happened before, it could happen again.

He debated whether to call her. But why? To let her know he was home in the hope she'd come back? Why should she? Just because he'd deigned to come home for an hour or two? When he should have been there all morning? Wherever she'd gone, they could have gone together. Their first family outing. But no, he'd put work first yet again. And what did he have to show for it? A limp.

His presence had been unnecessary. The investigation would have been just as far forward if he'd let Turner and the chief act on the new information about Dale Jessup's whereabouts. Pearson would have called Gina in and no doubt got Shore to do the door-to-door while he handled Dale, his family and the nurse.

Scott Yates. Why did the name sound familiar? Someone Becca had mentioned? He'd have to remember to ask her.

When they next saw each other.

He wandered back to the kitchen. Stood in front of the open door of the refrigerator and stared at the neatly labeled containers. His mother must have called by earlier. He scowled when he noticed one of the labels read guacamole, though the avocado ban didn't need to go into effect until Lotte was on solids. And really only at the meals where he was present. He'd noticed women seemed to have a much higher tolerance when it came to cleaning up messes, food-based or not, than most men. Certainly more than him. He still flinched at the sight of a dirty diaper. How could something so little make such a mess?

He slammed the door shut. Settled for a peanut butter and jelly sandwich. As he plastered the jelly on the bread he realized this was yet another food easy to smear. And by all accounts a firm favorite with kids. He shuddered. Damn, maybe he really wasn't cut out for fatherhood and all it entailed.

Then he pictured Lotte and smiled. For her, he'd do anything. He just hoped it didn't involve avocado, peanut butter or jelly.

Chapter 33

Becca had still not returned by the time Rigby's official shift started. He left her a note so she'd know he'd been home. Said he hoped she'd enjoyed whatever she'd been doing.

Back at his desk he cursed his stupidity. What if she'd gone for some invasive doctor's appointment or other essential errand? Then got home and found he thought she'd been out having fun—because she was at home and he was at work so she was obviously the one who had it easy. When actually it was the other way around. Much as he loved Lotte he'd go crazy being home twenty-four-seven.

He glanced at Harper, her fingers flying over the keyboard as she updated her case notes. Harper had no one to answer to outside of work as far as he knew. Nobody waiting at home. Didn't really have a home. Which reminded him.

"How did it go last night?" He swung around in his chair to face her. "With the apartment hunt?"

She stopped typing. Beamed at him. "Great. It was much better than I thought it was going to be. Definitely bigger than I expected."

Bigger? It was a stretch to call Pearson's apartment big. What had she been expecting? Though after almost a year in a room in a B & B maybe anything else would seem big.

"The landlady's going to check my references and all going well, I should be good to move in next week."

Rigby was surprised Molly had even asked for references.

"She does realize you're a cop, doesn't she?"

Harper gave him a strange look. "Of course. But why should that be a problem? In fact, she said she liked the idea of having a cop on the premises."

"Really?" Weird. Maybe Molly hadn't been too eager to rent the place out again, worried about who they'd get. "And it wouldn't bother you living there?"

"Why would it bother me?"

Rigby shrugged. It had bothered him. But at the time it had been the best of no other options other than moving back in with his parents. And to start it had been rent-free, which given he'd been suspended without pay at the time was the clincher for the deal. Then he'd got used to living there and didn't give a damn about anything or what anyone thought so he'd stayed. Longer than he should have. "Just, you know." He shrugged again. "Living so close to the chief."

Harper looked baffled. "What makes you think it's close to the chief?"

Molly mustn't have mentioned he'd been the previous tenant. He wondered why not. "Because I used to live there."

Harper burst out in a peal of laughter. He didn't think it was that funny but made no effort to defend himself. Thankfully, there was no one else in the office or they'd all want to be in on the joke.

Harper eventually managed to control herself. "You think I'm talking about Pearson's place?"

It was Rigby's turn to look baffled. "Well, aren't you?"

"God, no. I mean." Harper wiped tears from her eyes. "No offense to the chief, but who'd want their boss as their landlord?" She broke off. Gave him an uneasy look. "I mean it was obviously different for you."

How? Rigby didn't press her. "Pearson said they were looking to rent their place out again, and they had someone looking at it last night. That's why I thought...When you said it was an apartment over a garage."

Harper was still laughing. "No. This one's not far from your place actually. You know the white house on the corner of your road as you head out of town?"

Rigby nodded. He did. It was almost as grand as the one his

cottage had once been the gate house for, though most of the surrounding land had already been sold off for development. But the house had been kept in good condition, as had the four-car garage.

He whistled. "There's a studio above that garage?"

Harper nodded, a smile lightening up her face. "That's how she described it. And I suppose you could say it was one room with a kitchen and bathroom. But the kitchen's eat-in size, and the bathroom's bigger than any bathroom I've ever had, and the main room's got a double-sided shelf unit which effectively divides it into two."

"Sounds expensive."

Harper shook her head. "Not compared to what else I've seen."

"So what's the catch? A property like that, today's market, there has to be a reason it's not listed at full market value." He grinned. "Haunted maybe. Or the scene of a grisly murder?" He hesitated. Shrugged. "Though I can't think of one off the top of my head."

Harper rolled her eyes. "Mrs. Kinder is a sweet lady who, by the way, bakes excellent cookies, but is recently widowed and likes the idea of someone else living on the property with her. She has a large family. I lost count of how many sons and daughters, and the grandkids number way into double digits, but none of them live nearby. Apparently she has some of the kids stay with her during school vacations. She warned me it might get a little noisy then." She shrugged. "But given I'll be working, that's not going to be a problem. Besides, I like kids."

Rigby smiled. "You must be pleased to finally have found somewhere to live."

Harper stood up. "It'll be nice to be able to cook for myself again." She patted her flat stomach. "All the diner food and takeouts, not good for the figure."

Rigby didn't think she had anything to worry about but knew better than to comment. Instead he said, "I wonder how Molly got along last night. When Pearson said they had someone going over there, I put two and two together—"

"And got five." Harper turned off her computer. "Pearson

did ask me if I was interested in the apartment. Back when I first made detective." She grinned at Rigby. "Offered me a really good deal too, but I couldn't imagine living there."

"It's a nice place. It's pink." He wasn't sure why he added that fact. "And Molly used to throw in the occasional home-cooked breakfast."

Though that might have been because she was afraid he'd starve to death if she didn't. He'd been a basket case for most of the time he'd lived there. Looking back he wondered why Pearson had put up with him for so long Especially given he definitely hadn't acted as grateful as he should have been.

"To be honest, I think he was relieved when I turned it down. After all, he probably doesn't want one of us living on his property any more than we'd want to. It's just weird."

And with that she walked out.

Chapter 34

"Glad to see someone looking happy." Pearson strolled into the office and perched on the corner of Rigby's desk.

Rigby stared blankly at him. Was Pearson being sarcastic? Happy wasn't close to what he was feeling.

Pearson sighed. "No, not you." He gestured toward the door. "Harper. Passed her on the way in. Something's made her smile."

"She's found an apartment. Finally getting out of the B & B."

"That's a relief," Pearson said. "It bothered me she was still living in temporary accommodation. I thought she might decide to move on because she couldn't find anywhere decent to live. I'd hate to lose her."

Rigby had never considered that possibility. Harper had expressed her frustration over not being able to find a place she could afford on occasion but he hadn't seen it as a big deal. He smiled. Was that the reason why Pearson had offered his apartment to her? He wanted to make sure she stayed?

"How did your potential new tenant work out?"

Pearson's eyes narrowed before he broke out in a broad grin. "You mean the one you thought was going to turn out to be Harper?"

"No! What? Harper already told me you'd asked her about it." If he didn't say when, it wasn't really a lie. But his struggle not to laugh gave him away.

Pearson straightened up. "One of these days, Rigby. One of these days…"

Rigby knew better than to ask him to finish the sentence. Or to even speak at all.

Finally, Pearson continued. "All going well, she'll be moving in after the New Year. She's a teacher. Starts at the elementary school next term. I haven't met her yet, but Molly was impressed with her."

"And she doesn't mind living next door to the Chief of Police?"

"Why should she? It's almost a plus point, isn't it? I bet her parents will be pleased when they hear where she's going to live."

Her parents? Rigby frowned. Then he got it. "She's young?"

Pearson nodded. "Straight out of college."

"Good luck with that," Rigby muttered. He launched into an update on what he'd learned since Pearson had gone for his meeting with the mayor.

Which, unfortunately, was not a lot.

"If the tire treads come back as a match, we're going to have to come down hard on Dale. He's going to have to explain how his car sitting in his grandfather's garage could have been driven by anyone else," Pearson said.

"But what if he has changed the tires since the accident?"

Pearson grabbed Harper's chair, swung it around to face Rigby and sat down. "It's a possibility, but the level of planning required, having the spare tires, knowing how you were going to get rid of the originals, you go to all that trouble, wouldn't you also think of changing the license plate?"

"Tires are easier to get than license plates. Maybe we should ask around, see if anyone remembers selling four tires without fitting them on the vehicle."

Pearson stared at the whiteboard. "If Gina doesn't get a match we might have to do just that. But how would he have got rid of the tires? Without them we can't prove anything. All we'd be left with is the license plate match."

Rigby sighed. So much for hoping the case would be solved by the end of his shift. He looked at the board. He'd put the photo of the car in the garage next to the screenshot. Everything matched apart from the condition of the cars. The car in the screenshot looked far from pristine, but then the photo had been taken in the dark and from a greater distance than the one in the garage. Besides, it would be easy enough for Dale to return his car to a pristine condition if he had taken it out, and his comments to the nurse about not wanting to get it dirty could have been deliberate. After all, who cared about the state of their car when a relative was dying?

He voiced his thoughts to Pearson.

Pearson frowned. "You think he's used his dying grandfather as a cover to kill Gail?"

Put like that it did sound ludicrous. And given the comment was made before the hit-and-run it would imply premeditation—Dale setting up alibis in advance, knowing where Gail was going to be. But why would Dale want to kill Gail? She'd lived in Lewisville all her life. Dale was only a visitor. Gail was married. Dale wasn't. Was there something there? And even if there was, why would it lead to murder?

A shiver ran down his spine. He wished he could write this one off as an accident. He'd still want to catch the bastard who was driving the car but at least they'd understand the crime they were dealing with. Premeditation added an extra layer. Not only who but why? And when it came down to it there were only two answers to why. Someone had a grudge against Gail. Or the grudge was against someone connected to Gail—and Gail's death was a warning to them.

Chapter 35

Rigby pulled up outside the Cooper home, surprised to see the Christmas lights had been turned on. From the outside the house looked like all the others on the street, no indication of the sorrow within.

The driveway was clear of snow, likewise the path to the front door. A lop-sided toddler-size snowman stood by the steps, its carrot nose way out of proportion to its head. Even in grief, life went on. Add young kids to the mix and there was almost no choice but to carry on.

He'd spent the last hour on his computer, trawling through search results about numerous Martin Coopers—none of them the one he was interested in. The only mentions he'd found were an old college link in need of an update and the newspaper article about the fundraising. Martin either didn't do social media or used a false name.

Rigby wasn't sure what he'd expected to find. If Martin was involved in some criminal activity he was hardly likely to announce it online. It had been a waste of time, done to make him feel like he was doing something to progress the case because he was rapidly running out of ideas rather than in the expectation of finding a case-cracking lead.

Likewise with this visit to Martin. But he was now at a loss for what to do next. He sat in his car and tried to remember why he'd thought coming to reassure Martin he had the investigation into his wife's death under control had seemed such a good idea. What could he possibly get out of it? Could he get out of it? Slip away unnoticed? They weren't expecting him.

He saw movement at the window. Damn. Martin's mom closing the drapes. A slight hesitation, a glance back over her shoulder. Words spoken. His presence had been noted. The drapes closed. A light came on behind the front door.

Rigby got out of the car. Nodded a greeting at Martin who now stood in the open doorway.

"Have you found him?"

Rigby noted the assumption that the driver was male. "No, not yet." Then he added hurriedly, "But we're getting close." Damn, why did he feel the need to lie? All it did was raise Martin's hopes and the pressure to close the case.

"Oh." Martin's dull, disinterested stare suggested no hopes had been raised, that hope no longer existed, only grim reality. Faint traces of red still lined Martin's eyes but the dark circles under them had intensified. Had the guy slept since Tuesday? He'd definitely attempted to shave, but judging by the missed patches had not looked in a mirror since. And he'd also changed his clothes since Rigby last saw him.

Martin stood aside to let Rigby in. Then he glanced up and down the road as if he was expecting someone else.

"I hope I'm not disturbing you," Rigby said.

"No. It's just…" Martin sighed. "I still expect to see her. You know?" He closed the door. "Every time the bell rings, I think… she'd sometimes forget her keys when she went out on her own." He smiled sadly at the memory. "Never when she was with the kids. So when the bell rings—and it's been ringing so often—I forget and for a brief moment expect it to be her."

Damn, that couldn't be easy. Friends and neighbors, they'd want to rally round. The fridge was probably full of foil-wrapped dishes, delivered out of the goodness of their hearts. Nobody realizing the tiny darts of pain they were causing. "Maybe you should disable the bell?" It was all Rigby could think of to say.

Laughter and giggles erupted from the kitchen. Martin flinched.

"You okay?" Rigby said before he could stop himself. How

he hated that question. Usually asked only when it was obvious everything was not okay, but with the expectation the answer would be yes. Because no led to awkward silences and embarrassment. No was the truth that was hard to deal with. No required further action with no clue what that action should be.

Martin didn't seem to hear. He turned abruptly before he reached the kitchen door and gestured for Rigby to go in the living room.

Rigby winced as he opened the door to the blare of the evening news on the television. Despite the volume, Martin's father appeared to be fast asleep. Martin grabbed the remote, muted the sound, and then looked at Rigby as if to say "what can you do?"

Rigby sat in an armchair, furthest from the old man, still trying to decide how to start the conversation. In hindsight it had definitely been a mistake to come.

Martin flopped down on the sofa, leaned back and spoke to the ceiling. "I wish they would all just go away."

Rigby glanced at the old man to make sure he was still asleep.

Martin snickered. "Don't worry about him. He won't hear. You could fire a gun in here and it wouldn't wake him."

Rigby felt his chest tighten. He forced a grin. Took a deep breath. Tried to calm the unease Martin's words had sparked, push back the image of a gun pointed directly at him. He took another deep breath.

Fortunately, Martin hadn't noticed he was on the point of hyperventilating. "I know they mean well. And Izzy has been great with the kids, but I need some space. It seems every time I turn around, one of them is there. Every time I try to do something, make a coffee, deal with the kids, they rush to do it for me. It's as if they think I'm an invalid, incapable of looking after myself. I'm… I'm the same person I was on Tuesday morning. I'm not sick. I've just… I've lost my wife."

Wasn't grief a form of sickness?

"I need some space," Martin continued. "Space to grieve. Their presence isn't going to help me do that." He shook his head. "The opposite more likely. I need time. Time with the kids. We're the ones who've lost a wife and a mother."

Izzy had lost her sister, his parents their daughter-in-law. Helping Martin and the little ones was probably their way of dealing with their grief. But Rigby kept quiet. He remembered only too well the feeling of wanting to be left alone. The irritation at constantly being asked if he was okay?

He couldn't fault Martin for wanting to be alone but had Martin considered how he'd cope with his kids without help? The presence of the others might well distract them from their mom's disappearance. With just their father, their mother's absence would be all the more obvious. Would Martin know how to deal with it when they acted out? Because they would. And they'd take their young frustrations out on their father, day and night. Was Martin prepared for that?

Izzy stuck her head around the door. Rigby wondered how much she'd heard.

"Back again?" she said with forced jollity. She stepped into full view. "Would you like a coffee?"

"No thanks." Rigby waited for Izzy to leave but she didn't. She glanced expectantly at them.

Martin nodded toward the door. "Can you give us a moment, Izzy."

A slight scowl preceded her big grin and begrudging "of course," before she slunk out of the room, leaving the door open.

Martin heaved a sigh and got up to close the door. "See what I mean? They think I can't even handle a visitor on my own."

"It's your house. You could ask them to leave."

"Yeah, right. I can see how that would go down." He sighed again. "Mom and Dad, they only mean well." He hesitated. "Izzy too, but she sounds so like Gail, the way she speaks, her laugh. I hear her in another room with the kids and I think—" He looked down at his hands. "Then I remember."

Rigby didn't know what to say. It hardly seemed appropriate to launch into questions of whether Martin was involved in nefarious activities. At the same time, he was no psychologist and far from the best person to be offering advice on love and loss—unless it was an example of what not to do.

"I can't upset them, no matter how much they irritate me

now. I know I'm going to need them going forward. I can't do this on my own in the long run. Izzy's even offered to look after the kids for me when I have to go back to work. Until I can find them a suitable daycare, but with the hours I work that's not going to be easy."

"Daddy!" The door burst open and Martin's oldest daughter charged into the room and flung herself at her father's lap. "Izzy said it's bath time. But I want you to do it." She pulled on Martin's hand as if to make him stand up.

"Sorry." Izzy appeared carrying the younger child. "I told Martha you were busy and would see her later." Susie had her hands clasped around Izzy's neck in a tight hug but as soon as she saw her father she reached out for him. "Dada."

Izzy jiggled Susie in one arm and held out her other hand to the older girl. "Daddy's busy. He hasn't got time tonight."

The harshness in her tone surprised Rigby. He groaned inwardly. This was a complete mistake. He should have known early evening wasn't a good time to interview a parent of young children. He stood up. "I'll go. I can come back another time."

"No." Martin glared at Izzy. "Bath time can wait. It's not going to hurt the kids." Then he turned to Rigby. "You haven't told me why you're here yet."

Rigby scrambled for a good reason. His mind failed him. "I was passing and I thought I'd drop in and see how you were doing." The lamest of lame excuses.

Damn Pearson and his damn injunctions. What if Martin was the reason someone had wanted to kill Gail? Tiptoeing around him like this wasn't going to get them anywhere. And it wasn't as if they thought Martin was directly involved in Gail's death.

Though now he thought about it, maybe they shouldn't be ruling that possibility out. He watched as Martin enfolded his daughter in his arms and gently stroked her blonde curls. He noticed the look that passed between Martin and Izzy. A silent message?

Damn, he needed to get out of there before he said something he shouldn't.

Chapter 36

"Do you really think you'll be able to find the driver, Detective?" There was a hint of disbelief in Izzy's question. She removed her necklace from Susie's grip and, as the child made to protest, nuzzled up against her head until Susie giggled. "I mean, you said there were no witnesses, so how is it even possible?"

She spoke while still making Susie laugh, as if she felt the need to fill the awkward silence rather than genuinely wanting an answer.

"We have some leads." Rigby tried not to sound defensive. He wished she'd look at him while she talked. The child was a distraction. "Security footage from some nearby houses."

"Really?" That did get her attention. Fleetingly. Then she smiled back at Susie. "So how come you haven't arrested anyone yet?"

"We're working on it. We have to be sure we have the right person."

"Of course." She made a silly face at Susie. "But if you're looking at someone in particular, does that mean you think you've found the car that hit Gail?" She rubbed noses with Susie.

"I didn't say we were looking at anyone in particular." Rigby emphasized her words. "I said we had some leads. And I'm not in a position to divulge those leads."

"Even to us? The family of the victim?"

"Even to you." It came out harsher than he intended.

"Izzy." Martin lifted the older girl from his lap. "Can you

give us a moment? Take the girls to see Grandma."

Izzy hesitated. "Should I come back?"

"No, no need. I'd like to talk to Detective Rigby on my own."

Izzy glanced pointedly at Martin's father then took the older girl's hand and in a too chirpy voice said, "Let's go find Grandma."

"Close the door please," Martin called after her. When the door shut he sank his head back against the sofa again and closed his eyes. "Sorry about that. She can be intense."

"Not a problem," Rigby lied, hoping he could now ask questions rather than have to respond to ones for which he had no answer.

Martin opened his eyes. There were tears in them. "If she wasn't so good with the kids, I'd ask her to leave. But the kids love her. She's always made time for them." He scoffed lightly. "Too much time, I think. She should be out enjoying herself, making friends, but she spends a lot of her time hanging with Gail and the girls." He hesitated. "I mean, she used to."

He shook his head. "She's going to miss Gail. Almost as much as we are. She'd definitely say Gail was her best friend." He paused.

Rigby waited.

"Ironically, Gail would say Hannah was her best friend. Especially since the babies. They've got more in common. But I think she felt sorry for Izzy, found it hard to tell her not to come over so often." Martin wiped a tear from his right eye. "One of the few things we used to argue about. But that was Gail. Kind-hearted." He let out a long sigh. "Found it hard to say no."

He scoffed again. "And now I find myself in the same position. How can I say no?" He grimaced. "But it's not out of kind-heartedness. I need her."

Rigby had no advice for Martin. He suspected if he were in Martin's position he'd just tell Izzy to go. But then subtlety had never been one of his strong points. And until recently he'd only had himself to consider. But time to change the subject. He was a detective not an agony aunt.

"Does the name Dale Jessup mean anything to you?" he asked, watching for a tell-tale reaction.

Martin considered the name. "No. Should it?"

"Gail never mentioned it?"

Martin frowned. "Not that I recall. Who is he?"

The most likely suspect?

Rigby waved the question off. "One of the people we've spoken to. Said he thought he might have known Gail." Where would he be without little white lies?

Martin shrugged. "Gail grew up in Lewisville. We all did. Maybe he knew her from school. Although I don't remember a Jessup, not unless he goes back to elementary or junior high."

"He didn't grow up here. Just spent summers here."

Martin shook his head. "No. Definitely doesn't ring a bell with me. If he only spent summers here, it's possible he knew Gail from the town pool. Until we started dating in junior year I think Gail spent most of her free time in the summer at the pool."

Rigby waited for Martin to ask what someone who might have known his wife years earlier had to do with the investigation into her death, but fortunately Martin never made the connection. Instead, he said, "You should ask Hannah or Izzy. They would remember. You didn't get too many out-of-towners at the pool." He chuckled. "Chances are if he hung out at the pool, he'd have been a magnet for the local girls."

Rigby could see that. Assuming Dale hadn't undergone a drastic transformation since high school he'd probably turned a few girls' heads. Rigby reckoned he could guess the answer to his next question but asked it anyway. "Did you hang out at the pool?"

"No. I was the kid who spent too much time with his head in a book. You?"

Rigby smiled. He remembered long summer days at the pool, eyeing up the girls but never being brave enough to ask any of them out. His group of friends were mostly all talk, no confidence, especially when clad only in bathing suits.

Dale Jessup was several years younger than him so it was unlikely they crossed paths at the pool. Then again Dale would also have been younger than Gail so it was unlikely the connection, if any, stemmed from there. Unless it was through Izzy. She would be closer in age to Dale.

He shook his head. His thoughts were going off track. Even
if there was a link between Izzy and Dale, why would it be a factor
in Gail's death? Unless both Izzy and Gail had been involved in
something illegal. And what? Gail wanted out and had to be dealt
with? Couldn't be trusted to keep quiet? Needed to be made an
example of to keep others, like Izzy, in line?

Martin cleared his throat. Rigby realized he was still waiting
for an answer.

"Summer before senior year, I was one of the lifeguards."

"Bet that was fun."

"Yeah, it was." But his past was irrelevant to the
investigation. "What about you?"

Martin scoffed softly. "I worked in the library. Books and air
conditioning, I can't think of a better combination for the summer.
Although I actually worked there all year round. It's where I met
Gail. We knew each other from school but it was only through the
library that we became friends."

"Do you still work with books?"

"No." Martin paused. "Although I guess you could say yes,
seeing I spend most of my time researching cases, only mostly online
these days."

"You're a lawyer?" Could that be the link Rigby was looking
for? A dissatisfied client or clients?

Martin laughed. "I wish. No. Just a paralegal. Spend my day
with my nose to the grind, at the beck and call of the guys who make
the big money."

Rigby tried to hide his disappointment. It was unlikely a
paralegal would draw someone's wrath enough to justify killing their
wife. "What kind of cases do you work on?"

"Breach of contract, that kind of stuff."

"Not criminal law?"

Martin shook his head. "No. Strictly business law."

Rigby sighed. Business law in Lewisville. Most likely small-
scale cases. Lewisville didn't boast any multinational corporations
and even it if did, he suspected legal issues would be dealt with by
big city lawyers not family-run small-town practices. Still, just
because it was unlikely Martin had made enemies at work didn't

mean he hadn't run afoul in his personal life. There were all sorts of reasons an apparently upright citizen could get embroiled with the wrong kind—gambling, drugs, loan sharks. And once on that slippery slope, it could be hard to get off. And unfortunately for him, they were problems people were reluctant to own up to having, especially to cops.

And without telling Martin why he needed to know, he could hardly ask outright. Damn Pearson and his insistence they kept the possibility it was deliberate quiet until they had more evidence. It was hamstringing the investigation. How was he supposed to get the answers to questions he couldn't ask?

"Did Gail work?" Maybe if he got Martin talking about Gail, something would slip out that would help.

"No. She wanted to stay home with the kids. At least until they went to school. And even then, she said she'd only go back part-time."

"What did she do?"

"She was a nurse." Martin sighed. "It was all she ever wanted to do. Be a nurse and a mother." He clamped his lips together. Gave Rigby a pained smile. "I guess at least she got to achieve her ambitions." His voice broke.

Rigby waited. He didn't know what to say. He'd managed to upset Martin with a simple everyday question. Given Gail hadn't worked for four years, her time as a nurse was unlikely to have anything to do with her death. Four years was a long time to hold a grudge.

"Did she stay in touch with her coworkers after she left?"

"Absolutely. She met up with them every few months for lunch. Didn't want them to forget her in case she did want to go back. Anyway, she liked them. And they liked her." Martin hesitated. "Everyone did. It was hard not to like Gail. She was that kind of person, you know?"

As he'd been told so many times over the last few days. Was it possible he'd got this all wrong? It was a tragic accident, plain and simple. And someone, most likely Dale Jessup, was living with the guilt of what they'd done.

Not only had he upset Martin but he'd needlessly upset

Becca by his insistence on pushing forward with the case. He could have been patient and waited for Gina to do her work and confirm whether they were on the right track or wasting valuable time.

He should leave. Leave now before he upset Martin further. He wasn't going to hear from Gina that evening. It was too late now. And the next day was his day off. Whatever Gina found could wait until Sunday when he was back on the day shift. And maybe, just maybe, he could make it up to Becca for being so self-centered.

Chapter 37

Back at his desk Rigby discovered he'd missed two calls from Gina, but when he called her back he only got her voicemail. He left a message telling her he should be at his desk until the end of his shift or she could reach him on his cell phone at home. Not that he expected her to call him at eleven in the evening, but even if he was not supposed to be working the next day he could still take a phone call. Becca couldn't object to that, could she?

He updated the case notes, which didn't take long. His visit to the Cooper home hadn't provided any new insights. In fact the whole day had been somewhat of a write-off.

He slumped forward, resting his elbows on the desk, his chin in his fists, and stared blankly ahead. Why had he insisted on coming back to work? He could be at home now, snuggled up on the sofa with Becca and Lotte—his only concern whether to put another log on the fire. They could be making plans for Christmas, not only their first with a baby, but also their first when neither of them would be on duty or on call. Instead, he'd landed first on the roster for call out on Christmas Day. True, it was incredibly unlikely a call would come in, but the possibility it might would hang over the celebrations.

He sighed. He should have listened to Pearson. The chief had advised him to wait until the new year to return. But an additional three weeks had seemed like an eternity. He needed something to engage his mind. And in his defense, Becca hadn't objected too vehemently to the idea. If she had, no way would he have upset her. Secretly, he thought she was pleased to get him out of the house.

He grimaced. Though probably not for as long as he had been.

He straightened up. Well, there was no point brooding about it. He'd made the decision, now he had to live with it.

He spun his chair around to face the whiteboard. Went over again in his mind what he'd learned that evening. Nothing jumped out as being worthy of adding to the board. He scanned the scant information that was there. It didn't seem much for a week's work and not just his time, but also Harper and Brad Shore's input.

He stared at the copy of Dale Jessup's driver's license. Jessup was the link. He'd either driven the car or let someone else drive his car and for whatever reason didn't want to admit it even after being confronted with damning evidence. Why?

Was he so confident the police wouldn't discover any other evidence that would tie him to the crime? But how could he be? He couldn't have imagined Mrs. Henderson would have taken a photo of his car. And without that, they wouldn't have tracked him down to start with. But given they had found that one piece of evidence, how could he be confident there weren't other videos or screenshots out there as proof of his lies?

Of course there weren't, not at this point, but Dale didn't know that. Unless he assumed that if there were more damaging images, Rigby would have shown them to him to force a confession. Or arrested him.

Not one damn camera where they needed it. Only the blink-of-an-eye footage from Mr. Jenkins of a speeding light-colored car which, while most likely the car that hit Gail, might or might not be the same car as in Mrs. Henderson's photo.

He shifted his gaze to the two photos of the car. Two cars. Identical. Except one of them needed cleaning. No. He corrected himself. Not two cars. One car. Same make, model, license plate. Only the dirt set the images apart.

But the difference was considerable.

Rigby focused in on the photo of the dirty car. The nurse said Dale didn't want to take his car out in the morning because he'd just had it cleaned. But the dirt on the car wasn't the type you'd expect from a short drive, even if it was on slushy roads. This looked the kind of dirt that would accumulate over a long period of time where there were other vehicles spraying up slush as they passed. But the drive to the accident site from the grandfather's house was no more than a mile and on those residential streets the likelihood of being passed by another vehicle, let alone several, was minimal.

Rigby grabbed a pen from his desk, bounced it on the arm of the chair as he considered the possibilities. Had the nurse actually seen the car or was he simply repeating what he'd been told by Dale?

He stopped bouncing the pen. Damn, he'd messed up there. He should have clarified it. It was such an obvious point. He grimaced. It wasn't the kind of mistake he'd normally make. Was he slipping? Had the events of the last two months affected him more than he was willing to admit?

He scoffed. Last two months? In some ways the last year had been a nightmare, one thing after another. He wouldn't be sorry when the year was over. And yet, in a way it had been the most defining year of his life. It had brought him closer to Becca and blessed him with Lotte. He smiled. And Cocoa too.

Damn. See how easy it was to get distracted? The case, he had to concentrate on the case. If he'd slipped up once he might have slipped up elsewhere. Missed the obvious.

Dale had driven from Florida. While the recent snowfalls had been mostly north of New York City, it was hard to believe his car wouldn't show some signs of the long highway journey. Given the condition it was in when he saw it, it had to have been cleaned since Saturday. So when and why? The forecasts had predicted heavy snow over the next few days and into the next week so why bother getting the car cleaned when chances were it was only going to get dirty again immediately?

He bounced the pen again, slowly, as he tried to tease out justifications that he might be overlooking. Could Dale be one of those fanatics who obsessed about keeping their vehicles clean? Personally, he'd never understood them. Or had Dale known he wouldn't be driving his own car while he was in Lewisville so had made sure it was clean of any splattering of road deicer that might damage it while it was sitting in the garage?

Rigby made a note to ask the nurse whether he'd seen the car and to confirm with Dale when he claimed to have had it cleaned. He also wrote a request to Collins, the sergeant who'd be on duty the next day, to send an officer out to the local car washes and see if any of them cleaned the car on Wednesday morning. Just on the off-chance Dale had slipped up and run the car through a car wash rather than do it by hand. Given the amount of muck on the car, he could see how it might have been tempting.

He glanced back at the photo. The left rear brake light was almost covered in sludge, enough to cause a vigilant patrol officer to pull the driver over and issue a warning at least, if not a ticket. Too bad that hadn't happened Tuesday evening. Gail might still have been alive.

He leaned closer. Not only was the rear light almost obliterated but also what looked like a small bumper sticker next to it. Or was his mind playing tricks? He'd never noticed it before. White on white, it was almost invisible save for fragments of what he assumed were black letters peeping through.

He frowned. Turned back to his computer. Pulled the image up on his screen and zoomed in as close as he could get. He peered at it. Were they letters or just strokes of darker dirt? He wished he could wipe away the grime, tell for sure. Instead, he had to make do with a magnifying glass from out of his drawer. He held it up to the screen. It took him longer than it should have given how familiar it was, but it finally clicked—a round white sticker bearing three faded capital letters—LHS. Lewisville High School. It was a badge of honor for seniors who could drive to school, a signal to the world that they'd outgrown the school bus. Few people bothered to remove them even after they'd left school, gone to college and come back again. They were often there until the owner got rid of the car. Consequently they were a common sight in Lewisville.

Rigby spun toward the whiteboard. Just as he thought, there was no similar sticker on Dale's car. And why would there be? Dale was never a student at the local high school. Why would he have one?

Chapter 38

Pearson could hear the frustration in Rigby's voice. He let him vent without interruption. He could understand why Rigby felt that way, but he wished he didn't have to hear about it at eight-thirty on a Saturday morning when he had a long day of driving ahead of him.

Had he told Rigby he was going to pick up Sarah from college, bring her home for Christmas? Is that why Rigby was calling so early? To catch him before he left? But to what end? He wasn't going to cancel the trip. He couldn't cancel the trip. Sarah was expecting him and Molly had already left to fetch Annie from her college.

That evening all three of his girls would be at home for the first time in months. The mere thought brought a smile to his face. There'd been times in the turbulent years of raising three teenage daughters when he'd looked forward to them leaving home but the reality was he missed Sarah and Annie more than he'd expected. And next fall Emily would be gone too and family life as he'd got used to it would never be quite the same.

He almost envied Rigby. Hoped Rigby would appreciate what he had while he had it. Eighteen years seemed like a long time, but in hindsight it was fleeting. And there was no way of getting the time back. The job hadn't always made it easy, but he'd always tried to be there for the girls when it mattered—they and also Molly deserved that. And he liked to think he'd done a pretty good job of it and been something of a role model for the other family guys in the department. They knew he'd have their backs in times of family crisis. If they were happy at home, they were more likely to be happy at work, Trite but true.

Rigby finally shut up.

"Isn't today your day off?" Pearson said after a suitable pause.

An impatient sigh was the only response.

"You've just admitted we've hit a wall. That the little evidence we do have, or thought we had, doesn't make sense. One day isn't going to make a huge difference now. You've set all you can in motion. Now do me a favor. Go be with Becca and Lotte." Pearson emphasized his next words. "Be there for them. The case will still be there tomorrow. You, you need to make sure Becca is too."

There was silence from the other end of the phone.

Good. Maybe his words had hit home.

"Now I have to go. Enjoy your day off." He put the phone down. Exhaled hard. In years to come, all going well, he'd acquire sons-in-law. He could only hope they wouldn't turn out to be such hard work.

Chapter 39

Rigby put the phone down and glanced guiltily around the kitchen. The breakfast dishes were still on the table, the empty beer bottles from the previous night's post-work drink lined up next to the sink. Toast crumbs littered the countertop and scrapings of egg congealed in a pan. A hamper of dirty clothes blocked the door to the mudroom. Lotte seemed to produce as much laundry as he and Becca together. She was already on to her second outfit of the day having regurgitated her morning feed not long after Becca had dressed her.

Becca had had a rough night. Not helped by him accidentally waking Lotte when he went to give her a kiss goodnight. He'd bumped into the rocking chair by her bassinet and cursed out loud. Those babies that apparently slept through anything? Lotte wasn't one of them. Her wail had woken Becca who'd given him the evil eye and told him to go to bed in a voice that demanded obedience. So he had. And he'd slept solidly while Becca dealt with getting Lotte back to sleep. And, for once, also through Lotte's two additional demands for attention.

Which was why she was now back in bed and he was under strict instructions not to disturb her unless it was an absolute emergency. As if he would. Before she disappeared into the bedroom she'd also rattled off a list of chores she expected him to complete.

And Pearson told him to enjoy his day off? Fat chance. But Becca couldn't complain about him working on his day off if she didn't know about it. So he'd given her time enough to fall asleep and then phoned Gina.

Gina hadn't been too happy to hear from him. It did sound hectic in the background, kids yelling, doors banging, but he managed to keep her on the line long enough to find out that the tire treads at the scene were not a match for Dale's car. She'd expected him to be more disappointed than he was at the news but he explained about the bumper sticker.

He asked whether she would be able to tell whether there had ever been a sticker on Dale's car. Traces of the sticky stuff left behind after it was removed. She told him she'd look into it but not to get his hopes up. And she definitely wouldn't be able to do it that weekend.

He marked up a copy of the photo and sent it to her so she'd know exactly what and where he was talking about. He just hoped she didn't come back and say he was imagining it and all she could see was dirt.

Then he'd phoned Pearson who definitely hadn't been pleased to hear from him. He thought the chief would have been interested to hear the latest potential development but he guessed Pearson had other things on his mind. The last time Pearson had collected Sarah on her return from college, albeit that time only from the local train station, they'd almost lost their lives in a car accident. Not Pearson's fault in any way, but he'd noticed a wariness in Pearson's driving that hadn't been there before. Thankfully, there was no snow in the day's forecast so the roads should be okay.

Cocoa whined at the door.

"Not today, buddy. The snow's too deep out back."

Cocoa gave him a hurt look.

Damn dog. It knew how to get to him. Usually he'd give in, but not today. Not until he'd got through Becca's list.

"Sorry." He shook his head. So now he was apologizing to the dog? Could the day get any worse? He pushed that thought away. He knew only too well it could.

He picked up the hamper, took it into the mudroom and started throwing the clothes into the washing machine. He got halfway through the pile when he remembered Becca liked to separate the lights from the darks so he pulled the clothes out again and started to sort them. Cocoa padded over and poked his nose into the hamper. Rigby pushed him aside. "You do not want to smell these."

But Cocoa did. And it was all Rigby could do to stop the dog clambering into the hamper. He ended up holding Cocoa back with one hand and putting the clothes in with the other. As soon as he closed the machine door Cocoa jumped on top of the remaining laundry and curled up as if it was his bed. Luckily they were dark clothes and given his jeans were on the top he decided to let the dog be.

As he tidied up the kitchen he let his thoughts on what Gina had told him roam. The tire treads didn't match so it was either not the right car or, as he'd suggested earlier, the tires had been changed since the accident. But how to prove that? And now he had another possible reason as to why it was not the right car, albeit another reason which could be easily discounted. The sticker could have been added then removed. Though why would someone go to those lengths?

The overriding piece of evidence was still the license plate. Stealing license plates to conceal the car used in a crime was a well-known trick. But Dale's license plates hadn't been stolen. They were there. On his car. Plain to see.

Rigby scooped up the empty beer bottles and dumped them in the recycling bin. Cocoa raised his head as if to protest the noise and then slumped back down again.

He came up with two possibilities. Dale had used the plates on a different car or someone else had stolen the plates, used them and then put them back. All while the car was in a locked garage. And in either scenario the plates had been used on a car identical to Dale's. How likely was that?

He scrubbed furiously at the congealed egg on the pan. Why was it so difficult to remove? Wasn't this supposed to be a non-stick pan? He dropped the pan back into the sink. Why was this case so difficult to solve? What was he missing? Someone had to be lying.

No.

Dale Jessup had to be lying. He had to be involved in some way. That the license plate was his was the only evidence not in dispute.

He finished filling the dishwasher, wiped down the table and countertops and swept the floor, his actions automatic as his mind searched for the answers he needed.

Finally, pleased with his housekeeping efforts, he went to switch out the laundry.

Damn. He'd forgotten to turn the machine on.

Chapter 40

Midway through his shift on Monday, Rigby finally heard back from Gina. She confirmed that he hadn't imagined seeing the school bumper sticker but said she'd found no evidence there'd been one on Dale's car. Her verdict, although expected, disappointed Rigby. He could see the case slipping away from him. All they had was the license plate and supposition. Dale Jessup had a hefty dose of reasonable doubt on his side. Until they could squash that, no charges were going to be brought.

"Rigby, are you listening?"

Rigby tuned back into Gina. "Sorry, what did you say?"

Gina's loud sigh warned him to pay attention. "I said, I don't think they are the same car. It's hard to tell with it being so dirty but I think there's more than one ding on the back of the car in the photo and there's nothing similar on the car I've examined."

Rigby sat up straight. "You sure?"

That earned him another sigh. "No, I'm not sure. I would need to be able to examine the car in the photo to be sure or at least see a better photo of it, but I think you could well be looking at two different cars."

"How do you explain the license plates?"

"I can't." Gina laughed. "Fortunately, that's your job, not mine."

"Thanks," he muttered instead of what he really wanted to say. It wasn't Gina's fault. He couldn't take his frustrations out on her.

"Do you want me to tell you what I'm talking about or are you going to sulk?"

"Who's sulking?" Goddamn women and their intuition.

"It's all in the voice, Rigby. All in the voice." She paused. "And it helps I've seen you in action a few times."

Rigby scowled. She was probably teasing but he wasn't in the mood for it. "So tell me, what did I miss?" He'd stared at the goddamn photo for hours and never noticed any dings. But then he hadn't noticed the bumper sticker at first either.

He pulled the photo up on his screen and enlarged it until only the rear end of the car was visible. Now that Gina had confirmed she saw a bumper sticker too, he couldn't believe he'd missed it before. It was so damn obvious. But dings? He still couldn't see them.

She walked him through it. It would have been easier if they were both in the same room but Rigby didn't want to wait until she got over to the station house. He wanted answers right away. It took a while but finally he saw what she was seeing. What he'd taken for dirt on the bottom of the bumper could well be a scrape from a nudge by a darker colored car. To the inexperienced eye it looked much like another smear of dirt but Gina was experienced in analyzing the results of two objects making contact and if she said a particular mark was probably the result of a fender bender, he believed her.

But where did that leave him?

"Of course," Gina continued, "it's possible if the car was taken in for repair after the accident, the rear bumper could have been replaced at the same time which would explain why there was no sign of damage to the rear or of any sticker."

"Damn. So we're basically no further forward." He almost spat the words out. Out of the corner of his eye he saw Harper's startled reaction to his outburst.

"Sorry." Gina sounded as if she meant it.

Rigby raked his left hand through his hair. "I'm not... I didn't mean..."

"I should hope not." The levity in Gina's response reassured him she hadn't taken the comment personally. "I'm just telling you like I see it. No sugar coating."

"Wouldn't want it any other way." Rigby sighed. "Would just be nice if just one lead would turn out not to be a dead end. The photo was taken Tuesday evening. We saw Dale's car on Friday morning. How many body shops do you know that will turn a car around in that short a time? Besides…" He rummaged through the papers on his desk. Found the one he was looking for and read it over quickly even though he knew what it said. "Patrol checked all the body shops in the county. Only one of them reported having a white sedan brought in for repairs since Tuesday. It was the wrong make and model. And patrol had responded to the scene of the accident and filed a report."

"Unless someone's been paid to keep quiet."

Rigby groaned. "Then we'd be well and truly—" He swallowed back what he'd been about to say. "But more likely, the car's long gone from the county."

"Which would mean it can't be the car I've been examining."

Rigby nodded.

"Rigby?"

He sighed. "Which means, don't ask me how, but yes, we've probably been looking at the wrong car."

He slammed down the phone. Flopped back in his chair.

"Bad day?" Harper asked.

"Don't," he said. "Just don't."

"That bad?"

"Tomorrow is Gail's funeral. I really hoped by then I'd be able to give the family some answers. Instead I have nothing."

"You didn't make any promises, did you?"

"No." He hesitated. "But on Friday, I told them we were close." At Harper's expression, he added, "I thought we were. And I could tell they needed to hear something positive."

"So what you going to tell them now?"

"God knows. I've already had Gail's sister Izzy on the phone again yesterday asking how the investigation is going. Says the family really needs some answers. For closure."

"What did you tell her?"

Rigby shrugged. "Just that hit-and-runs, by their nature, are difficult. Not a lot of evidence to work with, especially when the victim is deceased. We were doing the best we could. What else could I say?"

Harper made a face. "And she was okay with that? After you'd told them you were close to wrapping it up?"

Rigby shuffled in his seat. "She used the word incompetent several times. So no, I don't think she was okay with it."

He'd been shocked by the vitriol of Izzy's outburst. Granted, he couldn't see her expression but her attitude had seemed at odds with that of the woman he'd spoken to in person. Then she'd been calm, collected, holding herself together, but yesterday she'd sounded almost unhinged. As if the reality of her sister's death had only just sunk in.

Her call had ruined the rest of his day. He was failing on all fronts, both as a detective and a father. When Becca woke up on Saturday she was in no better mood than she'd been earlier. She managed to find fault with everything he did and didn't do. Even his suggestion they bundled up and went for a walk around town was met with derision. You'd think he'd suggested they take Lotte for a hike in the Arctic.

This was a new Becca. One he'd never encountered before. And it scared him. Even his attempt to hug her had been brushed off as if his touch repelled her. Theirs hadn't been a perfect relationship by any means—whose was? —but this, this was something else altogether. And he had no idea what to do about it.

He glanced over at Harper. No good asking her, she didn't have kids, likely wouldn't understand what he was talking about.

Turner was seven kids in. Surely he'd experienced this… this schizophrenic-like behavior, and presumably survived it. Unfortunately, Turner wasn't back in the office until Wednesday. That left Pearson, but after Pearson's little speech about being there for Becca, he was reluctant to admit he'd failed miserably already.

Harper stood up and pulled on her coat. "There's still the question of the license plate. Switched or stolen? Your guy has to know more than he's telling. Maybe you need to scare him a little. Bring him in. See what he says or doesn't say."

"His grandfather is dying."

"So what?" Harper said harshly. "His grandfather lived a long life. Got to be a grandfather. Gail, she barely got to be a mother. And she's already dead." She hesitated. "I never took you for a walk-over, Rigby." She smiled but it didn't reach her eyes. "You can't let fatherhood color your judgment."

He glared at her. "Fuck off."

Startled, she raised her hands in surrender. "Just my advice. By the way, how are Becca and the little one?"

"Great." He forced a smile. "Everything's great."

Chapter 41

Dale Jessup flung open the door, his impatient expression morphing into a scowl on seeing Rigby. "You again?"

Rigby ignored the rudeness. He'd allow Dale some slack given what the guy was going through. That plus the fact he hadn't had to risk his neck getting to the front door—someone had finally cleared the icy path, meaning he only had to deal with the morning's fresh layer of fluffy snow.

"I just have a couple more questions." He brushed snow off his jacket as Dale reluctantly stepped back to let him in. "It shouldn't take long."

Dale led him into the kitchen. His mother stood at the stove stirring a pot. She smiled when she saw Rigby and nodded hello. Dale's father sat at the table reading the newspaper, the remains of a cooked breakfast in front of him. Though given the time maybe it was an early lunch. He glanced up and scowled. "Back again, Detective?"

Rigby merely acknowledged him with a nod. "Is there somewhere we can talk in private?" he asked Dale. He didn't want a family conference.

"My son's got nothing to hide," Mr. Jessup manage to make his words sound both defensive and threatening at the same time.

"It's okay, Dad." Dale gestured for Rigby to follow him. "We can go in the living room."

Rigby wondered why Dale hadn't taken him in there to start with. He must have known his parents were in the kitchen and it was hardly likely Rigby would want to talk to them.

The room was dark and somber even after Dale pulled back the drapes. The flocked wallpaper and high-backed armchairs were from another era. On top of a small bureau there was what Rigby took to be a shrine to the grandmother.

Dale noticed Rigby looking at the photos and said, "Grandpa never really got over Grandma passing. I think he always assumed he would be the first to go. He wasn't really equipped for living on his own, but he refused to move in with Mom and Dad. Said he could still sense her here. He didn't want to give that up."

"How's he doing?"

Dale gave a slight shrug. "Doctors say it could be any day now. But they said that last week too. So who knows?" Dale stared at the wedding photo on the bureau, a young happy couple just starting their life together. A couple who, unlike many of their contemporaries, had kept their "till death us do part" vows. Rigby wasn't sure whether there was an afterlife, but if there was he hoped the couple would be reunited.

Dale coughed. "I'm sure you're not here to ask after Grandpa's health."

There was bitterness in his voice. Sympathy was not going to work, time to be direct. Rigby showed him the photo of the car outside Mrs. Henderson's house again. "What I still need to understand is how a car with your license plate was seen minutes away from the accident site on Tuesday evening when you claim it was sitting in your garage."

Dale stared at the photo then up at Rigby. "I don't know."

Rigby resisted the temptation to roll his eyes. "You say you were here all evening?"

"Yes."

"You didn't go out at all? Maybe you were running out of beer?"

"I don't drink."

Rigby blinked. Of course the guy didn't drink. He should have seen that coming. "Snacks?"

Dale sneered. "In that weather? Who'd go out for snacks in the middle of a snow storm?"

It was hardly a snow storm, that came later, but not worth quibbling about. "So what did you do?"

Dale made a show of thinking about it. "The usual. Watched TV. Chatted to my girlfriend."

"You have a girlfriend?"

"Don't sound so surprised."

With Dale's good looks, it wasn't any surprise. It was the fact he was just learning about her now that surprised Rigby. "Where does she live?"

"Florida."

So unlikely to be driving around Lewisville in Dale's car, or to have somehow borrowed the license plate.

Dale's eyes lit up. "We were chatting, on Facetime. Same as every night since I've been away. Ten p.m. A chat before bed seeing we can't be together. It's a poor substitute but we're hoping it'll keep the relationship going until I finish my research." He grimaced. "The original plan was I'd spend Christmas with her before I left for my research, but that doesn't look as if it's going to happen now."

The chat should be easy to verify if necessary. And the timing could be crucial. Was it a coincidence it was at ten o'clock?

"She was taunting me about the weather," Dale continued. "It had been warm and sunny in Florida. She wanted to know what it was like here. Cold, dark and snowing, I told her."

"So your car was sitting in the garage all night? Could anyone else have had access to the garage?"

"Other than Grandpa? No." Dale smirked. "And I know Grandpa didn't take the car out. He was fast asleep when I checked to see if he needed anything before I called Shelly."

"Shelly being your girlfriend?"

Dale sighed impatiently. "Yes. Shelly is my girlfriend."

Rigby decided to move on for the moment. "Someone else must have had access to the garage. Or how do you explain this?" He pointed at the photo.

"I don't—" Dale broke off. "I told you. I can't." He shook his head, looking genuinely perplexed. "Could someone have faked the plates?"

Rigby stared at him.

"It happens, doesn't it?" Panic crept into Dale's voice. Rigby remained silent.

"Well, doesn't it?"

"Would be quite the coincidence if someone faked a plate that just happened to match a genuine one in the area they're planning to commit a crime." Rigby paused to let his argument sink in. "I'm no mathematician, but the probability of that happening has got to have a lot of zeroes in it." He paused again. "And for them also to get the correct state? Come on, Dale. Do I look stupid?"

Fortunately Dale took the last question as the rhetorical question it was meant to be. He sank down in one of the armchairs, so despondent Rigby wondered if he was about to get a confession.

Instead Dale said, "You think someone stole my license plate?"

"Or your car." He hadn't said anything yet about their belief it wasn't Dale's car.

Dale scoffed. "Why would anyone steal my car, kill someone with it, and then put the car back? Why not just abandon it?"

"Why indeed?" Rigby said. "There's only one reason I can think of for returning the car."

"It wasn't me!"

"And you didn't let someone borrow your car?" Rigby watched Dale's expression. "As a favor?" He paused. "Or because you couldn't refuse?"

Dale frowned. "What do you mean?"

Rigby shrugged nonchalantly. "Sometime people get themselves into situations they shouldn't. And the only way to get out is to do something else they shouldn't." He paused. "Only problem is, it tends to lead to them digging themselves a deeper hole rather than getting out of the one they're in."

"I did not, I repeat, did not lend my car to anyone." Dale's voice rose with indignation. "I don't let anyone drive my car. Not even my girlfriend."

Rigby nodded as if accepting Dale's statement. He pursed his lips. Scratched his head. "You went out Tuesday morning—"

"In my grandpa's car," Dale butted in before Rigby could finish.

"In your grandpa's car. But your car was in the garage at the time. Right?"

Dale smirked. "I think I would have noticed if it was missing."

"But would you have noticed if the license plate was missing?"

"The license plate? The car was locked in the garage. How would anyone get in to steal the license plate?"

Rigby raised his eyebrows. "You see our problem?" When Dale didn't respond he asked again if Dale would have noticed.

"I don't know. I think I would. So the fact I didn't notice, I'd have to assume it wasn't gone when I went to the supermarket."

"Is there any chance you left the garage unlocked when you went to the supermarket?"

"No."

"You sure about that?"

"Yes."

"You didn't think, I'm not going to be long, there's others in the house, why bother?"

"No."

Rigby stared at him. Dale wasn't helping himself with his blunt answers but neither was he helping the investigation. And maybe that was the point. Did Dale realize that whatever their suspicions, the police didn't have enough to arrest him so feigning ignorance was the smart way to go?

It was a stretch to think that if Dale had left the garage open, somebody just happened along who wanted to steal a license plate from a car that matched theirs. And then put it back. That night? The next day? Before Friday morning, for sure. But how did they get back into the garage? And why the hell would they bother anyway?

What would the benefit of putting it back be if it couldn't be traced to them? It would have to be a benefit that would outweigh the risk of being detected replacing it. Why?

He could only think of one reason. Because the absence of the license plate would have signaled a connection to Dale.

"How many people know you're here?" he asked.

"Just my parents and girlfriend. Why?"

Rigby didn't answer.

"And I guess some of the neighbors might have noticed I'm here." Dale seemed to need to fill the silence. "And of course, grandpa's doctor and the nurse who comes in every day."

The doorbell rang.

Dale glanced at his watch. "That should be the nurse now." He stood up. "I'll be back in a minute."

Rigby wondered why Dale's parents didn't answer the door. They knew their son was busy. He decided not to follow Dale out. He wanted another chat with the nurse—based on what Dale had told him he was one of the only other people in the house in the relevant time period—but he wanted to finish up with Dale first.

When he heard Dale's puzzled "Who are you?" he moved closer to the open living room door but remained out of sight.

"I'm Amy," a friendly female voice said. "I'm here to see Mr. Reed. I'm afraid the usual nurse had a family emergency and couldn't make it today so I was asked to cover for them."

Rigby cursed. Now he was going to either have to wait if he wanted to speak to Scott Yates or track him down in the midst of whatever family emergency had befallen him. Did Amy know how long Scott would be absent for?

He stepped out into the hallway to ask her but she'd already gone into the grandpa's room. Dale gently closed the door behind her and returned to the living room. Rigby followed him back in.

"That's unfortunate at this late stage. Although I think Grandpa is so fuddled now he won't realize Amy's not the usual nurse."

"He surely can't think she's Scott?"

Dale chuckled. "No, not Scott. He doesn't come on Monday. It's his day off. There's another nurse comes in then. A woman."

"So she was here last Monday?" Rigby swallowed back his impatience. "She was here at the house between your arrival on Saturday and Tuesday?" He was grasping at straws, he knew it, but why was he only learning this now? He'd asked Dale who else had been there. Barely concealing his anger, he asked, "Is there anyone else who's been here since you arrived that you might have forgotten about?"

Dale visibly flinched at the animosity in his voice. "No. I told you. Just Grandpa, me and the nurse. Okay, I should have said nurses. I didn't think. They come, they attend to Grandpa and they leave. You can't possibly think one of them crept into the garage and stole my license plate? It's not possible. I would have known."

"Not if it was done while you were at the supermarket."

Dale froze. A nervous grin spread across his face. "You think Scott might have done it?" He broke off. "That's ridiculous. Why would he do that?"

Rigby didn't answer.

"Why would he take it and put it back?"

Rigby still didn't answer.

"And when would he have put it back? I was here the rest of the time. I didn't go out again. Not until my parents arrived."

"Were you with him the whole time he was here?"

Dale looked exasperated. That made two of them, but Rigby knew antagonizing Dale wouldn't help so he had to dial back his own frustrations. Too bad the chief wasn't there. He was so good at putting people at ease, getting them to open up.

"Was I always in the same room as him? No, of course not." Dale gestured in the direction of the bedroom. "When they're attending to Grandpa, I leave them to it. He may be dying but he's still entitled to some privacy."

He pressed his lips together and blinked back tears. "It's hard to see him like this. There's not much dignity in the dying days, depending on others for everything. He was such a strong, vibrant guy. It's been tough watching him decline. And I know this sounds crazy given his age, I mean he was going to die sometime, wasn't he? But it all seemed to happen so fast. But not fast enough if you know what I mean?" Dale wiped tears from his eyes. "Grandma, she passed in her sleep. I wish…" He exhaled hard. "I wish he had too. So he didn't have to go through all this."

"I'm sorry," was all Rigby could think of to say.

Dale didn't appear to hear him. "I'm going to miss him so much. He was always there for me, always so supportive, no matter what I wanted to do. Not like…" He broke off again as if he'd just remembered who he was talking to.

Rigby scrambled for something to say. First Martin, now Dale, using him as a sounding board for their issues. When all he wanted was to get to the bottom of who was responsible for Gail's death. Not that he didn't feel sorry for them, but he was the last person they should be asking for advice on dealing with grief. Should he give them Nancy Tuccino's number?

Given Dale's embarrassed expression, Rigby decided to concentrate on what he needed to know and get the hell out of there as quickly as possible.

"Where would you be when Scott or the other nurse was in with your grandfather?"

"Mostly in the kitchen. Though sometimes I'd take the opportunity to have a shower."

"Where?"

"Where do you think?" When Rigby didn't respond, he added, "In the bathroom."

"Where's the bathroom?"

"What?" A slight smile appeared on Dale's face, disappearing quickly as he seemed to realize Rigby was serious. "I use... I used the one in the guest room. It's ensuite."

Rigby moved out into the hallway. "Which is the guest room?"

Dale pointed to the room at the end of the hallway, farthest away from both the grandfather's room and the door to the garage.

"Do you remember taking a shower last Wednesday or Thursday? While the nurse was here?"

Dale shook his head. "To be honest, I can barely recall what I did yesterday. The days just seem to roll into each other."

Rigby grimaced. That wasn't what he wanted to hear.

"But there's a chance at least one of those days, I did."

A chance.

Not great, but better than an outright no. And just maybe, enough to provide a new direction in their investigation.

Chapter 42

Tracking Scott Yates down proved harder than expected. Dale only had a work number for the nurse. Scott was employed by Lewisville Cares, a small private company providing nursing services for the sick and elderly in the comfort of their own homes according to the woman who answered the phone. Unfortunately, the woman quite rightly refused to give out any information about their employees over the phone even if Rigby did claim to be a detective.

He couldn't fault her, but it meant he was going to have to traipse all the way to Leyton—despite the company name, the offices turned out to be in a business park in Leyton—all for one telephone number and, if he was lucky, a current address. And to add to his frustration, the serene snowfall of earlier had increased in intensity and the forecast warned of worse to come.

He considered calling the station house in Leyton, asking for a patrol officer to get the required information. But a personal visit would give him a chance to ask other questions that might reveal more than an address and number. Background information to help connect the missing links, and he was the only one to know what links they were looking for.

The drive turned out to be a test of his patience. The wind had picked up, swirling the snow over the windscreen from all directions, the full-on wipers only just winning the battle for visibility. The few other drivers he encountered in town seemed incapable of driving more than fifteen miles an hour and when he finally turned onto the highway, tail lights stretched into the distance ahead. Stationery tail lights. He drummed his fingers on the steering wheel while he waited. The traffic started to move. One car's length and it stopped again.

He called the sergeant on the desk. Learned there'd been an accident a mile down the road, blocking both lanes of the highway. Best to avoid it, the desk sergeant told him, prompting Rigby to cut the call before swearing at the guy.

He gained another car length. And another. But the sight of a car passing in the opposite direction each time he inched forward told him he wasn't making real progress. Drivers ahead of him were giving up and turning around.

He checked the oncoming lane for traffic, signaled left and swung the car around just as a car behind him made the same maneuver. He hit the brakes. Felt the car slide but managed to get it back under control, his heart pumping hard at the near miss. Goddamn winter was beginning to get to him already and it was only December.

He took a circuitous route back through town and along minor roads until he could join the highway beyond the accident site. Not surprisingly the highway was virtually empty save for the occasional vehicle going in the opposite direction. Little did they know what lay in store, though maybe by the time they got there the accident would have been cleared. Collins hadn't said anything about injuries or fatalities, which Rigby hoped meant that the occupants of the vehicles had been able to walk away. There was grief enough in Lewisville so close to Christmas—and that was only the grief he personally knew about.

Finally, he arrived at the business park, a series of square, low-rise buildings around a large parking lot filled with cars, some almost hidden under a mound of snow. He pitied the drivers who'd have to dig out their cars before the evening journey home.

The office for Lewisville Cares was tucked away on the second floor of a building primarily occupied by doctors. An overly made-up middle-aged woman sat behind the reception desk. From her voice Rigby recognized her as the person he'd spoken to earlier. She was no more impressed by his actual presence than she'd been on the phone but he managed to persuade her to fetch someone who might listen to his request more sympathetically.

While she was gone he glanced around the sterile reception area. For an organization claiming to be caring it wasn't exactly welcoming. Two beige plastic chairs separated by an enormous rubber plant, which had seen better days, offered the only accommodation for waiting visitors. Behind the reception desk a series of diplomas and licenses hung on the wall around a large group photograph of smiling nurses flanked by several businessmen and women.

Rigby leaned over the counter in front of the receptionist's desk and scanned the faces. He spotted Scott Yates immediately, back row, center position. His smile made him look much more personable than the guy Rigby had met. No doubt because he was facing a camera rather than a cop. They all looked like one big happy team, which he guessed was the point. No doubt the photo was duplicated in all the company's marketing material, designed to convince potential clients their loved ones would be in good hands with Lewisville Cares.

What surprised him was there were almost as many male nurses as female. Just as he'd assumed Dale's grandfather's nurse would be a woman, he'd assumed most of the nurses would be female. For sure, at the hospital in Lewisville male nurses were a small minority. Maybe Lewisville wasn't so far behind the times as he sometimes thought. And now even the police department had their first female officer, although with her promotion to detective Harper would be less visible to the general public.

"Can I help you?"

Rigby turned at the question to find one of the businesswomen from the photo smiling at him. He introduced himself but before he could tell her why he was there Mrs. Grady gestured for him to follow her into her office and take a seat. He hoped this wasn't going to take longer than necessary otherwise he'd have to sweep his car off again.

She took her time settling into her executive chair, beamed broadly and asked again what she could do for him. The smile disappeared as he told her what he wanted. Hadn't the receptionist given her a head's up as to why he was there?

"Are you saying Nurse Yates is involved in criminal activity?" Rigby detected an element of disbelief in her question.

"I didn't say that. We think he may be able to help us in one of our investigations and we understand he's not working today, but we need to speak to him as soon as possible which is why I need his contact information."

"I trust the investigation has nothing to do with our work? Nurse Yates is one of our most popular nurses. His clients never have a bad word to say about him."

Rigby smiled. "No." Not that he'd admit it if it did, not at this stage. But now might be his chance to find out more about Scott. Just in case it proved relevant. "How long has he worked for you?"

Mrs. Grady gave the question some thought. "Two or three years," she said finally. "He used to work at the hospital but when he learned of the work we do when we looked after his dying father he decided to join us."

Rigby frowned. The guy was a nurse. Why not look after his own dying father?

Mrs. Grady must have read his mind. "He needed an income. Sadly, looking after his father wouldn't have covered his expenses and he's single so there was no partner to help support him. But he said it was a great comfort to know his father was getting the care he needed and that's when he decided that's what he wanted to do for others."

Saint Scott. No, that was mean thinking, but the unasked-for biography was a little much. And if most of Scott's clients were dying, when would they have a chance to say a bad word about him? He let that question go unasked.

He glanced out the window. The snowfall had intensified. Giant snowflakes pelted down. The damn forecast was proving accurate. If he didn't get out of there soon he'd be in danger of getting stuck. "So can you give me his contact details?"

She hesitated long enough to concern him then tapped on the keyboard in front of her. It took an inordinate amount of time. He guessed dealing with such data was way beneath her pay grade but she wasn't about to admit she didn't know what she was doing.

Finally, with a sigh that suggested she was doing him a huge favor, she gave him the address and number. He wrote it down and read it back to her to make sure he had it right. He'd wasted enough time without getting a silly detail wrong.

He thanked her and stood up. She leaned over the desk to shake his hand as if they'd just concluded a business deal. He dashed out through reception, but skidded to a halt as he cast another cursory glance at the group photo as he passed. The woman in the front row on the right caught his attention. Her mousy hair was pulled back severely from her face so she wasn't immediately recognizable, but the smile was the same.

He reversed direction and went back into Mrs. Grady's office.

Chapter 43

Rigby had planned to head straight over to Scott's address in the hope the weather would have kept the nurse homebound but after his second chat with Mrs. Grady he decided to go back to the office, give himself time to mull over what he'd learned—what it might mean, if anything.

"Spare a moment?" he asked from the open doorway of the chief's office.

Pearson motioned for him to enter. "By the look on your face, I'm guessing you're not bringing good news."

Rigby exhaled hard. "The Cooper case. Every time I think we're making progress it gets more complicated."

"Sit."

Rigby sat. Took a moment to try and get his thoughts in order.

Pearson raised his eyebrows. "I'm waiting."

"I'm not sure where to start."

Pearson scoffed. "Well, that's a first coming from you."

Rigby scowled. "The only potential lead we have is the photo of the car outside Mrs. Henderson's house and as you said, there's no absolute guarantee it's the car we should be looking for. While we've tracked down the license plate, we're being told the car it belongs to has been locked in a garage for over a week. Of course, that could be a lie, but now Gina believes the car in the garage and the car in the photo are different cars.

"Dale Jessup, the owner of the car in the garage, claims he

didn't go out on Tuesday evening, though his only alibi is a dying old man. But if we assume there are two different cars we have to ask, why would Dale take his license plate off his own car and put it on another identical car? That makes no sense at all."

Pearson nodded. "You think it was stolen and used by someone other than Dale?"

"Between the time of Dale's arrival on the previous Saturday and the Tuesday of the accident only two other people had access to the house according to Dale. Both are nurses, there to attend to the grandfather, but neither would have any reason to go into the garage." Rigby paused. "One is Scott Yates. He goes every day but Monday. And it turns out he was alone in the property—well save for the grandfather—on Tuesday while Dale went shopping."

"So he could have taken the license plate then?" Pearson said. "Have you checked his alibi for Tuesday evening?"

"Not yet."

Pearson frowned. "Why not?"

"Because it's Monday, so he wasn't at the house. I've been tracking down his contact details, about to head out there in a little while."

"So why are you sitting in my office?"

Rigby grimaced. Bounced his fingers on the arm of the chair. "Because I'm hoping you're going to tell me I'm over thinking this."

"Over thinking what?" Pearson's response was tinged with exasperation.

"That it's a strange coincidence that the other nurse, the one who covers for Scott on Mondays, just happens to be Isabelle Heaton."

At Pearson's puzzled expression, he added, "Gail Cooper's sister."

Chapter 44

Pearson stared at Rigby, a look of distaste spreading across his face. "You think Gail's sister is somehow connected to her death?"

It sounded ridiculous but Rigby had been on the job long enough not to dismiss the seemingly ridiculous out of hand. As had Pearson. Though in this instance, he'd have been delighted if the chief had laughed him out of the room. Instead, all the chief said was, "This close to Christmas?" As if the timing mattered.

But in a way it did. "If this wasn't an accident then it was premeditated. That would suggest whoever was driving knew Gail well enough to know she would be walking along that road at a particular time."

"Unless she was being watched, followed," Pearson interjected. "They saw her go to the party. Assumed she'd return home the same way. And waited. Hence the car outside the Henderson house."

Rigby shook his head. "That wouldn't work if they only were going to have the license plate for a limited period of time. They'd have to know she was going out that evening. Alone. Walking. And who better to know her movements than a sister, especially one who presumably knew about a party hosted by another sister. They must have talked about it. Even if only to explain why she wasn't invited."

"Why wasn't she invited?" Pearson asked.

"It was for moms. Izzy, as her family calls her, hasn't got kids."

Pearson shook his head. "I could see her being upset at being left out, but as a reason for murder? And why Gail and not the sister who was hosting the party?"

Rigby sighed. Tapped his fingers on the chair. Pearson knew it wasn't the lack of an invite to a party—at least they hoped it couldn't be something as petty—but by stating the obvious he was pushing Rigby to see beyond it. Take what he knew as fact, blend it with what seemed outrageous and come up with something worth following up.

Maybe the sleepless nights were getting to him or his underlying concerns about Becca were clouding his judgment, but Rigby couldn't make sense of it. Three people of interest. One, Dale, had easy access to the plate but nothing to gain by switching it to another car. Another, Izzy, who could potentially have had access to the plate before the accident but not afterward so how could she have returned it? And then there was Scott, who had an obvious opportunity to remove the plate on Tuesday and a potential chance to replace it the next day. An image of the guy talking to him outside the house came to mind. The messenger bag slung over his shoulder. A bag big enough to hold a license plate. Was that how he'd done it? Brought it back and waited for Dale to take a shower to sneak it into the garage and replace it? Took a gamble that Dale wouldn't notice it was missing in the interim. Given the weather, it wasn't much of a gamble. And if that was what had happened, it was a gamble that had worked—until the police arrived on the doorstep.

He recalled Scott's lack of interest in why the police were present. Had he read him wrong? Maybe it wasn't a lack of interest but a fear of saying something incriminating if he stuck around too long. So he'd made his escape, pretending his only concern was his dying patient. No doubt he'd had a chat with Dale later about the police presence. Learned what he needed to know. If Scott was involved, he'd probably thought he'd got away with it at this point so it was going to be a hell of a shock when the police turned up on his doorstep. Who knew how he'd react?

"Scott knows Izzy Heaton. That much we know for sure." He hesitated. "But if I hadn't recognized her in the photo on the wall, we might never have realized the connection."

"If there is one," Pearson said. "Other than they work for the same company."

"If there is one," Rigby conceded with a sigh. He wished

Pearson would just agree with him for once without nitpicking his thought process. Though he only had himself to blame. He was the one who'd come to see Pearson instead of going straight to Scott.

Assuming Scott was home, he could already have got Scott's side of the story re his links to Izzy and possibly even to Gail, and his alibi for Tuesday evening. True or not, and he suspected it would be the latter it would be something else to work with. Picking holes in a statement by a suspect often bore unexpected fruit.

Instead, as Pearson had pointed out, he was sitting in the chief's office, wasting time. Letting the unrelenting snow pile up again on his car in the lot. Snow he'd have to sweep off before he could get on his way, wasting more time. Why?

He sensed Pearson studying him, waiting for him to continue. Damn, he had nothing to add.

"How much do we know about Scott Yates?" Pearson eventually asked.

Rigby told him what he'd learned from Mrs. Grady. Pearson smiled. "I may be getting old and cynical but it seems the reviews are always glowing until we start digging."

"Mrs. Grady did seem overly concerned about the company's reputation if it got out their staff were involved in a police investigation."

"Who can blame her? A personal service like home care, you don't want anything that casts doubt on the integrity of your employees getting out. Another reason to keep our suspicions that this was more than an accidental hit-and-run under wraps or people will clam up before we get the answers we need." Pearson stood up. "And with that in mind, I think we should go and have a chat with this fine young man, see if we can figure out what he's hiding, if anything."

The suggestion took Rigby by surprise until it dawned on him this was what he'd been wanting. It wasn't going to see Scott per se he'd been putting off, but going to see him alone. His initial encounter with Scott had raised no alarm bells, but he knew only too well how quickly an innocent situation could turn bad. And this time he'd be on Scott's home ground.

For all he knew Scott could have less saintly roommates, a

vicious dog or two or—and he shivered at the thought—a friend with a baseball bat.

Damn, since when had he become this wary of going to interview a suspect? Was he turning into a wuss? He couldn't let one stupid mistake affect his decisions.

Chapter 45

Scott Yates lived in a large, well-kept, three-story house, which had been turned into apartments judging from the number of names listed next to the intercom. A large tree with multicolored lights sat in the window on one side of the front door while on the other, red and green bulbs draped around the frame flickered on and off.

The first two presses of the buzzer next to Scott's name went unanswered. Frustrated and fearing Scott had ignored the blizzard-like conditions and gone out anyway, rendering their trip a waste of time, Rigby held the buzzer down on the third attempt and then stepped back to eye the upper floors.

He could see lights on both floors. Not surprising given the gloom but unfortunately that didn't mean the residents were actually home. He swung around, looked at the row of snow-covered cars lining the street and smiled when he spotted Scott's green SUV. So if the guy had gone out, it would have to be on foot—which he somehow doubted. He pressed the buzzer again.

The door flew open. Scott stood there in baggy sweatpants and a grimy t-shirt; his blond hair ruffled as if he had just got out of bed. The look of annoyance on his face turned to surprise, whatever rebuke he'd been about to let out swallowed back. Whoever he'd been expecting to find on his doorstep, it obviously wasn't two policemen. He glanced frantically back and forth at them.

Rigby smiled. Flashed his badge. "Remember me?"

Scott's gaze rested on Rigby. "You're the cop from Mr. Reed's house?" He frowned, but not convincingly. "What can I do for you?"

"How about letting us in out of the snow?" Rigby widened his smile. "We've just got a couple of questions we want to ask you."

Scott's gaze flickered to Pearson and back. Presumably wondering why it took two plainclothes cops if that's all they wanted. As Scott took a step back, one hand still gripping the door, Rigby stepped forward in case Scott took it into his head to slam the door on them.

After a brief hesitation Scott ushered them in. They stomped the snow off their shoes on the doormat and followed him upstairs.

"The intercom doesn't work," Scott said over his shoulder. "That's why it took so long to answer. Pain in the neck having to run downstairs to answer the door. The landlord said he'll have it fixed but it's been a week already."

Only a week. A week of atrocious weather with so many plans and schedules delayed or canceled. Not being able to buzz in his visitors was hardly a hardship, especially from only the third floor. Scott should be grateful he didn't live in a high-rise. Then there might be a reason to complain.

Scott's apartment turned out to be the attic, taking up the whole of the third floor, much of the generous square footage seriously reduced by the sloping ceilings in every room. Rigby found himself wanting to duck even when he didn't need to.

The living room was neat and tidy, partly due to the sparse amount of furniture. A love-seat stood in front of the window centered under the peak of the roof, one of the few places near a wall where one could stand up without risk of bumping their head. A small coffee table, two low bookcases and two decrepit beanbag chairs were the only other furniture. There were no pictures on the wall, although the lack of suitable wall space might explain that, no photographs and, most surprisingly, no television or audio equipment. The only insight into Scott that Rigby could garner from the room was he liked mysteries and thrillers. And he didn't decorate for Christmas.

Scott slumped down on the sofa, taking up most of the space. "Have a seat."

Rigby glanced at the beanbag chairs. No way. Once he sat

down he might have problems getting up. He remained standing, allowing Pearson the option of squeezing onto the sofa next to Scott.

Pearson rejected the offer too. Instead he introduced himself to Scott, the young man's face losing much of its color on learning that the other cop was actually the chief of police.

A sign of guilt? Rigby was willing to read it as such. But guilt for what? For all he knew Scott could have stolen property or drugs on the premises. Maybe that was what had taken him so long to answer the door. He'd had evidence to hide.

Rigby glanced out the window. The view was of the side of the house next door. Most of the other windows would be cut into the roof which would mean Scott wouldn't be able to see who was outside the front door. He couldn't have known it would be the police so if he had hidden anything away it had to be something he didn't want anyone to see.

Pearson cleared his throat. Glanced expectantly at Rigby.

"When we spoke outside the house, you said you went to see Mr. Reed every day." Rigby hoped to put Scott on the defensive from the start.

"Yes." Scott grinned. "The patients like continuity, you know. They don't want someone different going in every day."

"But you haven't been today?"

"Monday's my day off."

"So you don't go every day?"

The grin slipped. Scott's eyes narrowed. "Of course I have a day off." His voice became indignant. "It should be two, but there's not enough nurses so I volunteered for the extra day." The grin returned but forced. "The overtime comes in useful. And I like the old guy. He's quite the character. Got some good stories to tell." He broke off. "Or he did have until recently. His family has got here just in time, I reckon. I mean, we knew he was sick. It's why I was going in the first place, but sometimes you'd hardly know he was, and then last week he started to decline rapidly. Only thing he talks about now is his brother. His dead brother. It's so sad." Scott hesitated. Frowned. "But why are you interested in Mr. Reed?"

"We're not," Rigby said.

Scott's frown deepened. "But... You asked..."

"Whether you were at the house every day." When Scott didn't speak, Rigby continued. "Do you know the nurse who goes in on Mondays?"

"Isabelle?"

Rigby nodded.

Scott shrugged. "Only as a work colleague. Obviously I don't see her on the job. I've met her a few times at company events and the like. But I wouldn't say I knew her well."

"Did you know she's the sister of the woman killed in a hit-and-run last week?"

"What?"

Together with the look of horror in Scott's eyes, Rigby took that as a no. He glanced over at Pearson but the chief wasn't giving anything away.

Scott gulped several times before managing to say, "How awful." He gulped again. "I heard about the hit-and-run. Didn't pay too much attention because the name didn't mean anything." He gasped. "Is that why you were at the house? Because you wanted to see Isabelle?"

"No. That was in regard to something else."

Another gasp. "Something else? Like what?"

"Where were you on Tuesday evening, Scott?"

The change in direction of questioning threw Scott off balance which was exactly what Rigby intended.

"Me? Tuesday evening? I… I…" His eyes lit up. "I was out with friends."

"All evening?"

"Seven until… Actually, I stayed out all night. A birthday party for a friend. We started at the bar then went to his girlfriend's place, but the weather was so bad by midnight and most of us had had far too much to drink so we crashed out on her floor. Got up early enough to dash home, change, and get to work." He chuckled. "But I doubt the birthday boy made it to work."

Rigby faked amusement at the story. Silently, he cursed. If the alibis held up, he could rule Scott out. He glanced at Pearson. The chief didn't look too happy either, probably realizing what a waste of time it all was. Though Pearson could hardly blame him, the chief was the one who'd suggested he came along to see Scott.

"Could you give us some names and numbers so we can confirm that?"

Scott gaped at them in turn. "Seriously? You think I might have something to do with it? Why?" He shook his head in disbelief. "That's ridiculous. I told you, I didn't drive home that night."

"It's just routine so we can eliminate you from our enquiries."

"Why am I even part of your enquiries? Because I happen to work with the sister of the victim? That's crazy. You said it was a hit-and-run. Anyone could have been driving. Are you checking on all the others who work at the company too? Or what about Isabelle's friends and families? Are you checking them out too?"

"Mr. Yates." Pearson's tone silenced Scott's rant. "Calm down. No, we are not checking everyone associated with Miss Heaton. The reason we're here now is that you are one of a limited number of people who had potential access to the vehicle we believe was involved in the hit-and-run."

Scott laughed. A scared laugh. "Me?" He leaped up from the sofa. "The only vehicle I've had access to is my own."

Pearson gestured for Rigby to hand over the photo. He unfolded it and showed it to Scott. "Recognize this?"

Scott stared at the photo. Shook his head.

"Think again," Pearson said.

Scott looked askance but the expression on Pearson's face silenced any further objections. It was a look Rigby wished he could emulate, though so far he'd only been on the wrong end of it. It was a look that made you shrivel inside and want to confess your sins and crawl into a dark hole. Or at least, that was the effect it had on him and by the look of it, it was having a similar effect on Scott.

Were they about to get a confession? Scott was hiding something. He was sure of it.

Scott took the photo from Pearson, studied it intently and then handed it back with a curt, "No, no idea whose car that is."

Before they could tell him, he pulled a phone out of his back pocket, pulled up his contacts and reeled off a series of names, addresses and numbers. Rigby scribbled them down in his notebook,

Scott begrudgingly repeating them to make sure he'd got them right. Then he told them to get out.

Chapter 46

Rigby eyed the line of cars parked on the street outside Scott's home. Two had been there long enough to be completely encased in snow but they weren't the right shape. Still, he went over and nudged a little snow away from the hoods in the hope he might catch Scott out in a simple lie. No such luck. One car was black, the other silver. Wherever the car was they were looking for, it wasn't on this street. Only the snow was white.

As he picked his way back over a mound of snow to Pearson's car he glanced up at Scott's living room window. Was Scott even now calling around his contacts to warn them the police might be in touch about an alibi and confirming what they should say? Though if Scott was going to create a false alibi why not pick just one person rather than a group? Safety in numbers didn't necessarily apply when trying to keep a story straight. One slip of the tongue could ruin everything. And the more tongues, the greater the risk of a slip.

Pearson already had the engine on and the heat blasting by the time Rigby got into the car. The snow had abated while they were indoors so a flick of the wipers was all Pearson needed to get under way. Typical. How come Pearson got all the breaks?

"What do you think? The girlfriend first?" Pearson pulled out onto the road. "If her version of events doesn't tie up then we'll know Scott is lying about something."

Rigby plugged the address into his phone. Pearson's offer to accompany him on the alibi checks was unexpected. And unnecessary. Was there a reason behind it? Since his accident earlier in the year, the chief had been mostly deskbound. True, he was still available as a sounding board but it wasn't the same as when they were active partners out in the field together on the more serious cases.

If Pearson had been with him on the last major case, the outcome could have been very different. Pearson would probably have stopped him running into the house, stopped him setting off a chain of events resulting in one man dead, one man imprisoned and Rigby missing one of the most important events in his life, the birth of his daughter. And there wouldn't be the nightmares and the fears which translated into a lack of confidence. He'd made a mistake, a serious mistake, and got away with it. Risk came with the job even in a small town. Desperate people did desperate things and part of his job was to stop them. He'd always accepted that. But he had new responsibilities now, ones that had nothing to do with the job, and they were changing him in ways he'd never imagined, making him more cautious. Had Pearson picked up on that? Felt he needed to keep an eye on him?

The girlfriend lived in one of the few purpose-built apartment blocks in Lewisville. A small complex of four-story buildings close to the hospital, the apartments had originally been built with hospital workers in mind, but as house prices had started to rise they'd become a magnet for those looking to get a foot on the property ladder. Rigby had viewed one during his search for a permanent home but even it had been out of his budget at the time. As they trudged up to the fourth floor and along a clean but drab hallway, he was grateful it hadn't worked out for him. It had none of the charm of the cottage he now called home.

A willowy young brunette waited at the door of one of the apartments for them. She made no attempt to invite them in even after they'd showed their ID. Instead she crossed her arms, leaned against the door jamb and smiled expectantly at Rigby.

Rigby explained why they were there without naming Scott in the hope she hadn't been warned the police were likely to turn up. Jane appeared puzzled by his question of what she'd been doing the previous Tuesday evening but after only a slight hesitation she confirmed she'd been at a bar with her boyfriend, invited several people back to her apartment and they'd all ended up staying over. When asked for names, Scott's was among them, neither first nor last and mentioned as casually as the others.

As much as he didn't want to—because where would that leave the investigation? —Rigby was inclined to believe her. He thanked her and made to turn away.

"He's not in trouble again, is he?"

Rigby glanced back. "What?"

Jane chewed on her bottom lip, refusing to look at either of them. "My boyfriend, Danny." She cast a quick glance back into the apartment.

"What makes you think he might be in trouble?" Pearson asked.

"Because you're here, asking questions about where he was."

"No. We asked you what you were doing that evening. Then we asked who you were with. It was you who gave us the names. Danny wasn't on our radar until you mentioned him."

That was a lie. Scott had given them Danny's name too.

"This has nothing to do with Danny." Pearson walked away, motioning for Rigby to follow. "Thanks for your help, Ma'am."

Rigby wanted to ask what kind of trouble Jane thought Danny might be in but she was already shutting the door on them. And why was Pearson being so dismissive of her concern?

As they exited the lobby doors, Pearson pointed out a camera on the outside wall. "See if you can get any footage from Tuesday night. I didn't get the impression she was lying but that would confirm it one way or the other."

Rigby cursed under his breath. How had he missed the camera? It was the first thing he should have looked for, visual evidence being so much more persuasive than verbal. Pearson had obviously spotted it on the way in and waited to see if he mentioned it. Wanted to see if his senior detective was still on the ball. Apparently not.

He crossed to the buzzer and reread the list of names. There was no mention of a superintendent but underneath the list was a small sign stating the name of a security company and a phone number.

He called the company as Pearson headed back to the car. Told the officious guy who answered what he wanted. The guy told him to get a warrant. Rigby cursed. The day was going from bad to worse.

Chapter 47

Rigby stood at the back of the church and watched the people file in. There were more than he'd expected. Had all these people really known Gail or had the news of the tragic death of the young mother so close to Christmas brought out onlookers? More importantly, was the driver of the car among the growing congregation, propelled by guilt to bear witness to the grief they'd caused?

On the left-hand side of the aisle, several young couples had gathered in the rows near the front. From the emotional hugs and kisses as they somberly greeted each other Rigby assumed the women were members of Gail's moms group. Some of the guys hung back slightly, presumably there more to support their partners than out of a close connection to the deceased.

Farther back there was a growing contingent of former high school students, some who'd arrived alone, others in pairs or groups. Rigby recognized one or two of them. Awkward handshakes were offered, the brief smiles on seeing someone for the first time in years fading on the acknowledgement of why they were there. Gail's death had touched a nerve. They were young, had their whole future ahead of them still. This was a timely reminder the future might not be as long as they'd expected.

On the other side of the aisle, the age range was more varied. He assumed the folks near the front were extended family members as young and old interacted as only families do. Behind them the people were more aloof, leaving empty seats between themselves and the others on the row. From their age he guessed they were friends and neighbors of Gail's parents. People who'd known her as a baby, watched her grow up, and now were watching her put to rest. One or two were already sniffling.

The quiet organ music faded away. Conversations stopped. The congregation straightened in their seats then, almost as one, stood as the somber notes of the funeral dirge filled the church.

Rigby fought an overwhelming desire to flee. He'd managed so far to block out the memories of the last funeral he'd attended. That had been personal—this was just part of the job. Damn, why hadn't he asked the chief if he'd be willing to represent the department? Pearson would understand why.

But it was too late. As the priest led the pallbearers down the aisle followed by the immediate family members, the memories came surging back. Another young woman, another untimely death. And a heap of guilt to go with his grief.

He pressed his lips tightly together. Blinked away the sheen threatening to obscure his vision. This was about Gail not Katy. Gail. The young woman in the coffin. The young woman whose family he'd yet to find justice for. The family he had to find justice for.

The sight of Martin walking behind the coffin was nearly his undoing though Martin seemed to be managing to keep it together. Maybe because he had no choice. He carried Suzie in his right arm, his left hand clutching Martha's hand. The children seemed incredibly young to be at a funeral, but after all it was their mother's. What was Martin supposed to do? Leave them behind?

Rigby had no idea what the protocol was when it came to children and funerals.

Izzy walked on the other side of Martha, her face partly hidden by the veil on her hat. Gail's parents followed behind and then Hannah and John. There was no sign of the latter's children.

As soon as the family was inside the church, Rigby slipped out the door. Hopefully, nobody would notice he hadn't stayed for the whole service. He could hardly be a sniveling wreck when he offered his condolences at the end. He made a dash for his car.

"Detective Rigby!" The familiar voice stopped him in his tracks. Damn, he was in no mood to deal with any reporters, let alone Josh Brook, but he could hardly ignore the guy. That would be asking for another snide dig in Josh's report on the funeral. Though why was the guy even there? He was a crime reporter. Didn't usually cover funerals or the like. Of course, this was a funeral linked to an unsolved crime. A crime Josh knew Rigby was investigating. Why wouldn't he be there? Any chance to needle Rigby, no matter the circumstances.

Rigby blinked hard. Hoped his eyes wouldn't give him away. The damage Josh could do with a photo of an emotionally distraught detective didn't bear thinking about. He turned, faked a somber expression, and looked expectantly at the reporter.

"You're not staying for the service?"

Several sarcastic responses came to mind, but instead he made do with "I have a job to do."

"But you took the time to come to the church. Why bother? Did you think the driver of the vehicle might have shown up?"

Rigby glared at him.

"Is that why you're rushing off? Do you think he did? Is there going to be an arrest?"

The gall of the guy. As if Rigby would tell him in advance. "Why don't you stick around and see?"

Josh laughed. "I intend to. This is my job. I'm just curious as to when the family can expect closure. It's been a week and according to the family the police don't seem any closer to finding out who the driver was."

Rigby cursed silently. What had they told Josh? And by family, who did he mean? Martin? Or Gail's parents or sisters?

"You been hassling the family, Josh? Because I know that's what you're good at. Never mind what anyone's going through, it's the story that matters, right?" He paused, but before Josh could speak he added, "Parasite," and headed for his car.

"Don't follow me. Don't follow me," he mumbled under his breath. There were so many emotions at play he couldn't be sure what he'd do if Josh came after him. There was only so much he could take.

Fortunately the reporter made the right choice and Rigby reached his car without doing anything he'd later regret. He slumped into the driver's seat, turned the heat on full and shivered as the blast of warm air engulfed him. The snow had finally stopped, the gloom replaced by a cloudless, brilliant blue sky, but the temperature was brutal. It wouldn't be long before all the soft fluffy snow blanketing the town was rock solid. Which meant the emergency services would be working overtime as people overestimated both their and their vehicles' ability to deal with the treacherous slippery conditions.

Luckily, this winter he didn't have to worry about Becca being out on the roads. Like all the emergency workers, EMTs didn't have the option of snow days. Emergencies didn't care what the weather was like, in fact the worse the weather the more emergencies, a simple fact of life. But what annoyed him most were the number of emergencies Becca attended caused by sheer obstinacy, the belief of certain individuals that they were stronger than whatever nature wanted to throw at them. That it was almost a badge of courage to say they ignored the warnings and survived. No thought for the people who might have to risk their own lives if nature got the upper hand.

He'd hated weather like this when he'd been on patrol. As a detective he had slightly more control over when and where he went, but lately he'd had Becca to worry about. The price of love.

He sighed. Looked back at the church. Inside, Gail's family and friends were paying the ultimate price. Grief. All the more profound because she'd been taken so young. Was one of the congregation also suffering guilt? As far as he could tell they all had a personal connection to Gail. Nobody stood out as an oddity, without a reason to be there. Neither Scott Yates nor Dale Jessup had shown up. But why would they? It appeared Dale had no link to the family and Scott's only link was through Izzy.

He frowned. Izzy. He'd been surprised to see her walking beside Martin and the kids. Presumably in case Martin needed help with the girls, but it had struck him as strange. It almost gave the impression they were a couple. Kind of inappropriate for the funeral of his wife. Surely if Martin needed someone by his side, his mother, as the kids' grandmother, would have been a better choice.

He remembered Martin's comment about wishing they would all leave him alone. Maybe it hadn't been Martin's idea, but he hadn't the heart to say no.

A knock on the window startled him. He turned ready to unleash his anger on Josh only to see Harper gesturing at him to roll down the window. Hunched against the cold, she stuck her hands deep into her pockets and stomped her feet as she waited for him to respond, her warm breath dissipating into the air.

"What are you doing here?" he asked.

"Thought you might appreciate some company."

He eyed her warily. Company. This wasn't a social event. He was there on the off chance somebody would do or say something in his presence that would give them a lead. It was a long shot but with so little to work with what else could he do? Much longer and he would have to turn his attention to other cases. The town didn't have the budget for long drawn-out investigations with no prospect of a result. And definitely not for two detectives to be working the case.

Still, she was there. And looking colder by the minute. He unlocked the car doors. "Get in." As she clambered in, he added, "You should try dressing for the weather."

She laughed. "I think I'm wearing my entire closet." She leaned back in the seat and closed her eyes. "Oh, that's nice."

He let her defrost in silence.

"So why aren't you inside?" she asked eventually.

"I was until it started."

"But now?"

He glanced away. Fiddled with the heating. "I don't like funerals."

"Who does?" Harper hesitated. "Been to many?"

"Only the one." He assumed she knew what he meant. He hadn't told her but he couldn't believe she hadn't heard the full back story by now. But she didn't push for more detail. He liked that about her. There was a lot he liked about her. "What about you?"

"Three. Two grandparents and a classmate from school."

If that was a sly attempt to get him to open up she was going to be disappointed.

She sighed. "He wasn't a close friend. I barely knew him. He died in a motorbike accident day after graduation." She sighed again. "The bike was a graduation present from his parents. Can you imagine?"

Rigby couldn't. How many times must those parents have thought "if only."

"I think the whole grade turned out for the funeral. Nobody could believe it. A day earlier we'd all been happy and excited for the future. Our lives stretched ahead, full of possibility. And then the news broke. And suddenly life seemed so fragile. It was a real wake-up call."

"I think there's a good number of people in that church who've just received the same wake-up call."

"Big turn out?" She answered her own question. "Front page stories of tragedy will bring out the crowds."

"There definitely seemed to be a lot more than just family and friends." He shrugged. "Or maybe Gail really was that popular." He frowned. "Her kids were there. Behind the coffin with Martin. Do you think that's right? I can't help thinking they're too young to be at a funeral. The oldest is barely four."

"It is their mom."

"But at that age? They're too young to understand what it means so why put them through it? There's nothing to be gained from it, is there? And it would mean Martin could grieve properly, not have to worry about putting on a brave face for them. The guy must be in agony."

"Maybe he wanted them there. As a source of comfort. Every family's different." Harper glanced over at the church. "I'd be concerned about them playing up during the service though. That age, you can't always just tell them to be quiet. I guess you'd have to have someone primed to bring them out if they start wailing."

"Maybe that's why Izzy was with them."

Harper grimaced. "Izzy? Isn't she the sister? She's not going to want to leave her sister's funeral mid-service."

Harper had a point.

"She walked into the church with Martin. Do you think that's weird? I mean, anyone not knowing might have mistaken them for a couple. They were both holding Martha's hands. Martha, that's the oldest girl. If I hadn't known I would have been wondering about their relationship."

Harper turned the heating down. "It does sound strange but I guess it's whatever Martin needed to get him through the day and appearances be damned."

He supposed she was right. Though it was one thing to think appearances be damned and another to see the result splashed across the morning tabloids by the likes of Josh.

"Is your sister inside?"

"My sister?"

Harper looked askance. "Didn't you say she knew Gail from school? Charity work?"

"Oh, Louise." He'd forgotten about that link. Hadn't got around to speaking to her yet. Had she been among the high school group? He'd only given them a cursory glance from behind. If she'd seen the news reports she'd know he was the detective on the case. Yet she hadn't reached out to him either. Which if she'd still been in contact with Gail would be unusual. But ten years was a long time and for most people the twenties were a time of great change, especially when it came to friendships.

Harper cleared her throat.

"I didn't see her."

"Was she still close to Gail?"

"She hasn't returned my calls." It sounded better than saying he'd forgotten to call her back. How had that happened? It had completely slipped his mind. Were there other points he'd forgotten to follow up on?

"You're not close to your sister?"

"No! We are. Close. But we've both got busy lives. Don't get to speak as often as we'd like." He shut up. He didn't need to justify his relationship with Louise to Harper. "Anyway, she'd be the first to call if she was still in contact with Gail."

"Do you want me to give her a call?"

He glared at her. "Why would you do that?"

He knew the answer. Wanted to hear her admit it.

"Because you're her brother."

He scoffed. Nice try. Harper was quick thinking, he'd give her that. The concern at stake wasn't a point of procedure—a detective couldn't interview his own family or friends—but whether he was too exhausted, too stressed to do his job properly. Whether he should be sitting in a therapist's chair not a church pew watching a funeral. Harper's presence was not random.

The chief had sent her.

Chapter 48

Pearson thanked Collins and put the phone down. He sat back in his chair and girded himself for the confrontation ahead.

He'd never had reason to doubt Rigby before. Yes, the guy had made mistakes. Who hadn't? And he'd got himself into a few messes, but he could always be depended on to be thorough. Little escaped Rigby. He picked up on nuances other detectives might overlook, his attention to detail and memory of those details second-to-none, which was why he was still in the department despite, to put it mildly, being an occasional pain in the butt.

But the attention to detail seemed to be slipping. Usually Rigby would be the first to spot the security camera outside the young woman's apartment, but he'd entered the building with barely a glance at his surroundings.

After Rigby had left for the funeral, Pearson had reviewed the case file. Again it wasn't up to the standard he'd come to expect. There were notations of potential leads which hadn't been followed up, including one involving his sister. In all their discussions about the case, she'd never come up. Maybe Rigby suspected it would be a dead end but given it was a relative he had no right to make that decision. The mere suggestion of the involvement of a detective's relative could blow a case apart if it wasn't handled correctly. No matter how incidental. And Rigby knew it and should have handed it over to one of his colleagues immediately so a decision could be taken on how to proceed.

All he could hope was whatever the connection between

Louise and Gail it proved irrelevant. What the hell was Rigby thinking?

More to the point, what was he thinking? He should have stood firm. Told Rigby he wasn't welcome back until the new year. Another few weeks for the guy to get some sleep—the shadows under his eyes grew darker by the day—and to process what he'd gone through both personally and professionally without the added stress of an investigation going nowhere.

He stood up. Paced his office. Debated his options. Neither offered a satisfactory solution. Though maybe if he didn't make it an ultimatum he could lessen the fallout. Instead of calling Rigby into his office he strode into the detective bureau, pleased to see it was empty save for Rigby and Harper.

Harper stood by her desk peeling off layers, her chair almost hidden by the discarded garments. At the back of the office, Rigby fiddled with the coffee machine.

"How'd it go?" Pearson leaned against Turner's desk. Folded his arms across his chest.

"How do funerals ever go?" Rigby slammed the lid on the coffee machine down and switched it on. He stared at the jug as if fascinated by the drip of coffee.

Not a good sign. Pearson glanced at Harper. She made a face as she shook her head.

"Anything worth noting?" he tried again.

"Lots of sad people." Rigby turned three mugs over. "Gail is… was a popular person. Some more than others—sad, that is. Lot of people wiping away tears as they left the church. Only close family went to the grave site. I… we didn't think there was any point in following them.

"The others dispersed fast. It was so damn cold. I'd been hoping I might get a chance to ask some of them if they recognized the car." He shrugged. "A long shot. But hell, what else do we have? I obscured the license plate in the photo, didn't want them focusing on that. But I only got to two or three of them." He shrugged again. "No luck."

"If we'd had another copy of the photo I could have got to a few more people," Harper said.

"If I'd known you were going to be there, I'd have made you one," Rigby snapped back.

Harper gave Pearson a "see what I mean" look. Pearson smiled. Rigby rarely used petulance but when he did it meant he was irritated with himself rather than others. No doubt, he blamed himself for the lack of progress on the case.

His smile disappeared when Rigby turned to face him. The pain in his eyes, the grief etched on his face, hurtled Pearson back to the days after Katy died. Emotions that should have been healed by time, a new love, a new life and a new future, but possibly had just been hiding, waiting to be dredged up again.

He should never have let Rigby go to the church. Should have ordered him to stay away. Gone in his place. They'd got nothing out of it, only thrown Rigby back into a morass of memories.

"Go home," he said.

Rigby frowned.

"Go home. Now. Sleep. Or hold your daughter. Or hug Becca. Anything but think about this."

"But…"

"One more day won't hurt." He gestured at Harper. "We've got this."

Harper nodded her agreement.

He waited for Rigby's next protest, but Rigby grabbed his coat and phone and headed silently for the door, only to stop and glance back at Harper. "Louise."

"I'm on it," Harper said and let out a huge sigh as Rigby disappeared from sight. "That was intense. Outside the church, I thought he was…" She frowned. "Is there something I should know?"

Pearson hesitated. If she was here for the duration, and he hoped she was, Harper had a right to know, especially when what they'd hoped Rigby had put behind him obviously wasn't.

The coffee maker gurgled and hissed.

"Coffee?"

Chapter 49

Rigby had every intention of following Pearson's orders but the chief had obviously forgotten what early fatherhood was like. He arrived home to find Becca in the living room feeding Lotte so he could neither hug her nor cuddle his daughter. Instead he made do with a kiss on the forehead and a genuine "Everything okay?" which prompted Becca to launch into a tirade of everything that was not okay.

Lotte had cried for most of the morning, wouldn't settle. Becca was tired of feeling like a cow, her only purpose in life to feed on demand. She hadn't been out of the house for days. She was a mess. The house was a mess. They were out of bread and milk again because he hadn't bought enough the last time he went to the store. What had he been thinking? He knew the weather was going to be bad. Knew she wouldn't be able to get out. But he wasn't thinking, was he? Not about her and Lotte at least. Work, work, work. He cared more about a dead woman than his family. It was almost Christmas and they still hadn't put up the tree. Hadn't even got the tree.

And she'd let Cocoa out into the yard because she couldn't take him for a walk and he'd trailed in a whole pile of dirt which was still there because she hadn't had time to clean it up. Why hadn't he taken Cocoa out before he went to work? She couldn't do everything. She was tired. And a mess. And the house was a mess. And what did he do to help? Nothing. Just left his dirty coffee cup in the sink for her to clear up.

She burst into tears.

Rigby stood open-mouthed. This was all sparked by a dirty coffee cup?

Lotte sensed her mother's distress, pulled away from Becca's breast, and let him know in no uncertain terms what she thought about it all.

He was tempted to flee. But he came to his senses. He had walked Cocoa. She'd told him how much bread and milk to get. He couldn't help it if she kept making coffee and toast and then let them get cold before she could eat them. The house wasn't a mess—well, not that much of a mess. And she certainly wasn't a mess. So what if she hadn't combed her hair or her shirt was covered in regurgitated milk stains. She was still beautiful to him.

He went to embrace her. She batted him away, wiped her nose on her arm, shushed Lotte and switched her over to the other breast.

He thought of all the things he could say and then decided silence was the best option. He wandered into the kitchen. Found a dejected looking Cocoa slumped in his crate. The trail of dirt had mostly melted, now only visible as tiny pools of grimy water. He mopped them up then unlocked the crate, blocking the door with his body until he could be sure Cocoa's paws were clean. The dog licked his face and snuggled against his chest, as much in need of a hug as he was. He shuffled back so he could lean against the wall, his legs stretched out in front of him. Cocoa sat on his lap, his head resting against Rigby's shoulder, their chins almost touching, their eyes meeting in sympathy.

"You had a tough day too?" Rigby scratched Cocoa's neck. "She loves you really. You just have to be patient. Things will get better." He sank his face into the dog's fur. Was he trying to reassure Cocoa or himself?

He was still there when he heard the front door open. They'd given his mother a key so her visits wouldn't disturb Becca if she was sleeping or feeding Lotte. He wondered what goodies she was delivering. Hopefully they might include bread and milk. His mother knew the contents of their fridge and cupboards better than they did.

She was at the kitchen door before he could get to his feet, her expression startled. She hadn't expected to find him home and certainly not sitting on the kitchen floor.

"What the—" She broke off. She never cursed because she said there were enough words in the dictionary without having to use bad language, but the sight of him had obviously made her forget them.

She dropped her bags onto the counter and approached with open arms as he eased Cocoa off his lap and stood up. It wasn't Becca or Lotte, but it was the next best thing. He let her enfold him in her arms, cradle his head—though he had to bend a little so she could—and it was as if the dam he'd been so busy building all morning to keep his emotions at bay broke.

She let him talk. He probably sounded to her like Becca had to him, the thoughts coming out random and unfiltered. No logical progression. Not necessarily based in fact. When he finally ran out of steam she asked him what he'd eaten that day—the answer was nothing—and ordered him to sit at the table while she made both him and Becca a sandwich. She didn't ask him what he wanted but produced one full of his favorite foods. She hadn't forgotten even after all those years.

She took Becca's sandwich through to the living room and then returned and sat opposite, dispensing advice while he ate. Her reassurances that the hiccups he and Becca were experiencing were normal buoyed him. It was always tough, she told him. Anyone who said otherwise was lying.

Babies took up time, energy and patience, especially the first one when the changes to daily life were so enormous. She could still remember the sense of frustration she'd felt after he'd been born. How the image she'd been sold of motherhood didn't tie up with her experience the majority of the time. And she said, with a twinkle in her eyes, he'd been one of the "good" babies. She'd often wondered how some of her friends had coped with babies that wouldn't feed, wouldn't sleep, or were constantly colicky. It was tough enough with a good baby.

"Be patient with each other, do your best and this phase will pass." She chuckled. "And down the line you'll barely remember it." She paused. "Until you have the next one."

Rigby was fairly certain there weren't going to be any more. Not now they knew what it was like. Did that make him a wimp? His parents had gone through it four times. Four! And yet somehow they'd weathered it. He wondered how his father had felt at the time. How he'd coped. Maybe he should get together with him over a beer and pick his brains. His father would like that. He liked dispensing advice to his son.

Rigby sighed. He probably should have taken it more often.

He cleared his throat. His mother had a soft smile as if she was on a trip down memory lane, one of the pleasant lanes. "So Mom, in terms of this good baby scale, I mean, how would you rate Lotte?"

His mother's face lit up. "Oh, you've got a real sweetie, Paul. You don't know how lucky you are."

Her words left Rigby speechless. They were one of the lucky ones? How much worse could it get?

Chapter 50

No one said a word when Rigby strolled into the office two hours late the next morning, although Gaines made a point of checking his watch. He ignored the gesture, determined not to get riled up.

He'd woken at his usual time but instead of his normal routine when he was on first shift, which was basically up and out in the shortest possible time, he'd made breakfast for Becca, amused Lotte while she ate it, and cleaned up the kitchen while she had a shower. Then he'd taken Cocoa for a walk. He'd have taken Lotte too if the temperature hadn't still been so brutal. Lotte was asleep when he got back and Becca much more cheerful than the day before so they had one more cup of coffee together before he left the house—after he'd put the dirty cups in the dishwasher.

Someone—he suspected Harper because no one had bothered before—had put a small fake Christmas tree with lights on the counter near the coffee machine. It reminded him that he'd promised Becca he'd pick up a tree on the way home.

"I spoke to Louise yesterday," Harper said as he brought his coffee to his desk.

"And?"

"She hasn't spoken to Gail in years. Said they'd worked together on the school project but weren't really friends and there were no trips to Africa for any of them. Gail was a year ahead of her in school. Once she left there was no reason to keep in touch. She'd seen the news about the accident. Hadn't realized Gail and Martin had got married but she said she wasn't surprised. She described them as crazy about each other in high school."

So Louise was a dead end as far as the case was concerned. That was a relief. Pearson's patience had its limits. If Louise had had valuable information, he'd really be in the dog house.

"She's nice," Harper added. "Your sister. Very friendly."

He faked a smile. He hoped not too friendly with Harper. The stories Louise could tell. He didn't want any of his colleagues hearing them.

"She was surprised you didn't call her yourself." Harper hesitated. "Said she hadn't seen you since the day after Lotte was born. I explained that as a relative you couldn't interview her." Harper smiled mischievously. "You know what she said in response?"

He hated to think.

"She couldn't see why that would have stopped you."

It almost hadn't.

"Anyway, she said to say she'd see you at Christmas, if not before."

"Thanks." He picked up the case file. Wanted to read what Harper had written about the interview.

"By the way, I think she's hoping to be godmother."

Rigby frowned. "We're not religious."

"You're not going to have Lotte baptized?"

Rigby scowled. The grandparents were all in favor of it, but he and Becca thought it was hypocritical if they were never going to take Lotte to church. Surely it was better to let her make her own decision when she got older.

"You should at least name guardians. Just in case…" Harper didn't need to finish the sentence. Lotte had come within a hair's breadth of being fatherless from the moment of birth. But she would still have had a mother. A guardian, that would only kick in if… He shuddered. Had Becca thought about it? They'd never discussed it. Hadn't really discussed how close that day had been. She didn't need to know the exact details. What good would it do? What she did know was bad enough. He'd been held hostage by a man with nothing to lose.

His phone rang. Grateful for the distraction he snatched it

up.

"I think I'm going to make your day." Gina's upbeat voice made him smile.

"Go on. Try."

"After we spoke, I ran some more tests on Dale Jessup's car, specifically the license plate. Given you suspected it might have been switched, I thought I should look at the back of the plate too. Previously I'd only examined it while it was on the car."

"You found something?" He couldn't keep the excitement out of his voice. Of course she'd found something. She'd said she was going to make his day. "And?"

"Two prints. One full. One partial. And they're in the system."

"Yes!" Rigby punched his fist in the air. "Let me guess. Scott Yates?"

"Who?"

"What?" Rigby's enthusiasm temporarily deflated. "Not Scott Yates?"

"No. Whoever that is." Gina paused. "They're a woman's prints. Isabelle Heaton. She works as a nurse—"

Rigby cut her off. "I know. Gail Cooper's sister."

"Oh my God." Gina went quiet. Presumably as stunned as he was. "Her sister? You think? No!"

Rigby ignored her.

Izzy. First he learned of her link through work to the Reed house. And now this. But why would Izzy be involved in stealing the license plate? Did she know what it was going to be used for? She was only at the house once before the accident after Dale arrived and she hadn't been back as far as he knew. If she stole it, she couldn't have returned it. There had to be someone else involved and as far as he could tell there were only two possibilities—Scott Yates or Dale Jessup.

"Are you positive they're Izzy's prints?"

"Sure as I can be."

Damn, how could that be? It made no sense. Her own sister? Randomly killed in the process of some crime that Izzy had been involved in? The woman must be devastated. He pictured Izzy with the kids. Was it guilt that had made her so eager to lend a hand, to take time off work to help Martin?

He drummed his fingers on the desktop. Frowned. But unless Scott or Dale had told her, Izzy wouldn't know they were looking at Dale's license plate. They hadn't told the family about it yet. So if she'd been involved in stealing the plate on Monday, she'd have no reason to connect it to Gail's death unless she was also involved in the hit-and-run. The thought turned his stomach. What possible reason could she have for wanting to kill her sister?

"Rigby? You still there?" Gina's voice startled him from his thoughts.

"Yeah. Sorry. Thanks, Gina. Good work. I'll get back to you."

He put the phone down, his mind still trying to make sense of what he'd heard. He grabbed the case notes and shuffled through the pages until he found the one where he'd summarized his conversation with Izzy. She'd told him she'd gone straight around to her sister's house when she'd heard the news but there was no record of where she'd been earlier.

He hadn't asked the basic question even though at that point he'd had suspicions the accident might have been more than a simple hit-and-run. Not that he'd expect her to have admitted she was sitting in a car on a street corner waiting for her sister to pass by so she could knock her over. But if she was involved, Izzy would have had to lie to him. And once there was one lie, others usually followed. And the more lies the easier it was to find the lie that would catch the teller out.

Izzy hadn't been asked any questions yet that would require her to lie. In fact, most of what he knew about her had come from third parties rather than Izzy herself. She'd talked at length about her sister and at the time that's what he'd been interested in. And he'd been acutely aware of asking any questions that might suggest to the family they were looking at the case as anything other than a random hit-and-run. Damn Pearson and his edict.

Though if he'd wanted to he could have found out where Izzy had been before she heard the news about Gail without raising suspicion. Getting people to talk was one of his skills. And Izzy had talked. He recalled his surprise at her description of Gail as lucky so soon after the woman's death. He'd put it down to shock but could it have been jealousy pure and simple? And all the calls from Izzy asking whether they'd found the driver, as if the family wouldn't be the first to hear when they did—were they not out of frustration at the police ineptitude as he'd assumed, but as a way of tracking whether the police were honing in on the truth?

But why would Izzy want her sister dead? What possible— Damn! His mind flashed back to the church. Izzy walking alongside Martin. Holding Martha's hand. As if they were a couple.

Were they a couple?

Chapter 51

Pearson's face fell as Rigby brought him up to date on the case, the boost to the investigation the new evidence brought outweighed by the dark direction it was leading them.

Izzy provided the answer to several questions they had if indeed the hit-and-run had been deliberate. She would likely have known Gail was going out that evening, would have known the route her sister would take between Hannah's house and home. Would have known the approximate time and where would be a good place to wait for her.

She was one of the few people who'd had access to the license plate and her fingerprints on it confirmed that she'd played some part in its removal, presumably the day before the hit-and-run when she was tending to Dale's grandfather. But how had she got it back? As far as they knew she hadn't been back to the house since that visit.

Rigby highlighted that question on the white board. It had to be answered. He wrote Scott and Dale's names with a question mark next to it, convinced it had to be one of them working with Izzy though he came up blank as to why they would be.

Harper, who had been invited to sit in because three minds were better than two, especially when at least one of them was female, pointed out that if Izzy had been planning this for a while she could have found some way of copying a key or leaving a window unlocked so she could sneak back in and replace the plate.

"That's a hell of a risk to take," Rigby said.

Harper shrugged. "Hell of a risk taking it in the first place. She presumably knew the layout of the place well, knew which rooms they slept in. She could have watched the house for a few nights, figured out their routine, when would be the best time to go in."

"But if she took the plate on Monday, wasn't there a risk Dale would have noticed it was missing before she could get it back?" Pearson turned to Rigby. "Didn't you say he went out on Tuesday? And both cars were in the garage then, right? She couldn't know he wouldn't take his own car."

"It was a risk she had to take, I guess." Harper glanced over at Rigby. "Which way were the cars parked?"

Rigby pictured himself walking into the garage. "Dale's car had been reversed in. The other had been driven straight in. Why?"

Harper smiled. "Florida cars only have a rear plate. If the car was backed up to the rear wall, Dale's hardly likely to notice if the plate was there or not."

Rigby cursed silently. He hadn't even considered that. And Dale hadn't thought to mention it. Was that telling? If Dale was involved there'd be no need for Izzy to sneak around. But why the hell would Dale let her use his license plate for what had to be an illegal activity? If he was willing to let her use the plate, why not let her use the car? Maybe because he was afraid it would be damaged?

He let out a loud exhale. "The more we learn, the less sense it makes."

"If your theory's right and Izzy and Martin are in it together, why would you expect there to be any sense in it?" Pearson shook his head. "If they wanted to be together why didn't Martin just split up with Gail? Why kill her?"

"I can't see that going down well with the rest of the Heaton family." Harper said. "Divorcing one sister and taking up with another. And what about the kids? There'd be joint custody at least. Very messy. And maybe he didn't want Gail but he wanted the kids."

"They were supposed to be crazy about each other," Rigby said.

"And maybe they were. At the beginning. But marriages, babies." She cast a cautious glance at Rigby. "It can take the shine off a relationship. They'd been together, what? Ten years? A lot of relationships that start off with the couple being crazy for each other don't last that long. Married or not,"

Rigby studied Harper. She sounded as if she was speaking from experience. Despite looking as if she could still be in college, she was of an age where she could have had a serious relationship gone wrong. Was that what had brought her to Lewisville? An escape from the memories? So far, she'd always been vague about the move and he didn't like to pry. No matter how curious he was.

Or how uncomfortable she'd made him feel.

"Okay, let's move on." There was a hint of impatience in Pearson's voice. "There seems to be a lot we still don't know." He paused. Glanced from one to the other grimly. "Including whether the license plate is even connected to the hit-and-run."

"It has to be," Rigby said.

"You could prove that in court, could you?"

Rigby scowled. There was no need for Pearson to be snarky. Or for Harper to look as if she was about to laugh.

"We don't even know who the car in the photo belongs to," Pearson said. "Let alone why it's got the wrong plate on it."

"Patrol has been on the lookout for any car fitting the description. They've come up blank. Not a single sighting of a similar car. It's either long gone from the area or it's hidden in a garage somewhere. And if it's the latter, unless you'd like to order a house-to-house search of garages belonging to everyone who's got that model of white car, we're not going to find it."

Pearson picked up the photo of the car and studied it. "Get this out to the public. Flyers around town, asking if anyone recognizes it." He half smiled. "Who knows we might hit lucky with a nosy neighbor. And get it into the press. That might shake out a few leads. But obscure the plate otherwise all the tips, assuming we get any, will probably only lead back to Jessup." Pearson put the photo down. "I assume you've checked Izzy doesn't drive a white car?"

Rigby grimaced. He hadn't officially. But when he'd visited Martin there'd been three cars outside the house. A silver SUV with kid seats in the back, an ancient blue sedan and a yellow car with a bumper sticker about nurses.

"Not unless she's got more than one car," he said to cover himself.

Pearson glared at him. "Harper, check it out. But first I want you to bring her in. Let's hear what she has to say about her fingerprints being on the back of the plate."

Harper stood up. Rigby hesitated, annoyed that the chief was handing her this element of the case. His case. He got to hand out flyers while she got to arrest a suspect? The chief must be well and truly pissed with him.

"You coming?" Harper said.

"Am I?" He glanced at the chief. "I thought—"

Pearson heaved an exasperated sigh. "As the lead detective, why wouldn't you go?" He shook his head at Harper. "Try and keep him out of trouble this time."

Chapter 52

As expected, Izzy was at Martin's house. She even answered the door. Rigby wondered whether she'd already moved in on the pretext of helping out, then chastised himself. He had no proof yet that her presence was not purely to help.

Her surprise at seeing them on the doorstep quickly changed to a welcoming smile and she invited them in without being asked. The smile soon faded as Rigby ignored the offer and told her why they were there.

"But I can't come with you now. Martin's not here. He had some business to take care of. I can't leave the girls."

Rigby made a point of looking at the two cars in the driveway. "His parents are still here?"

"Yes, but—"

"I'm sure they're capable of looking after their granddaughters until he gets home."

She hesitated. He waited for the next excuse. But it didn't come. Her shoulders slumped even as she forced a smile back on her face. "Let me get my coat and tell them I have to go out."

Rigby signaled for Harper to shadow her. But there was no need. Izzy merely went to the kitchen door, had a brief conversation with Mrs. Cooper during which she told her she had a work-related matter to deal with and wouldn't be long, then returned to the entrance, swapped her sneakers for boots and grabbed her coat from a rack by the front door.

She noticed Rigby's bemused expression. "Yes, okay, I lied

to them. But they've got enough to worry about. Why give them anymore?" She finished buttoning her coat. "Especially when it's all a big mistake. It has to be." She shook her head. "You'll see."

Rigby was eager to hear how she would explain away the fingerprints but he kept quiet all the way back to the station house. He didn't want to read Izzy her rights until they were in the interview room which meant they couldn't ask her any questions. But sometimes the strained silence, combined with guilt, fear and the knowledge of where they were headed, was enough to bring forth spontaneous outbursts, damning in nature. And if Izzy said anything, he had Harper there as a witness.

Unfortunately, Izzy sat tight-lipped and furious the whole journey. Harper took her to the interview room while Rigby let Pearson know they were back. Pearson declined to sit in on the interview, indicating he'd watch from the viewing room. The chief rarely did that, so Rigby took it as a warning. He was the one who'd be watched. But first he was going to do some watching of his own.

Izzy had taken her coat off and flung it over the back of her chair. She glanced around the room as Harper left, obviously less than impressed with her surroundings. She combed her fingers through her hair, checking her image in the one-way window. Did she know she was being watched? With nothing else to do she studied her fingernails then began tapping her right foot. Impatience or nerves? He suspected the latter when she started pulling at the collar of her cream turtleneck sweater.

They made her wait until Harper checked the DMV database. Izzy had a clean record and only one car, a yellow Beetle. She glanced at her watch as they entered the room. "Is this going to take long? I'd like to be back before Martin returns."

Rigby ignored the question. He sat down, switched on the recorder, and identified the date and time and who was in the room. Then he read Izzy her rights.

"Why would I need an attorney?" she said indignantly. "I haven't done anything wrong."

Rigby didn't mind. It made his job easier. Attorneys tended to tell their clients to shut up. He asked Izzy to sign the waiver. Made it clear she could change her mind at any time. He hoped she wouldn't.

They'd told her only that they wanted to question her in connection to a burglary at the Reed house. Didn't specify what had been taken. Rigby pushed a copy of the photo of the car in the garage across the table. "Recognize this?"

"It's Dale Jessup's car," she answered without hesitation.

Rigby glanced at Harper. Could it be that easy? Had she slipped up already? Dale kept his car in the garage. There was no reason for her to go in there. "How do you know that?"

Izzy looked incredulous. "Because the last time he was in Lewisville, he kindly gave me a ride home when my car broke down."

That would be easy enough to confirm. Rigby scribbled a reminder down on his pad.

"Has his car been stolen?" Izzy scoffed. "Is that why I'm here? You surely can't think I had anything to do with that."

"No. It's not his car that was stolen."

"Then what?"

He made sure he had her full attention. "The license plate."

Her expression never changed. She stared back at him. He would have loved to know what was going through her mind. Then she cracked a grin. "You think I stole a license plate?"

"I never said I thought you'd stolen it."

"Come on, Detective. We both know that's what you were implying."

He held her stare.

"Why would I steal a license plate? I already have two."

"I don't know. Why would you steal a license plate?" he parroted back.

She dropped the stare. Glanced down at her hands. He waited for her to ask for an attorney. Instead she looked up and in a firm voice said, "I wouldn't."

"Then perhaps you can explain how your fingerprints are on the back of the plate."

She still didn't blink. "It's not possible. It must be a mistake."

"Fingerprints don't lie."

She scoffed again. "Is that right?"

"Yes, it is." Her calmness under pressure was impressive.

Too impressive. A truly innocent person would be a little frantic by now, and rightly so. What greater fear was there than to be accused of a crime you hadn't committed? Rigby had once had the misfortune to be on the wrong side of the table in a murder inquiry and would never forget how scared he'd felt despite his innocence. He sure hadn't been able to remain calm and collected.

"What can I say?" Izzy said. "I did not steal the plate."

"You never went into the garage?"

She shrugged. "Why would I? I was only there to tend to Mr. Reed. I was in and out within an hour."

"What about when Dale gave you a ride home? You didn't go into the garage then?"

"No. He brought the car out before I got in."

Rigby made a note to get Gina to check for prints on the garage door. Though as a nurse Izzy would have had easy access to gloves. In fact, given the prints were only on the back of the plate, it suggested that at some point while it was in her possession she'd slipped up and touched it barehanded. If she'd realized what she'd done she would surely have wiped away the evidence.

"So you never went into the garage. And you didn't steal the plate?" Harper said, emphasizing the "you."

Izzy smiled at her. Nodded. "No. I didn't."

"And yet your prints are on the back." Harper shook her head as if she was trying to figure it out then casually asked, "Did you get someone else to steal it for you?"

The smile disappeared. Izzy gaped at Harper, her calm and collected composure gone. "No! What possible reason can you have to think I'd want to steal a license plate?"

Rigby waited a beat before replying. "Mostly they're stolen to avoid detection during another crime. Throw the police off if the vehicle happens to be seen or picked up on camera." He picked up the photo taken outside the Henderson house, laid it in front of Izzy. "Like in this instance."

As she studied the photo, he tried to determine whether the deepening frown on her face was driven by confusion or panic.

"I don't understand." She looked up. "Isn't that Dale's car?"

"That's what the driver would like us to believe."

"It isn't his car? It looks like it. How can you tell?"

Rigby smiled. "We have our ways. When you look closely you can see the differences. It's like the puzzle you probably did as a child. Spot the differences, between two pictures. They'd tell you how many there were and you had to find them."

"Is that how you solve crimes, Detective? By playing games?"

"Whatever it takes."

"Well, whatever you're playing at the moment, I'm sorry to tell you, but you're not going to win. I didn't steal a car, a license plate, or anything else from the Reed house. And I resent the insinuation."

"How do you explain your fingerprints then?"

"I can't. I told you. You must have made a mistake."

"Where were you last Tuesday evening?"

"Last Tuesday evening? I was…" The color drained from Izzy's face. "Last Tuesday? You're asking me where I was when… How dare you?" She blinked away tears. "Have you no compassion. I've just lost my sister and you're… you're…" The tears became a torrent. She brushed at her cheeks with the back of her hand. Sniffed hard and glared at him as if expecting an apology.

When none was forthcoming, she sniffed again. "This is disgraceful. I want an attorney."

Chapter 53

Izzy didn't have an attorney. Or at least not one who dealt with criminal law. Why would she, she spluttered? She'd never broken the law. She made it sound as if that fact alone should be enough for them to realize they'd made a big mistake. Being accused of being a thief was bad enough but to suggest she'd played any part in her sister's death was simply outrageous.

She offered all this without any encouragement from Rigby and, fortunately, before the tape was turned off so there could be no later claim he'd continued asking questions after her request. And he refrained from pointing out he had merely asked her whereabouts that particular evening and it was she who'd jumped to the conclusion it was connected to Gail's death. It was a fine line but he'd stayed on the right side of it.

He asked the desk sergeant to help her find an attorney. He hoped Izzy realized it could be some time before one arrived and she wasn't getting out of there before then, regardless of who might need her help. Unfortunately, it also meant the process might run way past the end of his shift. Damn her, why didn't she just answer the question? Then they could all have been out of there by three.

He went back to his desk. Checked his phone. Found a message from Nancy Tuccino reminding him he had an appointment with her that morning. As he was already ten minutes late, she assumed he wasn't coming, which didn't bode well for their agreement. If she hadn't heard from him by the end of the day, she'd have no option but to speak to the chief.

Damn. Damn. Damn! He called her back. Got her voicemail. She must have been in with another client. He decided to grovel in the hope it would give him more leeway. Told her the pressure was on with a big case and he couldn't get away. Maybe next week instead? "Things are great," he added to make her feel better about the delay.

He wished. He ended the call. Stuck his phone in his pocket. His desk phone rang.

"My office," Pearson said and hung up.

Harper was already there, laughing at something the chief was saying. She stopped abruptly when he walked in. Was it something about him? Not that he'd done much to laugh about recently.

"How do you think it went?" Pearson asked.

Rigby considered the question. Nixed the first thoughts that came to mind. Settled on "much as I expected."

"Really? You were expecting it to be such a disaster?"

Rigby scowled. "I'd hardly call it a disaster. I wasn't expecting an immediate confession about the plate, though that would have been nice. And I'm definitely intrigued by her response to the question of what she was doing Tuesday evening." He glanced at Harper. "We never mentioned there could be a link. She jumped to that conclusion."

"Damn easy one to draw from where I was standing." Pearson shuffled in his seat. "The girl's grieving her sister. A sister who by all accounts she was very close to. First she's accused of stealing then she's asked where she was when her sister was killed. How else was she supposed to read the situation?"

"No. She was asked where she was that evening, not at ten when the accident occurred."

Pearson shrugged. "In her mind, it's probably all the same. Grief works in strange ways. In some it illuminates what they were doing when they got the bad news. Others, it makes them numb, wipes out everything but the news. You should know that."

He did, but he didn't want to get into it in front of Harper. "You're defending her now?"

"No. I just don't want us jumping to convenient conclusions.

Missing the broader picture because we're so focused on evidence that could turn out to be a red herring."

"For God's sake, it's the only evidence we have! That plate number and Izzy's fingerprint on it. And I refuse to believe that the car parked around the corner from the accident only minutes before it happened is not connected in some way."

Pearson ignored the outburst. "So what's your next move going to be?"

Rigby didn't know. He'd been hoping he would get something to work with out of the interview, another lead to follow up on. He was more convinced than ever Izzy was involved, however obnoxious the idea was. There was a reason why they looked at family and friends first in crimes against the person. More often than not the culprit proved to be in the victim's close circle of contacts. It was only because of the nature of the crime—a hit-and-run, usually a random accident—that they hadn't looked at the close family immediately.

Normally, the first person they'd look at would be the spouse or partner. And Martin's appearance with Izzy at the funeral raised his suspicions, but Martin couldn't have been driving the car. He'd been at home looking after the kids, watching a documentary, having a beer. He couldn't have sat in the car all that time waiting for his wife to pass, knocked her down, drove home and then acted so devastated when the police turned up on his doorstep to deliver the news. Could he?

He would have had to hide the car on his return. And from memory Rigby was sure there was only the SUV in the driveway when he and Docherty turned up. The house had a single garage but assuming they were a two-car family, the second car was presumably in there.

He froze at the thought. Voiced his concerns. Could the second car be the one they were looking for? Could it actually have been on the premises as they spoke to Martin?

"He surely wouldn't have left the kids alone," Harper said.

"She died only two blocks from her home. He wouldn't have been gone long. He could have been in and out while the kids were asleep."

"Not if he sat in the car for an hour or more waiting for her." Pearson leaned back in his chair, studying Rigby. "Unless you are now suggesting the white car wasn't linked to the accident after all, was merely a coincidence?" He paused. "Problem is, that's the only link to Izzy."

Rigby crossed to the window. Leaned against the frame and stared out into the street. It was snowing again. Not even mid-afternoon and already gloomy as night, the Christmas lights on the tree in the middle of the common the only splash of color in the gray day.

Christmas tree. He mustn't forget the Christmas tree. Assuming there was anywhere still open by the time they'd finished with Izzy.

Izzy. Of course.

He pushed away from the window. "Maybe Izzy was there. While Martin was out. That's why she didn't want to tell us where she was. She wasn't expecting to be asked. Hadn't come up with a cover story." He sighed. "She's probably making one up as we speak."

He paced across the room, invigorated by his thoughts. "Maybe when he got back, she took the car away, hid it. They were in this together because that's what they wanted, to be together."

And all Martin's "love of my life" and "what will I do without her" laments were just spiel. Distractions.

"Sticking with your latest theory for a moment," Pearson said, which meant he wasn't buying it. "It's possible when you and Docherty turned up both the car was in the garage and Izzy was still in the house hiding until you left."

Rigby glared at Pearson. The chief was merely goading him, forcing him to justify his thoughts, but he also had a point. He'd just assumed Martin was alone with the kids. A perfectly reasonable assumption. He'd never asked so Martin didn't even have to lie. He remembered how Martin kept looking up at the ceiling. How he assumed Martin was thinking about his kids. Could all the answers he needed to solve the case have been right there? Damn.

"One question," Harper said. "About your theory. What makes you rule out Izzy as the driver?"

"Because." Rigby broke off. Thought through the logic. "If Izzy was the driver then there'd be no need for Martin to be involved. Or at least no direct connection back to him. And if the whole idea was for them to be together as a couple afterward then I would think Izzy would want Martin to be as equally involved as she was, for her own protection. In case he got cold feet. He was the one with the kids to worry about. If one went down, then they'd both go down."

"Compelling stuff," Pearson said sarcastically. "But no proof. And if you don't get anything more from Izzy, what do you suggest we charge her with? Stealing something nobody has reported stolen? No prosecutor is going to touch that one and Izzy probably knows that. So even if she is involved in something nefarious, she's not going to offer it up, is she?"

Rigby stayed silent. The chief was right again, but that didn't abate the fury building inside. He could sense what was coming.

"What other evidence do we have?" Pearson continued, not expecting an answer. "We can't keep coming up empty. I'll give you until tomorrow end of shift. No new leads by then, the case has to go on the back burner."

"Just like that. A young mother dies and we just shrug it off."

"We're not shrugging anything off. You've done all you can. Bar accusing people of crimes you can't prove, what else are you going to do? And face it—it's still possible it was a tragic accident."

"A tragic accident that turned into a crime because the damn driver didn't stop. A crime that nobody's going to pay for. There's a guilty person out there, whichever way you look at it. And you're just prepared to let them get away with it!"

Harper looked aghast. Pearson sat seemingly unperturbed; a danger sign Rigby knew only too well. He knew he'd gone too far but he'd be damned if he was going to walk away from the case.

He stormed out of the office.

Chapter 54

Rigby stared blindly into the bathroom mirror, his grip on the lip of the sink so tight his knuckles turned white. Anger roiled inside, pounded through his veins, the temptation to lash out overwhelming. He tried counting to ten. Got to six and cursed out loud. The chief couldn't just shut down the investigation. Gail deserved justice. Murders didn't happen often in Lewisville, thank God, but so far he had a hundred percent record for solving those cases he had been involved in. And this was going to be no different. Her family deserved answers, the innocent members, at least. This was no accident. It was cold-blooded murder and the culprits deserved to be behind bars. No matter who they were or how much grief they claimed to be suffering.

Put it on the backburner? Ha! They might as well admit it would never be solved. Whatever potential leads were out there would dry up, forgotten with the passage of time and lack of interest. The guilty would get what they wanted rather than what they deserved. And he, he would be haunted by it. By his failure to close it. He had enough demons ruining his sleep. He didn't need any more.

The bathroom door opened. He froze, hoping his vibe would deter the entrant.

"Izzy's attorney is here," Harper said.

"Last time I looked this was the men's bathroom," he muttered to the sink.

"It still is. But, um… The chief told me to tell you." She

cleared her throat. "To get your ass out of there and back into his office. Pronto."

"The chief didn't say pronto."

"No. You're right. I added that. But his tone suggested it."

Rigby washed his hands, pretending that's why he'd been standing there. He turned to face her. "You should have knocked. I might have been busy."

She rolled her eyes. "I doubt I would have seen anything I haven't seen before." She stepped back and let the door swing shut behind her. "Pronto!"

Without thinking he washed his hands again. Checked his reflection, surprised by how haggard he looked. It had to be the lighting. He splashed water on his face. Patted it dry with a paper towel. It made no difference.

He took a deep breath. Straightened his tie. Might as well get it over with.

He knocked on Pearson's door.

The chief stood by the window looking out onto the common. "Come in," he said without turning around. "Shut the door."

Rigby grimaced. Understood Harper's comment.

"Well?" Pearson spoke to Rigby's reflection in the window.

His reflection looked as haggard as it had in the bathroom. So not the lighting then. Most likely the job. Having to live up to the demands of the chief, meet his expectations. He used to think it was a big deal, having the chief as a mentor. And it was at first. But now he wasn't so sure. Better the chief was just the chief, not some quasi father-like figure who knew him better than he knew himself. The boundaries tended to get murky. Especially in the heat of the moment. Or at least they did for him. Pearson seemed to have no problem handling it.

Which was why the chief remained silent. He wanted Rigby to acknowledge, without help, that he'd not only crossed a line but done it in front of a colleague.

Rigby recalled Harper's quote. Would a little humor lighten the atmosphere?

"My ass is sorry."

Pearson glared at him. "What?"

Okay, humor, not a good idea. "I'm sorry for my outburst. I wasn't thinking."

"Obviously not."

The retort annoyed Rigby. "No, actually, I was thinking. I meant every word."

Pearson's eyebrows shot up.

Rigby rushed to finish. "But I shouldn't have said it the way I did and especially not in front of Harper."

"In front of anyone."

Rigby nodded. Tried to look chastised. "In front of anybody."

"It can't happen again. You might have been acting chief while I was out but I'm back now and I can't have you undermining my authority and the others hearing you got away with it."

Undermining his authority? That was taking it to an extreme. All he'd said was… Damn, he couldn't remember exactly what he had said.

"I'm not stupid enough to think that you all don't grouch about my orders between yourselves from time to time. I'm the boss. I have to make hard decisions. There's bound to be resentment, times when you don't agree with those decisions. But if the department is to function efficiently, there's got to be respect for rank.

"You of all people know that I'll listen to dissent, offered in a respectful manner, and if it's rational I'll take it into account. But what I will not do, will not tolerate is having it flung in my face during an uncalled-for rant in front of colleagues. Especially not from you."

Rigby gulped. He'd seen several versions of Pearson. Never this one.

"Do you understand?"

Rigby gulped again. "Yes."

"You have until three o'clock tomorrow to work the Cooper case. Then it's got to be as and when a lead comes in. If a lead comes in. Got it?"

Rigby nodded.

Pearson looked dissatisfied.

"Yes. Sir."

That brought a hint of a smile to Pearson's eyes. As Rigby turned to leave, he said, "And Rigby, Becca and Lotte come first. They have to. So no thinking you're going to work the case in your free time. Family comes first or none of this is worth it. You're not single now."

Wasn't that a fact? Rigby acknowledged it with another nod. He headed for the door. Hesitated. Turned back. "Just so you know, there's not a lot of grouching goes on out there. Not about you at least."

He left, pulling the door gently to behind him.

"Not usually," he muttered.

Chapter 55

Rigby groaned inwardly when he saw who Izzy's attorney was. He'd come up against Sue Woodward before. Despite her grandmotherly appearance, she was smart and tough. Just his luck Izzy should have landed her rather than a less seasoned public defender. He'd be lucky to get anything more than "no comment" out of Izzy now.

Izzy stared at him defiantly as he sat down. No doubt Sue had told her there was little the police could do with the information they had. Which left him with trying to rattle her with his questions. There had to be a reason why being asked her whereabouts the night her sister died had prompted the request for an attorney.

He started to ask the question but Sue cut him off. "Was this also the night the so-called burglary took place? Otherwise I can't see how it's relevant."

Rigby glared at her. "We don't know exactly when the burglary took place. What we do know is the stolen license plate was used on a car that evening." He pointed at the photo. "And given your client's fingerprints are on it, I think it's very relevant where she was that night."

"I was at home." Izzy's interjection startled them both but Sue's dagger-like glance at Izzy told Rigby the attorney was not pleased. Good. Maybe the interview wouldn't be such a waste of time after all. Although why Izzy couldn't have told him that when he first asked was beyond him.

He curbed his impatience. Repeated, "Home?"

Izzy nodded.

"Can anyone confirm that?"

Izzy pursed her lips. Scrunched her face up. "No. Just me on my lonesome. A quiet night in." She held Rigby's stare. Blinked away tears that suddenly threatened and with a catch in her voice added, "Until Hannah called. And told me about Gail."

"You were at home alone when you got the news?"

"My client has already told you she was," Sue said sharply, but Izzy was already nodding.

Rigby pushed on. "So you heard about the accident from Hannah but then you rushed around to Martin's?" He frowned. "Why didn't you go to your sister's or your parents' home?"

"I knew Martin would need help. With the children."

"In the middle of the night?"

"Detective," Sue interrupted. "I don't see what any of this has to do with the reason you brought Miss Heaton in."

Rigby shrugged. "She seems willing enough to answer my questions now."

The attorney whispered in Izzy's ear.

"No comment," Izzy said.

"I haven't asked you another question yet."

The attorney smirked.

"Might anyone have seen you leave to go to Martin's? A neighbor, say?"

Izzy shook her head. "No comment."

"But you shook your head. Is that a no?"

"Miss Heaton said no comment, Detective."

"Only after she shook her head." Rigby shrugged nonchalantly. "Which usually means no." He smiled at Izzy. "So you've got no alibis for that evening until you arrived at Martin's house?"

"No comment."

Rigby exhaled hard. "You're not helping yourself here. All I'm trying to do is establish whether you have an alibi for the evening. Why would you not want to help us?"

"Miss Heaton has told you she hasn't."

"Only while she says she was at home. She might have passed someone on the way to Martin's who could confirm her movements." Rigby knew he was nitpicking but without being able to tie down Izzy's whereabouts that evening he couldn't rule her out as the driver. He made a note to check whether there were any cameras in the vicinity of Izzy's apartment and to get Martin to confirm exactly what time Izzy had shown up. Though he wasn't sure what that would prove. But he wanted to make sure he'd checked every possible angle. No one would be able to say he hadn't done his best.

He glanced at Harper, hoping she'd have an idea how to move forward. The tiny shrug of her shoulders and her glum look told him she didn't.

It had been a complete waste of time. Time he didn't have to waste. He asked a few more questions about the visits to the Reed house, the plate, and how Izzy had spent her evening alone, but all he got in response was "no comment."

He wrapped the interview up. Told Izzy she could go. Added, "For now," as he noticed her fleeting smug smile. He wanted to keep her on edge, deny her any sense she'd got away with whatever she was hiding.

He let Harper usher them out. He stared into the mirrored window. Had Pearson watched the fiasco too? He'd rather not know. He scooped up the file, wandered back into the detective bureau, tossed it down on his desk and cursed out loud.

"No luck?" Turner said.

"Nope." He slumped down in his chair, swung his legs up onto the desk. "She denies touching the license plate." He scoffed. "She has to be lying, but because we can't directly link the plate to any crime, let alone the hit-and-run, we don't have anything to hold her on. We need the car. If we could find the car that would at least give us the owner to follow up with."

"Unless it was stolen."

"But we haven't had any reports of stolen cars fitting the description. Likewise, the body shops, the car washes, have all been dead ends. We even put signs up in the neighborhood asking if anyone recognized it. The photo's been in the papers. We've had a few calls in but nothing came of them." He sighed. "Without the correct plate number it's almost impossible."

"Which is obviously what the perpetrator was thinking. Strikes me as a well-planned operation. They could have just concealed the plate in some way. Didn't you say the car was dirty? A streak of mud would do the job. As long as they didn't fall foul of patrol. Swapping out the plates would solve that problem provided they didn't get stopped for another infraction where the officer could see the plates and vehicle type didn't match with what was in the system. But stealing from a similar vehicle, that's being ultra cautious." Turner paused. "Though even then, if they did get stopped the registration docket would be different. So they hadn't covered every eventuality."

Rigby drummed his fingers on the desk. "I don't think they were worried about getting stopped. I think it was all done for the cameras. In case they showed up on one. They probably guessed we'd canvas the nearby houses and there was a chance there'd be some footage of the car, if not the entire plate. Making sure the model and plate matched would send us off on a wild goose chase, which it has, and then we'd be forced to give up, which is apparently what the chief wants us to do."

"No evidence, no case. What else can we do?"

"But there is evidence!" Rigby swung his legs down.

"Conclusive evidence. You know, that joins the dots, makes a whole picture. What have you got? A couple of unconnected lines, if that."

Rigby scowled. "So you agree with the chief. We should let it go. Let the family believe it was random, tragic. Gail happened to be in the wrong place at the wrong time."

"You can't win them all."

Rigby stood up. "I'm not losing this one."

Chapter 56

The footage from the camera outside Jane's apartment turned up just before Rigby's shift was due to end. He opened the file and skipped through to nine p.m. Scott had been hazy about the exact time they'd left the bar, guessed it was between nine and ten, and Jane had agreed that sounded about right, but not a soul went in or out of the building during that hour.

Rigby recalled Scott's comment about them being too drunk to drive home from the party. But what about to the party? Were they drunk before they even got there? Not that any of them would admit it now. He checked the map. The apartment was in the opposite direction to the bar from where Gail was hit. But what if not everyone in the gathering at the bar had gone to the party? He called Jane. For once his luck was in and she picked up immediately. She confirmed all of Danny's friends had gone back to the apartment. The bar was too noisy and crowded so they decided to decamp.

She went quiet when he mentioned he'd watched the camera footage from the door and had yet to see them turn up. He'd already got to ten-thirty while they talked and still hadn't seen anybody.

Jane apologized and said it must have been before nine. They hadn't paid much attention to the time but now she thought about it, it made sense because they'd only had a couple of drinks in the bar, mostly beer. They'd hit the hard stuff at home.

Her apology sounded genuine but it was fortunate she couldn't see his expression. Still, at least it sounded as if he could rule them out for drunk driving.

He found them at eight-forty-two. Ten of them, three females and seven males judging from their clothes, though most were so bundled up he had to zoom in on the individual faces before he was able to pick out either Scott or Jane.

He sat back in his chair, raked his fingers through his hair. Scott's story held up. He'd seen him go in. Nobody had come out before ten-thirty. Just to be sure Rigby ran the footage onward. A couple went in. Nobody left. The only other exit to the building was a fire door, which would set off an alarm if opened. He could rule Scott Yates out as the driver.

Yet Scott had lied about knowing anyone with a white car. Why? Had he genuinely forgotten about Dale's car? After all, Dale was hardly a friend and if they'd only talked about his car Scott may not have actually seen it.

That reminded him. He wanted Gina to check for prints on the internal garage door. He called her, but it turned out she'd beaten him to the idea. The only prints she'd found were Dale's and the grandfather's. She'd emailed him her report. Hadn't he seen it?

He checked his inbox. And there it was. He apologized for disturbing her and she laughed and said it was a welcome distraction from refereeing childish disputes.

A loud crash at her end of the phone was followed by an indignant wail. "Gotta go," she said hastily and hung up.

He printed off Gina's report, added it to the file. He spotted the note he'd made about confirming Izzy's time of arrival at Martin's and whether there was any camera footage near her home showing her movements.

He couldn't figure out a way to ask Martin about Izzy without generating more questions than he wanted to answer so he decided to hold off on that point. He looked up Izzy's address on a map. Smiled when he saw where it was—a side street three blocks south of the station house, primarily of small shops and offices with apartments above. Hopefully some of the businesses had security cameras.

He sent Becca a text. Told her he'd be a little late but definitely back for dinner. Then he bundled up for the walk. Parking around the area was never easy so it would be pointless to take the car.

"Off home?" Harper strolled into the office.

He told her where he was going.

She glanced at her watch. "Want me to do it for you? I haven't got any plans this evening. And it's already gone past the end of your shift."

He hesitated. She was right. But this could be a vital piece of evidence if they could find proof Izzy wasn't at home. Of course, they might as easily find proof that she was, but he had a feeling about this. This was going to be the break they needed. He needed.

"No, I've already told Becca I'll be late." He grinned. "But if you want to come with me, I won't say no."

Chapter 57

Izzy's apartment was above a realtor's office sandwiched between a hair salon and what Rigby assumed was a high-end boutique. He certainly couldn't imagine Becca wearing the kind of clothes they had in the window. Though her mother might.

It was the only one of the three that had a camera, but purely for internal use. He guessed shoplifting was more of a concern than someone breaking in. The rather snooty assistant pointed out the premises had an alarm and any intruders would be caught on the internal camera so what was the point of having one outside?

He smiled politely and left. Harper had gone to the bakery café and the dog grooming store on the opposite side of the road. He doubted she'd have any more luck. Why couldn't Izzy have lived near a bank or a jewelry store?

Mid-afternoon and the street was reasonably busy, but presumably after the businesses closed there wouldn't be as much pedestrian traffic. A nearby sign informed him that between the hours of seven p.m. and six a.m. parking on the block was for residents only.

How often would Izzy be able to find a space outside her place? The buildings on Izzy's side of the street were three stories, so at least two apartments above each business. Which meant her car could have been parked anywhere along the street that night. And it was a long street—two blocks of stores, one a mix of professional offices and residential, and then several more blocks of homes.

Harper appeared at the bakery door clutching two cups. He

waited for a break in the traffic and jogged across the road.

"Hot chocolate." She handed him a cup.

He wished it was coffee, but he thanked her anyway.

"No luck, I'm afraid," she said between sips. "There's a bank one block up. The girl in the grooming shop thought they'd probably got a camera, but it's going to be too far away to pick up Izzy's place."

He told her his thoughts about the parking.

She blew a raspberry. "You're not going to suggest we canvas the whole street?"

He pushed away the temptation to say yes. It would be an act of desperation and one that could—no, probably would—come up empty. But if Izzy was telling the truth then her distinctive yellow car would have to be parked somewhere nearby until she went to Martin's. And if her car was there all evening then she couldn't be the driver who'd hit Gail.

He froze. Unless…

He eyed the parked cars, looking for a white sedan. A dirty white one. Though chances were it had been cleaned by now. Then again, why bother when the weather was so bad? And cleaning wouldn't take away the paint scrape or the dings.

Harper shuffled her feet. "What?"

"What if the car was stolen but put back before the owner noticed?"

Harper frowned.

"Like the plate. It's not missing so it was never reported stolen. We know there were no similar cars reported stolen, right? But what if that's because it was taken, used in the hit-and-run, and returned all in the space of a couple of hours? This time of year who's likely to notice?"

Harper looked doubtful.

"I'm not talking about someone driving off in a car parked in a driveway, though God knows we know it happens, but if it was parked on a street like this, not necessarily outside the owner's residence."

"So what? The owner just happens to leave the keys in the car?"

Good point. "Or hot-wired it. Or… or something."

Harper shivered. Glanced back at the café. "How about we have this conversation inside?"

"What? No. I need to…" Need to what? Rush off and do what? Better to talk it over, get it straight in his mind. And who better than Harper to discuss it with? What difference would half an hour make?

"Good idea." He led the way. Once inside, he headed for a table in the far corner away from the other patrons so their conversation wouldn't be overheard. The warmth of the café was welcome. They peeled off their coats and piled them on a spare chair. He wondered whether it would be rude to go and get a coffee, but decided against it when he noticed the line at the counter.

"You want me to pick holes in your theory?" Harper smiled. Took a sip of her drink.

He'd rather she just agree with him. "Fire away."

"We've had signs up about the vehicle, it's been in the media, so do you really think there could be someone out there who hasn't realized it could be their car we're looking for."

"The signs weren't in this neighborhood. Not everyone will have seen them or watched the news or read the papers."

"But you've had no report of sightings either, right? No calls in to say there's a car like that parked on our street. Or I saw it outside of wherever."

"We had a couple but they came to nothing."

"And haven't patrol been keeping an eye out for a white sedan?"

He scowled. "They can't be everywhere. And with all the snow we've had the car could be hidden under a mound." He broke off. Had a drink as he let the thoughts percolate. "What if it is? Under snow. What if the owner is away? A snowbird or visiting family for Christmas. Have no idea their car was taken or about any of the publicity over the hit-and-run. Won't know there's been any damage to the front of the car until they return and then," he shrugged, "have no idea how it happened."

Harper pouted her lips. Nodded her head. "That would work. Except for the part about the keys. And the sheer coincidence that their car happened to be the same as Dale Jessup's?" She exhaled hard. "And that it all fell into place the night Gail was going to her sister's party."

Put like that, Harper made sense. He leaned back in his chair and crossed his arms. "You think it was just an accident too?"

"I don't think you're going to be able to prove it was anything but."

Damn. First Pearson, then Turner, now Harper. Was he the only one who cared? "What about the fingerprints? How the hell did they get onto the back of a plate on a car the plate didn't belong to?"

Harper sighed. "I don't know. But apart from beating a confession out of someone, I don't think we're ever going to find out."

Rigby stood up. Pulled on his coat. "I'm going to the bank. If they have footage, I need to see it. Even if there's no sign of her parked car, there's a chance she drove past the bank at some point that night. It's a distinctive car, should be easy to spot. Not like trying to find a black SUV. Car like that goes past, more likely than not it's Izzy's."

Harper grimaced. "But if you see it, what will that prove? She could be going anywhere."

"Depends on the time. She said she was home until she got the call from Hannah. If we see the car moving between, say, seven and ten-thirty, we'll know she was lying. Again."

Harper sighed. "It's a long shot."

"It's the only shot I've got."

Chapter 58

They got to the bank just before it closed. A solitary teller sat behind the counter busy dealing with a customer while another waited in line. No sign of a manager though Rigby knew there had to be one somewhere. He waited impatiently while cash was counted and deposits made in a leisurely fashion.

When they finally got to the counter, the teller glanced at the clock and told them to make an appointment to see the manager the following morning.

Rigby flashed his badge. "No. We need to see him now." His tone sent the clerk scurrying into a back office.

The manager turned out to be a woman. And an old friend of Mrs. Heaton. She'd heard about the tragic accident, she told them. Had been at the funeral service, which explained how she'd looked vaguely familiar though he'd never met her before.

He told her why they wanted the footage without mentioning Izzy's name. They were following up on a lead, a long shot, but they'd be grateful if she didn't mention their request outside of the bank for now. Rigby specifically meant talking about it to the Heatons but could hardly tell her that.

She agreed without question. Said she knew how much comfort it would bring the family to know the driver had been brought to justice.

Rigby forced a smile and nodded. If he was on the right track there'd be little comfort for the family. Devastation more likely.

She did ask why the footage from outside the bank could be

linked to an accident that had happened on the other side of town. Rigby gave her the boilerplate answer of "we can't discuss details of an ongoing investigation at this time," and she seemed satisfied.

She led them into the back office and showed them how to access the footage. Rigby had hoped he could have it sent to his computer but the manager said she thought she'd need a warrant to do that but she had no problem letting them watch it on the premises.

He tried arguing, but lost. He glanced at his watch. He was in danger of being late for dinner. But they knew the timeframe they were looking at and it wasn't too long. And they could fast forward until they spotted the yellow car. Assuming they spotted the yellow car.

Or he could leave Harper to go through it. She'd said she had nothing planned for the evening. But he didn't want to leave it to her, he wanted to see for himself. He decided to compromise. He'd stay as long as he could and if they weren't done by then, he'd leave Harper to it. He wondered whether the manager was now in her office changing her plans for the evening. Wondering why the police couldn't have turned up during normal office hours. Still, it couldn't be helped.

They decided to start the recording from five o'clock. If Izzy had come home from work they figured it would be around then. Harper annoyed him by pointing out that if Izzy had driven home via Main Street, the most likely route, she wouldn't pass the bank. Didn't she realize he knew that? But Pearson's deadline loomed in his mind. He was getting desperate.

They watched as parked cars were driven off and others took their place. A constant stream of traffic passed the bank until six-thirty when it thinned out. By seven there were periods when there was no traffic at all, which made sense given there were no bars or restaurants to attract evening customers and the threat of heavy snowfalls would keep locals indoors.

But there was also no sign of Izzy's car either parked or passing. By eight, frustration set in. The long shot was proving to be just that. By eight-thirty he was prepared to admit it had been a crazy idea. He sensed Harper felt the same way too—though maybe she'd always thought it was a crazy idea and was merely humoring him.

He glanced over to see if she was paying attention. She hadn't spoken for some time and watching footage could be sleep-inducing.

"There!" she said, startling him. She pointed at the screen. Hit pause.

He looked back. Frowned. The frozen screen showed only parked cars. Was this Harper's idea of a joke? Her broad grin suggested as much.

She rewound the footage at the slowest speed possible. A yellow Beetle reversed into the picture from the right side of the screen. It was eight-thirty-seven and Izzy was heading in the opposite direction to her apartment.

Rigby beamed. They'd caught her in another lie.

Chapter 59

Rigby winced as he reached up to untie the Christmas tree from the top of his car. He hoped the sight of it would go some way to lessen Becca's wrath at how late he was for dinner. He'd got halfway home when he'd remembered his promise and in a tossup between being on time with no tree or late with a tree, he decided the latter was the more sensible option.

He thought he'd seen trees for sale outside the hardware store on Main Street but by the time he got there it was already closed. A quick search on the internet told him there was a nursery ten minutes outside of town, which, if he was lucky, he might just reach before it too closed. For once, luck was on his side, though the owner didn't look too pleased as he sped into the empty parking lot and leaped out of the car with two minutes to spare.

The trees on offer didn't quite match his expectations but given he'd left it so late he could hardly complain. He eyed the choices. Would Becca prefer a tall, sparse tree or a short bushier one? He had no idea. He hadn't bothered with a tree the previous year, despite Becca's protests. They weren't officially living together then and given they'd gone to his parents for Christmas Day and his mother always went all out with decorations, he hadn't seen the point. But this year was different. Their first as a family. Sometimes he still found it hard to believe.

The tree earned him some goodwill though Becca's enthusiasm for the specimen he'd chosen, the short bushy one, seemed a little forced. He understood why when after dinner she brought out the boxes of lights and decorations she'd bought earlier. He should have definitely chosen the taller tree. He wasn't sure whether Becca saw it as a challenge or whether she was making a point but she was determined to use every single bauble. By the time they'd emptied all the cartons and switched on the lights, the tree itself was almost invisible.

They stood back and surveyed their handiwork. Rigby put his arm around Becca, pulled her toward him and kissed her cheek. "I'm sorry," he whispered.

She pulled back, looked up in alarm. "What for?"

What for? For all the ways he was failing. As a father, as a partner. For putting work ahead of family, for allowing his desire to get justice for one family to take precedence over his own. He was a cop, had been most of his adult life. It's what drove him and deep down, he knew he was good at it. But could he be a good cop and a good father? When even at home with his loved ones, listening to Christmas music and creating memories together, his mind was still on work? Becca deserved more. As did Lotte.

"For being late again. Leaving you alone with Lotte." He wasn't ready to share his real fears yet.

She snuggled up against him. "One of us needs to earn a paycheck."

That was true. But some paychecks came with less of an obligation, the ability to switch off after hours until the next shift. Live a life separate from work. For him there was no separation. Work consumed him. His cases were always there, in the back of his mind, ready to demand attention at inappropriate times. Single, he could get away with it. As a family man, he wasn't sure it would work.

Harper had offered to deal with the warrant for the bank footage. She pointed out there was no urgent need to call Izzy out on her lie, if it was indeed a lie, that evening. She was hardly likely to disappear overnight.

Rigby wasn't so sure. The conversation at the station house might have spooked her, but he had to concede they couldn't drag her back in again without more evidence than a single sighting of her car. What if she'd merely been looking for a parking space further down the block? Though he'd got the impression the car was speeding up not slowing down.

He'd taken a photo of the frozen screenshot with his phone, proof of what they'd seen in case anything went awry with the footage before they could watch it again. He wanted to leave nothing to chance.

Then he'd realized that if Izzy had been looking for a parking spot she'd have to walk back to her apartment—pass the camera on foot. The answer could be right there if they watched a little more of the footage.

Harper pointed out the time. Hadn't he said he had to be home for dinner? She told him to go. She'd stay on. Let him know what she found.

So why the hell hadn't she phoned?

Lotte wailed. Becca sighed. She pulled out of his embrace. "At least we got the tree done."

He pulled her back. Kissed her hard. She responded. The wail grew louder. And louder. Then Cocoa joined in to remind them they were being derelict in their duty.

Becca pulled back again. Wiped at the damp patch blossoming on her T-shirt. "I can't believe I used to worry whether I'd have enough milk. Seems like she only has to whimper and out it comes." She hesitated at the door. "Still, shouldn't complain. Some of the other moms are really struggling to breastfeed. I've got it easy by comparison."

Easy? If this was considered easy he'd hate to think how the others from the childbirth class were coping. He hadn't seen any of them in person since the births, only photos of the proud parents and their bundles of joy. Becca met up with all the other moms weekly to compare notes on all things baby-related and presumably other topics too. Did they grouch about their partners? How they couldn't possibly understand what it was like to be a walking source of food? Or did Becca listen with envy to tales of supportive dads who weren't obsessed with work?

He really needed to try harder.

He heard the creak of the rocking chair as Becca settled into it. Cocoa who'd followed her out padded back into the room, waited for Rigby to sit down, and then curled up on the sofa next to him.

"Got to do better," he muttered, stroking Cocoa gently. He admired the tree. Glanced at his phone. Still no message from Harper. He put the phone down. Picked it up again. One quick call to satisfy his curiosity. Had Harper spotted Izzy walking back to her apartment or not?

One quick call—it could hardly be classed as working. Besides, Becca need never know. The call went to voicemail.

Damn, what was Harper playing at? He decided not to leave a message. He sent a text instead.

He got no answer.

Chapter 60

Rigby arrived at the office the next morning refreshed and raring to go. He'd actually managed a six-hour stretch of uninterrupted sleep and woken without the help of either Lotte or a nightmare. He'd almost forgotten what it felt like to wake rested.

He managed to get out without waking Becca or Lotte. From the dishes left on the kitchen table, he assumed Becca had not been so lucky in the sleep stakes, and given she hadn't put them in the dishwasher he also assumed she wanted him to know that. Damn, nowadays even a good night's sleep came with guilt.

There was still no response from Harper. Not that he expected her to contact him in the middle of the night but a quick message to say whether she'd made any progress would have been useful. Give him an idea of how the day might pan out. Pearson's deadline weighed heavily on his mind. He didn't have time to waste. But he had no choice. Harper wasn't in the office.

She strolled in at eight, unfazed by his demands to know what had kept her. "What's the hurry?" She dropped a document onto his desk. "The manager said she wouldn't be back at the bank until eight at the earliest."

Rigby glanced at his watch.

Harper laughed. "At the earliest."

"What about Izzy though?" He pulled on his coat and grabbed the warrant. "Any further sightings?"

Harper grimaced. "I don't think so."

Rigby glared at her. "What does that mean? You either saw

her or you didn't."

Harper glared back. "What I mean is that the only passersby were so bundled up I could barely tell whether they were male or female, let alone whether one of them was Izzy. Maybe Turner can work with the images, give us more to go on." She paused. "But I also think there could be a blind spot on the other side of the road. She could have passed by there and we'd be none the wiser."

"You couldn't have told me this last night?"

"What good would it have done?"

She was right. Not that he wanted to admit it. He was the one creating the urgency. He made a dash for the door. Stopped abruptly. What the hell was the matter with him?

He turned. Waved the warrant. "Thanks. For this." He managed a smile. "And for last night. For the help."

He got a tight-lipped smile in return. But the "you're welcome" came out as a heavy sigh. Still, it was more polite than he deserved.

On his walk to the bank, he mulled over the implications of what Harper had told him. He should feel elated. It was good news. For them. As long as none of the passersby turned out be Izzy. How would she explain where she was going? True, it was another unconnected dot but given the commonality was Izzy, he didn't believe it was a coincidence. And the more discrepancies in her story he could confront her with, the greater the likelihood of getting her to break. She already had to be on edge about her fingerprints.

He scanned the street while he waited for the bank manager to let him in. Watched as pedestrians hurried by, their heads bowed against the icy breeze, their movements cautious, and their identities concealed by heavy coats, hats and scarves. Harper was right. They'd need Turner's help on this and even he couldn't work miracles.

The manager offered him a brusque "Good morning," took him through to the back office, quickly read the warrant, watched as he downloaded the file and then ushered him out, all without breaking a smile. Either she was not a morning person or they'd really messed up her plans for the previous evening.

Back in the office there was no sign of Harper. Rigby poured a coffee and sat back to watch the footage from the point when

Izzy's car appeared. Harper had probably noted the times when she'd spotted pedestrians but he wanted to go through it himself. It only took a moment of distraction to miss a vital clue.

He froze the screen each time he saw someone and compared the image with his recollection of Izzy in her coat on the way to the station house. A dark-colored, knee-length padded coat— which unfortunately ruled out only one of the individuals he saw. He tried to eliminate the others based on size but gave up when he realized how pointless it was. Now he was the one wasting time.

He needed to speak to Izzy. She could clear this up immediately. She should want to clear it up if she was telling the truth about being home.

But would she speak to him without a lawyer?

Chapter 61

Both the SUV and dark sedan were gone when Rigby pulled up outside the Cooper home. And there were no lights in the windows to brighten the overcast day. Another snowstorm was in the forecast. It seemed a strange day for the whole family to go out. Still, Izzy's car was there so maybe, just maybe, the trip wouldn't be wasted after all.

He trudged up to the front door, noticing the two small pairs of snow boots were missing from the lineup. How long would it be before Gail's were removed?

He rang the bell. Knocked on the door. Turned to scan the street in the hope he'd see them returning, though given the time, it was more likely they'd just left. If he hadn't waited to see the footage they might still have been home. He knocked again, releasing his frustration in the effort. Then he pressed on the bell.

He cursed. Stepped off the porch, ready to admit defeat and go back to his desk. And do what? This was the only lead he had, if it could be called a lead. Maybe he'd be better off sitting in his car, waiting for them to return.

"Can I help you?" The male voice startled him. He turned to find Martin's father standing at the door. "Oh, it's you again. I'm sorry, you caught me..." Mr. Cooper gave an embarrassed grin, raised the newspaper in his hand. "I was in the bathroom."

"Is Izzy here?" Rigby raised his voice, remembering the guy had a hearing problem.

"No. Sorry. Just me. Izzy took the girls to play at her sister's.

Martin had some business to deal with in town, and my wife, she's gone to the supermarket. Said she needed to stock up before the next snow." He glanced up at the sky. "Hopefully, they'll all be back before it starts. Don't like the idea of them driving in bad weather. But Izzy and the girls, they were on foot." He broke off. Shuddered as if he'd just remembered that was no guarantee of safety. "Would you like to come in and wait?"

Rigby was about to say no but reconsidered. Izzy had lied to Martin's parents about where she was going the previous day. Had she told them afterward about the interview? This could be his chance to find out. He nodded and followed Mr. Cooper into the house.

"Come into the kitchen. I'll make us some fresh coffee." Mr. Cooper tossed his newspaper on to the table. "Have a seat."

"Thanks."

"You're lucky I had my hearing aids in, or else I might not have heard you." Mr. Cooper grinned at Rigby. "I usually wear them all the time but the last few days I've found myself taking them off. Those girls are little darlings, but boy, can they make a racket. I feel for my wife. She can't turn the noise off. I don't know how she stands it." He set the coffee brewing and sat down opposite Rigby.

"Martin, he says you get used to it. Me, I'd rather take my hearing aids out. Maybe if we'd had more than one child, I'd have got used to the noise, but Martin, he didn't have anybody to fight with at home so we didn't have to deal with all the sibling squabbles and upsets." He hesitated. "I know Martin has found it a strain since Suzy was born. Not that he'd admit it." He shook his head. "I don't know what he's going to do without Gail."

He stood up abruptly, turned his back on Rigby and fiddled with the mugs next to the coffee machine, surreptitiously brushing at the corner of his eyes with the back of his hand.

"Did you get along well with Gail?" Rigby asked as Mr. Cooper brought the mugs to the table.

Mr. Cooper swallowed hard. "She was like a daughter to us. From the moment we first met her we knew there was something special between them. They seemed so right for each other." He shook his head again "I can't believe she's gone. So young, so much life ahead of her, ahead of both of them." He picked up his mug. Put it down again without drinking. "She was so good to us too. Even before they were married, she was always there if we needed help. We've both had spells of illness and each time she's stepped in, even at one time when Martha was little more than a baby. I said I don't know what Martin's going to do without her." He gave a hollow laugh. "I'm not sure what we'll do."

"At least Izzy seems willing to help."

"Oh, Izzy." Mr. Cooper grimaced. "Yes, she means well. I'm sure."

Rigby frowned. Not exactly a glowing reference. "What? She hasn't been helpful?"

"Izzy's not Gail."

"No." How else could he reply to such a blatantly obvious comment?

Mr. Cooper fiddled with the handle of his mug, seemingly lost in memory. "But at times she sounds like Gail and some of her mannerisms are like Gail. And I think Martin, not just Martin, all of us, find that hard to handle. Because she reminds us of Gail." He scoffed uneasily. "But she's not Gail. Not by any means. And, yes, she's been helpful, but almost too helpful. I told him to tell her she needs to go home and he says he has, but he's either lying because he doesn't want to upset her, after all she's lost a sister, or she's just not listening."

Rigby gulped, not sure how to respond. What if there was a third reason why Izzy was still there? A reason Mr. Cooper hadn't grasped.

What if his son's protestations were a ruse and Izzy was right where he wanted her to be?

Chapter 62

Rigby had no problem keeping Mr. Cooper talking about Izzy. It didn't sound as if much goodwill existed between the pair. Rigby recalled the disdainful way Izzy had referred to Mr. Cooper and the older man didn't seem to be any more enamored of her. And, much to Rigby's surprise, he seemed to suggest Martin didn't hold Izzy in any higher regard.

As he debated how to bring up Izzy's role at the funeral, Mrs. Cooper arrived back, deposited two bags of groceries on the countertop, and asked her husband to help bring in the rest. Rigby offered to assist, expecting to be told there was no need, but his offer was met with enthusiasm. He understood why when he got outside. The trunk was stuffed full of shopping bags and there were more on the rear seat. There was enough for a siege never mind a snowstorm.

"Martin has no idea when it comes to food." Mrs. Cooper placed a bowl piled high with apples, peaches and bananas on the table. "He might be able to survive on takeouts, but the little ones can't. They need good home-cooked food. None of this instant or prepackaged stuff."

Rigby smiled. Mrs. Cooper would get on well with his mother. She continued to make small talk while she unpacked the bags as if it were perfectly normal for a detective to be sitting in her son's kitchen early in the morning. Though he guessed there'd been nothing normal about the last few days.

Finally, she sat down at the table with a cup of coffee. "We've told Martin we'll stay until the new year and then we'll come over to look after the kids while he's at work until he decides what he wants to do long term. If we weren't so old, I'd offer to do it full-time." She smiled sadly. "Or if they were a little older, at school part of the day, but I don't have the energy to cope with two little ones full-time."

"I thought Izzy had offered to look after the girls when Martin went back to work," Rigby said.

Mrs. Cooper gasped. "Why would she do that? She has her own job. She's young. Why would she give up her work to look after someone else's kids?"

"They are her nieces."

"But what would she live on? I doubt Martin could afford to pay her a salary. Since Gail gave up work after Martha was born it's been a struggle for them."

But if Izzy moved in, she'd basically be replacing Gail. Financially, Martin would be no worse off. Rigby held back that thought. Whatever his suspicions, the senior Coopers obviously had no inkling of them and even the suggestion their son might have played a part in his wife's death would probably blow his chances of getting any useful information out of them. He shrugged. "Just something she said the other day."

"Oh, that." Mr. Cooper sneered. "Martin shut that one down straight away. Told her that while it was kind of her to offer, he needed to get himself sorted out, make a life without Gail for him and the girls as soon as possible. For the girls' sake. And he's got us to help in the short term. As I said earlier, I'm not sure why she's still here."

"Now, now." Mrs. Cooper scowled at her husband. "She's only trying to help. And the girls are comfortable with her. Probably know her better than they know me."

"But they're our grandkids."

"And Gail's parents' grandkids too," Mrs. Cooper scolded. "Maisie told me that knowing we were here to help Martin was a great comfort to her and Jack. Gave them a chance to grieve their daughter without having to keep up appearances for the girls."

"Izzy doesn't seem to have a problem keeping up appearances," Mr. Cooper muttered. "Haven't seen her shed a tear.

Not even at the funeral."

Mrs. Cooper tut-tutted.

"Martin must have been grateful for her help with the kids at the funeral." Though what Rigby really wanted to ask was why it was Izzy rather than a grandparent.

"I questioned the wisdom of it." Mrs. Cooper got up, fetched the coffee pot and offered them refills. "It's not as if the girls will remember. They're so young. But the Heatons, they insisted. And Martin, he didn't want to upset them more than they already were."

"So Izzy offered to help?"

"She was the one doing the insisting if you ask me," Mr. Cooper said.

"You don't know that," Mrs. Cooper snapped. "She said she was passing on her family's wishes."

"Except Jack told me after the funeral that Izzy told them Martin asked her to help at the last minute. He wanted the kids to be there and would she help him?"

The comment intrigued Rigby. Why would each side of the family get a different story? "Did you mention it to Martin?"

Mr. Cooper scowled. "Why would I do that? He was upset enough without embroiling him in whatever game she was playing. And the funeral was over so what good would it do?"

"You think she's playing a game?"

Mrs. Cooper rolled her eyes. "Ignore him. He's never liked Izzy. Not since he first met her when she was dating Martin. He thought she was too—"

"Sorry." Rigby gulped. "You're saying Martin dated Izzy? I thought Gail and Martin had been together since high school."

"That's right. Senior year. But before that, Martin had met Izzy and they dated for a few weeks. I thought she was too young at the time. She was only about fifteen. But that was how he got to know Gail."

"He dropped Izzy for her sister?" Rigby's mind raced at the potential implications.

"Oh, no. Martin would never behave like that. He and Izzy broke up after a few weeks. We knew it wouldn't last, didn't we, dear?" She smiled at her husband. "There was no spark between them. And I don't think Izzy ever read a book unless she had to for school." She leaned toward Rigby as if she was about to tell him a secret. "To be honest, I think it was more of a convenience, wanting to be seen to be dating. Not be the only one without a girlfriend or boyfriend. Though as I said, I thought she was too young. She's a couple of years younger than her sister and Martin was Gail's first boyfriend apparently." She sat back in her chair. "It was a while before we realized Izzy was her sister. They are so different in many ways." She broke off. Added in a choked voice, "Were so different."

Damn. Why was he only learning this now? It could be irrelevant, but based on what he'd learned in this conversation alone, it could be pivotal. Had the time Izzy spent with the couple over the years rekindled an old flame? And if so, was the flame one of mutual love or unabated jealousy?

Chapter 63

The front door slammed. Mrs. Cooper got up and poked her head out into the hallway. "The detective's here, Martin."

"I figured that was his car outside." Martin's disgruntled response was accompanied by the ruffle of garments and the thud of shoes being taken off before he appeared in the doorway. "Tell me you've got the bastard."

"Martin!"

Martin ignored his mother. He loosened his tie, pulled it over his head and threw it over the back of a chair then slumped down into the seat, braced his arms on the table, and glared at Rigby.

Rigby cursed silently. Just what he needed. Belligerence. Though Martin's stance conveyed one of defeat rather than anger. He looked like a man who'd been tested and found wanting.

"No, not yet," he said. "I actually came to speak to Izzy. I had a quick question after our talk yesterday."

"Izzy? What's she got to do with anything?" Martin glanced at his parents, a frown spreading across his face. "Where is she?"

"She took the girls over to Hannah's," Mrs. Cooper said.

"What?" Martin thumped his hand on the table. "I told her I would take them when I got back from the bank."

"She wasn't sure how long you'd be and the girls, they were getting restless."

"But I promised the girls I would take them."

"You can go over there now. Join them."

Martin exhaled heavily. "That's not the point. She knew my

plans. She had no right to usurp them without asking me first."

"But you were at the bank. And you were longer than you said you'd be."

"Damn bureaucracy. You'd think they'd have some compassion for the bereaved. I felt like I was erasing Gail's existence, taking her name off the mortgage and our accounts. Oh, they offer their condolences, but it's still just a job for them. Check the documents, delete a few entries on a computer screen. It's all so impersonal. And all the while I feel as if I'm being torn apart inside."

Mrs. Cooper put her hand on Martin's shoulder. "At least it's done now."

Martin sat back. "This is just the beginning. There're so many other matters to deal with. Her car. Her phone." He sighed again. "And all I want to do is to be with the kids." He glanced angrily at Rigby. "And I get home and find you here again."

"I'm doing all I can to track down the driver."

Martin scoffed. "You're not going to find them here, are you?" He pointed at the empty cup of coffee in front of Rigby. "Sitting here, drinking coffee, and asking pointless questions. How's that going to help? Or do you do it so that we'll think you're working hard to get a result, make yourself visible to us so if you don't get one you can say you did everything you could?"

"Martin!" Mrs. Cooper looked shocked. "I'm sure the detective is doing everything he can."

"Pah!" Martin shrugged his mother's hand off his shoulder. "It's been over a week. If they were going to track down the driver, they would have by now. They don't want to admit it. So instead they come around asking us irrelevant questions. I mean, Izzy? What can she possibly tell them that would make a difference?"

Rigby thought fast as three pairs of eyes focused on him. He made a snap decision. One Pearson would no doubt have plenty to say about, but Pearson wasn't the one who had to answer to the Coopers. "In the course of our investigation, we came across potential evidence, and I stress it is only potential evidence—we can't say for certain it had anything to do with the accident. But Izzy's name came up in connection with it. And so obviously we wanted to speak to her about it so—" He paused. "So nobody could claim we hadn't done a thorough job."

Martin looked guarded. "What is this evidence?"

"I'm afraid I can't discuss that."

"Don't we have a right to know, Detective?" Mr. Cooper said. "We're family of the victim."

"As I said, this is only potential evidence. We can't release information that could cast suspicion on someone without significant proof."

Martin's eyes narrowed. "Sounds like Izzy's the one you might be casting suspicion on."

"No." Rigby said a little too forcibly. "I just needed to clarify something she told us yesterday."

"You spoke to Izzy yesterday?"

"Yes. Didn't she mention it?"

Martin looked at his parents in turn. "You never mentioned Detective Rigby came by yesterday."

"He didn't." Mrs. Cooper looked at Rigby for confirmation. "Leastwise, I don't think so. Someone came to the door but Izzy said it was work-related. And that she had to go out for a while."

So Izzy had kept quiet about her ordeal the previous day. Interesting. Rigby studied Martin for signs he was lying. If Martin was involved, Izzy could easily have told him but not his parents, but Martin looked genuinely confused.

After a few minutes silence, Martin said. "I guess she didn't want to bother us with needless concerns." The words were uttered without conviction, but Rigby decided to leave it there and get away before he got bogged down any further.

Chapter 64

Rigby shivered. Turned the heating up high as the radio announcer informed him this was as warm as the day would get and snowfall forecasts of two to three inches were now more likely to be three to five. Damn weather. Couldn't something work in his favor for once?

He put the car into drive. Was about to pull away when he noticed the gray sedan in the spot where the SUV had been parked. Presumably Martin's car, which on previous visits must have been in the garage. The garage he'd parked in front of, blocking access. No wonder Martin had been so grumpy when he returned. But if Martin had taken the sedan that morning, where was the SUV? Mr. Cooper said Izzy and the girls had gone out on foot.

Decision time. He could go back to the house and ask or he could mind his own business. Maybe Martin had put the SUV in the garage. Maybe he was seeing anomalies where none existed. But it was an anomaly and it would nag at him unless he resolved it. So at the risk of annoying Martin even further, he had no choice.

He turned off the engine and got out of the car. As expected, Martin was not pleased to see him. His expression turned to incredulity as Rigby asked the question. "Izzy will have taken it. It's the only one with child seats."

"Your father said Izzy was walking."

Martin scoffed. "In this weather? I doubt it very much. I've never known Izzy walk any further than she absolutely has to." He frowned. "And why are you even asking?"

Rigby didn't really have an answer, at least not one he could say out loud. "Just curious." He grinned. "Thanks."

"Why don't you worry about finding the driver who killed Gail rather than asking us all these stupid questions?" Martin's voice broke. "Or at least admit it's like looking for a needle in a haystack and you're never going to find him."

Rigby stared at him. Tried to determine whether it was a genuine sentiment or an act. There were so many contradictions in what he'd been told, he wasn't sure who to believe.

"Oh, I'm going to find him, Martin. You can be sure of that."

Martin stared back, no indication of whether he took that as a reassurance or a threat.

Whatever. It worked both ways.

Rigby hurried back to his car.

Assuming he could pull it off.

Chapter 65

There was no sign of the SUV outside of Hannah's house, but the noise that greeted Rigby when Hannah opened the front door suggested there were more than her own kids there. She looked taken aback at the sight of him.

"Detective Rigby." Her smile was forced. "What are you doing here?"

"Actually, I was hoping to speak to Izzy." He kept his tone light. He didn't want to stress Hannah any more than she already looked.

Hannah made a face. "She's not here right now."

A loud shriek emanated from a back room. Hannah glanced anxiously over her shoulder. "Can you excuse me a moment?" She made to move away. Gestured at him. "Come in. It's freezing out there." She rushed off into the room the cry had come from.

Rigby stepped inside and closed the door. He could hear a resigned patience in Hannah's voice, presumably not the first squabble she'd had to sort out that day. He only hoped he could be as tolerant when it was his turn. And that Lotte took after Becca more than she did him. His mother didn't need to remind him he'd been a handful as a small kid. But she did. And with an unbecoming sense of glee since Lotte was born.

Hannah reappeared with a toddler in her arms. The child's tear-stained cheeks and snotty nose identified him as the injured party. Rigby smiled at him. The boy instantly hid his face in his mother's chest. Rigby decided not to take it personally.

Hannah rolled her eyes. "You were saying?"

"I was told I might find Izzy here."

"She was earlier. She came over with the girls. Martin was supposed to be bringing them but she said he'd some legal stuff he had to deal with and was probably going to be late so she thought she'd bring them instead."

Rigby frowned. He hadn't passed the SUV on the way over. "So they've been and gone?"

Hannah laughed. "No. The girls are still here. But after she got here Izzy got a work call. Said it was an emergency, asked if I could keep an eye on the girls while she dealt with it."

"I thought she'd stopped working for the time being?" Then he remembered how Izzy had used a work-related excuse the previous day. Was this another one? Though yesterday it was to cover going to the station house. Where could she be going today that she needed an excuse for?

"Me too." Hannah swayed as she spoke, gently stroking the toddler's back. "But I think this was one of her regulars who'd apparently caused a fuss when the substitute nurse turned up. So Izzy said she'd deal with it."

It sounded all above board.

"She said she should be finished by twelve. If not, she'd get Martin to pick up the kids." Hannah hesitated. "But given she's got the car with the kid seats I don't know how he's going to manage."

"Mr. Cooper said Izzy told him she was going to walk here."

Hannah snorted. "Walk? Izzy? No way would she walk. And with the girls in this weather? It's only a twenty-minute walk but that's a long time to sit in a stroller when it's cold."

"Mr. Cooper might have got it wrong."

She smiled. "You know he takes his hearing aid out when it gets too noisy for him. Which according to Izzy is most of the time. Then he turns the TV up to the maximum. It drives her crazy. But Martin won't say anything to his dad about it."

It was beginning to sound as if Martin wouldn't say anything to anybody. "So why does Izzy stay? Martin's got his parents there to help."

Hannah shrugged. "She seems to think she's got some

responsibility because Martha's her godchild. But to be honest, I think she's crazy. I know it's sad and hard for Martin, but we're all going to have to move on and for Izzy to give up her job to help him out, I'm not sure she knows what she's doing."

She leaned toward Rigby. "Gail used to complain sometimes about how often Izzy would go over. I told her to tell her she had to stop, but Gail was too nice. She didn't want to upset her. Especially knowing Izzy couldn't have kids of her own."

Before Rigby had time to process that information Hannah continued. "But as I said to Gail, Izzy's never come running around here to spend time with my kids like she has hers." She finally paused. "But then to be honest, I'd have no problem telling her it had to stop. We might be sisters, but we're also adults and we have our own lives."

She paused again. "And Izzy needs to get her own life together. Stop living through Gail."

She bit down on her bottom lip. Hugged the toddler tighter. "And I guess now, she's going to have to."

Chapter 66

Rigby pushed his plate to one side and slumped back in his chair. He hadn't realized how hungry he was until the food had been put down in front of him. The sated feeling went some way to easing his frustration but he knew it would only be a temporary relief.

He stared at his phone on the table, willing it to light up. Hannah, calling to let him know Izzy had returned. Or patrol, saying they'd spotted the SUV. Putting a BOLO on the car was an act of desperation borne of a fear that maybe they'd spooked Izzy the previous day and she'd used the excuse of taking the kids to Hannah's place as a cover to flee. Give her a few hours before anyone realized she was missing, long enough to get out of the county, possibly out of the state.

"If she was going to flee," Harper said between mouthfuls. "And I say if, why would she take the SUV?" Finished her food, she wiped her mouth and tossed her napkin onto her plate.

Rigby raised his eyebrows. "Because it's slightly less visible than a yellow Beetle."

Harper rolled her eyes. "Obviously. But it's not like we don't know the registration number of the SUV."

"Unless she swaps it out for another. It sure looks as if she's done that before."

"But not spur of the moment like this. Taking Dale's plate had to be a well-thought-out operation. Besides…" She scrunched her nose up. "The kids' car seats are in there. Leaves Martin in the lurch."

"I think that would be the least of her concerns. She needed a vehicle. Her own was too obvious. What's the alternative?"

"A rental?"

Rigby considered that. "It would be too easy to trace. She'd need her driver's license, a credit card." He grinned. "And she'd need some way of getting to the rental office." His grin widened. "In the heat of the moment, all she's thinking of is how to get some transport and get out of Lewisville. Maybe doesn't realize we'd be able to trace the rental. So she drives the SUV to within walking distance of the rental office. Knows it will be spotted eventually and returned—with the car seats—to Martin."

Harper looked dubious.

He leaped to his feet. "Can you get the check? I'll pay you back later."

"Where you going?"

"Where do you think? To check out the car rental places."

"But you don't even know whether Izzy has fled. She might be with a client like she told Hannah."

"It's gone twelve. She told Hannah she'd be back by twelve. And Hannah hasn't called. At this point I don't believe a word Izzy says and if there's any possibility she's gone for a rental car, I want to know now, not in several hours' time."

"But—"

Rigby snatched his phone off the table. Headed for the door. He didn't want to hear "buts." He wanted to take action. And as tenuous a lead as this was, it was better than doing nothing.

There were only two car rental companies in town. Rigby started with the one nearest to Hannah's house, an office in an outdoor mall two miles to the west. Unfortunately, the mall also housed an enormous supermarket and the fear of inclement weather to come had brought out the shoppers in their droves. Mrs. Cooper wasn't the only one preparing for a siege. Any hope he had of spotting Martin's SUV outside faded. Even he ended up parking at the opposite end of the lot to his chosen destination.

He weaved across the lot, dodging reversing cars and badly controlled trolleys. Halfway across a familiar voice caught his attention. "Paul!" He turned to find his parents, each with a laden trolley.

"What are you doing here?" he said, only realizing the stupidity of his question after the words left his mouth.

"More to the point, what are you doing here?" his father said. "If it's food you're after, we've already got you covered." He nudged his trolley toward Rigby.

Rigby glanced at the contents. Enough for a week by his reckoning.

"I called Becca," his mother said. "Told her we were coming out. Asked whether she needed anything. Save her the trip. We knew you'd be at work."

"Thanks, Mom." Way to make him feel guilty. He hadn't even considered whether they might need any supplies before the storm. When he'd lived on his own, keeping the fridge or pantry stocked had never been a concern. And he'd never starved. Though he guessed now he had a family to think about, it was different.

"We were going to drop it off on the way home," his father added. "But now you're here do you want to take it?"

Rigby grimaced. "I'm here on business actually. Don't know how long it'll be until I get home. Do you mind?"

Judging from their expressions, they did. But what could he do? He was working. And if he hadn't bumped into them they would have dropped the shopping off so what difference did it make? Except, it wasn't the shopping that annoyed them, more likely the hours he'd been working. His father had always had a nine-to-five job. Home in the evenings and weekends, helping with the kids and the household chores. So much easier for him to be a good father and husband than with a job where you never knew when you might have to work late or give up days off.

"It's fine," his mother said. "We'll see you on Christmas Day then?"

He smiled. Nodded. Headed toward the car rental office. Had he warned his parents he was on call on Christmas Day?

A bored-looking young man sat behind the counter of the car rental. As Rigby pushed open the door he could see the relief on the guy's face at the prospect of finally having a client to deal with. When he showed his badge, excitement lit up Justin's eyes only to

257

dim when Rigby mentioned the name Isabelle Heaton.

No. Nobody of that name had been in earlier. In fact, he confided, apart from one family, Rigby was the only other person to come in all day and there were only a couple of reservations for later that afternoon.

"What's she done?" Justin asked.

"What?"

"If you're looking for her. She must have done something. Right?"

"I'm not at liberty to say."

Justin's face fell further.

"And our conversation needs to stay between the two of us, okay? No gossiping about it with pals. Right?"

Justin didn't respond.

"Understand? If her name gets out in public, I'll know where to look. And I'll be back."

"Yeah, yeah. I hear you."

"You'd better. That would be obstructing an investigation," Rigby added for emphasis. Hopefully, that would scare Justin into keeping his mouth shut. Pearson would go ballistic if Izzy's name appeared in the paper or was bandied around in public.

And the chief would know exactly who to blame.

Chapter 67

The second rental office was attached to a garage on the east side of town. Rigby scanned the vehicles waiting for repair but saw no sign of the SUV. The young woman behind the counter gave him a broad smile as he entered but continued an animated phone conversation that sounded more like gossip than work, and bitchy gossip at that.

When she finally hung up, she asked him sweetly what she could do for him as if he hadn't just heard the other side of her personality. He guessed she was about the same age as Izzy, which probably meant she'd been in school with her and might recognize the name so he decided to tread carefully.

Without mentioning Izzy's name he asked if anyone had come in unexpectedly needing a car. The woman switched her attention from his badge to his face and gave a coy smile as if he'd asked a personal question.

He coughed.

She gave a little laugh. "There's been several rentals today. The weather, you know? Fender benders. And people have to have a car."

"Could you give me their names?"

The woman looked stricken. "I don't think I'm supposed to do that. Not without the manager's say-so."

"Could you ask the manager?"

The sweet smile returned. "He's gone for the day."

Rigby raised his eyes to the ceiling. Let out a huge sigh. "Could you at least tell me if there were any rentals under the name of Heaton?"

Her eyes lit up. "Ooh, I went to school with someone called Heaton."

Rigby froze. Damn.

"He was a real cutie." She sniffed. "Not that he paid me any attention." She shrugged. "Just as well. He got a classmate pregnant. He married her but then he joined the military. I wouldn't want to be a military wife. Living on a base. Your husband being sent overseas. What kind of life's that?"

Rigby coughed again.

"He definitely hasn't been in renting a car. Or his wife. I guess she's a Heaton now." She frowned. "Though I think I heard they got divorced."

Rigby spoke slowly, partly to prevent his frustration from erupting. "I don't need a family history. I only need to know whether you rented a car to someone called Heaton."

The woman scowled at him and consulted her computer screen. Tapped at the keyboard with fingernails akin to talons. After what seemed an eternity she glanced up and uttered a surly "no."

"Fuck."

Her eyes widened.

"Sorry." He shook his head. "Thanks." He turned to leave.

"Merry Christmas," she called after him.

"Merry Christmas," he replied, trying to put some enthusiasm in his voice.

It had been a long shot. Another long shot. And another dead end. He glanced at his watch. Only two hours until Pearson's deadline.

Chapter 68

Rigby sat in his car outside the garage. He didn't want to go back to his desk. Back to Harper to tell her she was right, it had been a waste of time. He called into the duty sergeant. Checked there were no messages for him. There were, but nothing related to the case. He'd have plenty of time to follow them up the next day.

He drummed his fingers on the steering wheel. There had to be something else he could do. Something he'd missed. Though if Izzy had fled then that surely had to be a sign of her guilt. Why else would she run?

So all the focus had to be on finding her. He wished he'd never let her go after the last interview. Technically, they could have held her longer but based on the evidence he had at the time it would have been tough to defend. And maybe he shouldn't have tried to unnerve her with his comment of "for now" when he told her she could go.

Damn. If she thought she'd got away with the interview would she have assumed she was in the clear with no reason to run? She would have been at Martin's that morning and right now they'd be sitting back in the interview room challenging her movements on the night of Gail's death.

He sighed. But if she kept saying no comment, they'd still have no solid evidence to use against her. Just hunches and speculation.

He thumped the steering wheel. Her disappearance was the biggest indication they had of her guilt. She could of course keep silent as to why she'd fled, but her family would want answers too. And if he caught up with her—no, when he caught up with her—all the pussy-footing around the family would end. He'd tell them in no uncertain terms what evidence they did have suggesting Izzy's involvement and see how that played out. Especially between Martin and Izzy. She'd have to be one tough lady to deal with the fallout from the family. Even tougher to protect Martin if he was indeed involved.

He leaned back against the headrest. Family. A source of joy. A source of agony. And you didn't get to choose them. They were inflicted on you for better or worse. And in his job, he'd seen a lot of the worse. Happy families on the outside, a morass of insecurities, jealousy and resentment on the inside.

He was one of the lucky ones. His parents hadn't caused him any more grief than good parents should—though they might have a different opinion about the grief he'd caused them—and he got along well with his sisters, especially now they were all adults.

His phone rang.

He straightened up at the sight of the name on the screen. "Hello, Hannah?"

"Hi. You asked me to let you know when Izzy returned. She's just got back."

What? Izzy was back? He turned on the engine.

"I'm on my way over."

"No. Don't come here. She was in a hurry. Apparently her client was being really difficult. And then the woman's daughter turned up and complicated matters. That's why she was away so long. She said she had to get the kids home so she's already left. If you want to speak to her you'll have to go to Martin's."

"Okay. Thanks," he muttered, still stunned by the news. He ended the call. So Izzy hadn't fled. Where did that leave him?

Right back where he started that morning, that's where. Except now without anything to persuade Izzy to explain her actions.

And to make matters worse, a flurry of snowflakes against the windscreen announced the beginning of the storm.

Chapter 69

Sure enough, when he got back to Martin's house there were four cars outside. This time it was the SUV that blocked the entrance to the garage. He parked outside the house next door and hurried up onto the porch. Even before the front door opened, he could hear yelling.

"It's not a good time, Detective." Mrs. Cooper glanced back over her shoulder in the direction of the heated conversation.

"I'm only trying to help." Izzy sounded petulant and aggrieved.

"You want to help, the best thing you can do is go home," Martin snapped back.

"Oh, dear." Mrs. Cooper gave Rigby a nervous grin. "Tempers are a little frayed today."

That was an understatement. The momentary silence ended with Izzy's stunned, "You don't mean that."

"I do. It's for the best. We need some space."

"After all I've done?"

There was another silence.

"Just go, Izzy." Martin hesitated. "Please. Go."

Izzy stormed out of the living room and dashed up the stairs, paying no heed to Rigby.

"Oh, dear," Mrs. Cooper said again. "Are you sure you want to come in?"

Martin appeared in the doorway. "What do you want now?"

"I still need to speak to Izzy."

Martin looked puzzled. "You didn't speak to her at Hannah's?"

"She wasn't there."

Martin frowned. "Of course she was there. She called to say Hannah had invited them to stay for lunch. Was it okay?" He spluttered. "What was I going to say? Just because I was furious with her didn't mean I should take it out on the kids. They're the ones that matter."

Rigby took a deep breath. "Hannah said she'd got a work call out."

"Izzy's not working at the moment."

"An emergency, apparently."

"She forgot to mention that too."

"You didn't give me a chance to tell you," Izzy said from the top of the stairs. She stomped down the steps, a small bag in her hand. "I'll pick up the rest of my stuff later."

She eyed Rigby cautiously. "What do you want?"

She had to know. Hannah must have mentioned he'd called by. "I have some follow-up questions after our talk yesterday."

If looks could kill.

"Seems you didn't get a chance to tell me about that either," Martin said.

"It had nothing to do with you."

"That's what I told Detective Rigby," Martin said with even less conviction than before. "But you're both here now. If you want to use the living room, go ahead."

"I don't think so. I know when I'm not wanted." She smiled insincerely at Rigby. "How about I drop my bag at home and call by the station house after?"

No way was he letting her out of his sight again. "How about we go straight to the station house? I'm sure your bag won't come to any harm in your car."

"You want to go in my car?"

"No. I'll follow in my car."

That seemed to amuse her. "I'm not that bad a driver."

"Protocol. We either do it this way or I call for a patrol car to take you in. Your choice."

She hesitated. "Am I under arrest?"

"I just want to clear up a few points about what you said yesterday. That's all."

She considered that. Her eyes narrowed. "I think I want to call my lawyer."

Martin gaped at her. "Why would you need a lawyer?" He hesitated. "Why do you even have a lawyer?"

Izzy ignored the questions. Pulled out her phone and stepped into the living room to make the call. A heated conversation ensued. Sue Woodward was probably busy with other clients and couldn't drop everything to rush to Izzy's side. Izzy seemed to be having a problem understanding that.

Rigby groaned. He'd either have to arrest Izzy and make her wait at the station house until the lawyer turned up or get her to commit to turning up with the lawyer later. Despite his fears, she hadn't run yet but she must surely realize the stakes were higher now. He didn't want to let her out of his sight again.

He glanced at his watch. Maybe he wouldn't have to.

Chapter 70

Because Izzy lived so close to the station house it was perfectly natural for Rigby to follow her most of the way home. As they got closer he deliberately dropped back so he could see her turn onto her street before he would have to turn into the parking lot. Fortunately, the now heavy snow meant there were fewer cars on the road than normal and it wouldn't seem too strange that he was driving so slowly. As soon as Izzy made the turn, he sped to the corner and peered down the street. He spotted her reversing into a space two blocks down from her apartment.

He made the turn and immediately pulled into a no parking space and watched. He grew concerned when she didn't get out of the car even after the engine had been turned off and the headlights went out. What was she doing?

Finally, she did get out. He watched her retrieve her bag from the trunk and hurry back toward her apartment. As she disappeared inside a light went on in the room above the realtor. Izzy appeared at the window. She stood staring out into the street before drawing the drapes.

Hopefully, she'd stay there until her short journey to meet with Rigby and her lawyer at six as arranged, but just to be sure he was going to keep an eye on her. He drove along the road looking for a parking space but there was nothing close enough so he returned to his original spot.

He called Harper. Asked her if she could sit in on the interview. She agreed, but told him Turner hadn't been able to get any clearer images from the bundled-up pedestrians, though he reckoned two of them were male. He brought her up to speed on the events of the day only to be disappointed by her despondent, "so no further forward really."

Next he called Becca and told her he'd be late again. She sighed loudly, said, "Okay. See you later," and ended the call.

He could have gone home. Spent a couple of hours there and then come back for the interview. But Izzy must be feeling the pressure of her lies and if she was going to do anything stupid in response, now would be the time. He couldn't risk the case for a few hours with his family.

A patrol car pulled up alongside him, the red and blue strobes filling his car. The passenger window rolled down. A patrol officer, Sommers, peered across at him as he lowered his window in response. "Sir, you can't wait— Oh, it's you."

"Just keeping my eye on someone."

"Damn stupid place to do it. Right on the corner without your lights on."

"That would be a giveaway, wouldn't it? Might as well have a large sign on the side of my vehicle saying police."

Rigby didn't catch the muttered response but given the look on Sommers' face it was probably just as well.

As Sommers pulled away, Rigby felt a pang of guilt. The guy was only doing his job. There'd been no need to be so snarky. Sommers was right, there was a reason there was a no parking sign on the corner. And as soon as a spot opened up, he'd take it. As long as it wasn't right outside the realtor's office.

He turned the radio on. Christmas music filled the car. Two days until Christmas Eve. He let the thought sink in. Only two days. That might explain the crowded stores and loaded shopping carts. Not the threat of a snowstorm per se, but the need to be ready for Christmas accentuated by the threat of bad weather. He tried to remember whether Becca had mentioned plans for food shopping. Had he let that chore slip by too? No wonder she was in a bad mood with him.

The door next to the realtors opened. A figure stepped out. In the growing dusk it was hard to make out their features but they looked about the same size as Izzy. The only differences were the color of coat, a vivid red, and matching knee length leather boots. It was both too early for a trip to the station house and an unlikely choice of outfit for the occasion. He watched as the person gingerly made their way along the snow-covered sidewalk toward the yellow car. His hand on the key, he readied to start the engine. But the figure stopped by a red sedan three spaces down and got in.

To follow or not? The car was pointed in the opposite direction to his so he wasn't going to get a closer look at the driver. But what was the likelihood it was Izzy? Different style of clothes. Different car. More likely the tenant of the third floor. Or maybe Izzy had a roommate.

Decisions, decisions. Stay or follow? He looked up at the window where he'd seen Izzy. Light still leaked through the thin gap between the drapes.

The red car pulled away. It was now or never. He looked back up at the window. Decided the odds were against it being Izzy. He should stay.

He changed the radio station. More Christmas music. And again. And again. The same music on every channel. He checked his watch. More than two hours to go. He wished he had a coffee. And a partner. And he hoped he didn't have to pee. And that there was something other than damned Christmas music on the radio.

He jumped as the passenger door opened. Pearson climbed inside, brushing snow off his coat onto the seat and floor.

"What are you doing here?" Rigby dreaded the answer.

"I could ask you the same question." The chief gave him a piercing stare.

Rigby didn't answer.

"I hear you have a six o'clock appointment with Isabelle Heaton. And her lawyer."

"Harper?"

Pearson nodded. "She has this novel idea of keeping me informed about what she's up to. You should try it."

"Seems like I don't need to. You've obviously got your sources."

"I'll pretend you didn't say that." Pearson said sharply and continued to stare at him until Rigby felt obliged to look away. "The rules are there for a reason. How are we supposed to know if you get yourself into a sticky situation if we don't have any idea where you are?"

"Ah, so that's what this is about? You're worried I'm going to mess up again?"

"No." Pearson hesitated. "At least, not me."

Rigby frowned. "Then who?"

"Nancy Tuccino said you missed your appointment. The one that was part of the deal for her signing you off as being fit for work."

Damn, he'd forgotten all about it. Though he had called her back, hadn't he? She was the one who hadn't returned his call.

"And Becca."

"Becca!" Rigby stared open-mouthed at the suggestion. "Becca's been in touch with you?"

"Not quite." Pearson hesitated again. "But Molly called her to see how she was doing and to invite you over on New Year's Eve and I think she may have caught Becca at a bad moment but let's just say Becca had a lot to say."

"Like what?" If Molly had shared it with Pearson, it couldn't be good.

"That she'd hardly seen you since you came back to work. That you seemed distracted, obsessed with a particular case to the exclusion of pretty much anything else."

"Wanting to catch Gail's killer is not being obsessed."

"You don't think what you're doing right now is obsessive? You could easily have asked Izzy to come in tomorrow morning."

"What? And given her the night to disappear?"

"Her whole life is here in Lewisville. I doubt she's going to leave it all behind because you've asked her some awkward questions." He paused. "Besides, if you'd presented a compelling case and asked, I could have had one of the guys from patrol keep an eye on her. Given you a chance to go home."

Rigby scoffed. "You'd be willing to put someone on her all night? What happened to those budget concerns?"

"If the forecast is right, and so far it looks like it might be, it's going to be a quiet night. Everyone hunkered down." Pearson laughed. "This snow keeps up, Izzy's car will probably be snowed in by nine. She won't be going anywhere without having to dig it out first. It shouldn't be hard to keep an eye on her."

As he spoke, a car pulled into the spot vacated by the red sedan. When the headlights went out, the warning lights flashed briefly.

"That's Weldon," Pearson said. "He's going to sit there until Izzy comes out for her interview. I told him to wrap up warm and bring plenty of coffee. You, I want you to go home. Spend a little time with Becca before you have to come back."

Rigby's phone rang.

Collins sounded upbeat. "Thought you might want to know. We've just had a call. About the white sedan we're looking for. A lady reckons she might know where it is."

Chapter 71

The address Collins gave them was on the same side of town as the accident site. Rigby tried to balance his excitement about the lead with the need for caution on the snowy roads. He'd already noticed Pearson tense as he'd take a bend a little faster than he should. But he knew the roads. He'd driven them in all weathers. He knew how to handle them. Then again, so did Pearson but that hadn't prevented him from being involved in a serious crash.

He slowed down. Sensed Pearson relax. When Rigby had relayed Collins' message the chief had simply said, "Let's go." Then he'd called Molly and told her he'd be late. His smile as he ended the call told Rigby that Molly had been more accommodating than Becca. So much for Pearson's lectures on family first. Though when was the last time the chief would have worked late? Molly had little to complain about on that score.

He pulled up outside an enormous colonial in pristine condition. The house was considerably larger than its neighbors with a detached double garage on the left of the property. But unlike its neighbors, there wasn't a single Christmas decoration. Nor was there any sign of a white sedan.

"Do you think the car's in there?" Rigby gestured at the garage.

Pearson chuckled. "That would be too easy."

"It's about time I had some luck."

Rigby's phone buzzed. A text. No message. Just a photo. "Shit!"

"What now?" Pearson asked warily.

Rigby held the screen out for Pearson to see the photo of Lotte in a red and green plaid dress and a tiny Santa hat. "I'd forgotten Becca said a friend of hers, a photographer, was coming over to take some holiday snaps. She wants to make a tradition of it. Apparently it was something her mom did when she was growing up."

Pearson gave him a sly smile. "Don't tell me you have to wear one of those ugly Christmas sweaters."

Rigby grimaced. "I wouldn't say ugly. But they are matching."

Pearson laughed out loud. Slapped him on the shoulder. "No wonder you're in the doghouse." He opened the car door. "Come on. Let's see what we've got here."

An expensively-dressed middle-aged woman opened the door to them. "I hope I'm not wasting your time," she said as she ushered them in. "But when I saw the story in the paper, I couldn't help noticing the car looked like Mommy's." She laughed nervously. "Silly, isn't it. There must be hundreds of similar cars and Mommy hasn't been out in hers for..." She exhaled hard. "I'd say over a year now. But then I thought what if it had been stolen? Nobody would know. And you do hear about so many cars being stolen." She laughed again. "Not that I need to tell you that."

Rigby glanced at Pearson, wondering if he was having the same thoughts. If it was stolen, Marie, as she'd introduced herself, was unlikely to know where the vehicle was. "And you discovered it was stolen?" he said to hurry the interview along.

"No, no. It's there. That's why I called." She broke off. "I mean I would have called to report it stolen too, if it had been, and I was so happy to see it hadn't, but then I noticed something odd."

She looked back and forth between them.

"Go on," Rigby urged her, a familiar sense of anticipation replacing his temporary disillusionment.

"As I said, Mommy hasn't driven the car for over a year now. Since she became so frail. She was so upset when she was told she had to stop driving. She loved her car, the freedom it gave her, especially when she couldn't walk so well anymore."

Once again she looked at both of them, nodding and smiling as if looking for reassurance they understood. Rigby just wanted her to get to the point.

"She looked after her car. Had it cleaned inside and out every month or so. She knew all the guys at the car wash."

"So the car in the garage was dirty?" Rigby said to distract her before she could launch into the guys' names.

"Yes. That's what I'm trying to tell you. Mommy would never have left the car in such a state."

"Can we see it?" Rigby asked.

"Of course. I'll get my coat and boots. We can go out the back door. It's slightly nearer the garage."

Pearson turned to Rigby. "If this is the right car, it's going to raise more questions than answers."

Rigby merely nodded. They'd almost be back to square one. If it was locked away in the garage who knew it was even there? Who had access? And how did it end up with Dale Jessup's license plate?

When Marie returned, dressed as if she was off on a long walk rather than a dash across the yard, Rigby asked, "Do you know someone called Isabelle Heaton?"

Pearson gave him a sharp look.

"Is that the poor woman who was killed?"

"No. It's her sister."

"No. Sorry. I don't live here anymore. I only came over this morning. I'm taking Mommy to my place for Christmas. That's why I didn't call before. I hadn't heard about the accident. I was tidying up, throwing away some old newspapers—Mommy does tend to let them accumulate—when I saw the story on the front page. Such a sad thing to happen, especially so close to Christmas. I don't usually bother with the local papers but the photo of the car caught my eye, it being the same as Mommy's. And when Mommy said they still hadn't found the driver, I thought I should check her car was where it should be." A guilty look crossed her face. "I haven't mentioned this to Mommy yet. I don't want to upset her. I mean, she'd be upset enough to hear the car was damaged."

"Damaged? Or dirty?"

Marie scrunched her face up. "The front does look a little

misshapen. But Mommy did have one or two little accidents before she stopped driving altogether. Misjudging the distance to the garage wall, that kind of thing, so it's possible she'd had some scrapes she didn't tell us about. She's quite proud. She wouldn't want to admit that's why she stopped driving. And nobody's had any reason to use the car since." She paused. "I doubt anyone's even been in the garage since."

She led them through to the back of the house, unlocked the back door and gestured outside. "Shall we?"

Rigby let out a huge sigh. About time.

Chapter 72

The garage had the air of a space that hadn't been opened for a long time. Half of it was filled with boxes, furniture and sports equipment, the other with the white car.

"Mommy doesn't like to throw anything away. She says you never know when it might come in useful. I think all our childhood toys might be in some of those boxes." Marie sighed. "When she does finally pass it's going to be a huge task."

Pearson nodded sympathetically. Rigby didn't care about the boxes. The car was all he was interested in. It was definitely dirty. He pulled up the photos he had on his phone, enlarged the close-up of the rear, then crouched down at the back of the car to compare them. He smiled. Barring a huge coincidence, he was looking at the car from the photo. The half-hidden high school sticker, the scratches Gina had pointed out--they were all there. He pointed out the similarities to Pearson.

"A high school sticker on an older person's car—that's not something you see often," Pearson said.

"Mommy was a teacher. Didn't retire until she was in her seventies. We thought we were going to have to carry her out. She loved the school so much." Marie grinned at Pearson. "If you went to the high school you might remember her. Mrs. Carmichael."

Rigby couldn't be sure in the dim garage light but Pearson seemed to blanch.

"English. Literature," Pearson said.

"And deputy principal at the end. Which is why she's always

proud to have the sticker on her car," Marie added. "She still remembers a lot of her students. I'll have to ask her if she remembers you."

Pearson gave an uneasy smile.

Rigby stored that nugget away for later. He moved to the front of the car. Winced at the sight of the damage. The left headlight was cracked and the hood had a substantial dent in it. He was no expert and they'd need Gina to confirm it, but the back of the car matched the car outside Mrs. Henderson's house with Dale Jessup's license plate and the front looked as if it had had an encounter with a body rather than a fixed object.

He smiled up at Pearson.

Now all he had to do was figure out the connection to Izzy.

Chapter 73

Marie sat slumped at the kitchen table, her head in her hands. "I don't believe this. How is it even possible?"

Rigby wished he knew.

"Our forensic expert will be here soon to go over the car. Confirm whether it's the vehicle we're looking for and if it is, to check for fingerprints," Pearson said. "And we'll need to get your prints and your mother's so we can eliminate those from any we find."

"Is that really necessary?" Marie looked up. "I'd prefer my mother knew as little about this as possible. We're leaving to drive back to Virginia tomorrow. The family's gathering there."

Pearson glanced around the large kitchen. "Your mother lives here alone? At her age?"

"She won't leave. Says all her friends are here. Not that there's many left. She's outlived most of them." Marie sighed. "She might be frail physically but there's nothing frail about her obstinacy. We take it in turns to visit every month and she has a cleaner come in two or three times a week, and a gardener to look after the outside. Then there's an aide who comes in regularly. And she had various alarms around the house in case she needs help when she is alone."

"So there's several people who've had access to the house?"

Marie thought for a moment. "The cleaner has a set of keys. The gardener, no. All the tools he needs are in a shed out back. I guess the aide would have one too. But you can't think they had anything to do with the car?"

"Somebody took the car and put it back again which suggests they have a familiarity with the house. Most stolen cars don't get returned, unless it's by the police." Pearson said. "Is the garage normally kept locked?"

"There's an automatic garage opener in the car and a pin pad to open the main doors from the outside." Marie looked sheepish. "There's also a side door but the lock's been broken for a while."

"Forensics will check the door. I assume there's no reason why any of the people you mentioned should need to go into the garage?"

"Not unless Mommy asked them to fetch her something." She hesitated. "Though I can't think what. She probably doesn't remember half what's in there."

"The cleaner and the aide," Rigby interjected. "Can you give us their names and addresses?"

"Maria Lopez is the cleaner. Lovely woman. Been working for Mommy for years. A real gem. I wish I could find someone so loyal as she is. It's so hard to find good help nowadays."

"And the aide?" Rigby wanted details not references.

"There, we haven't been so lucky. We did have a lovely lady until recently but she moved away to be close to her family. But since then it seems to have been a string of different people. The agency says Mommy's fussy, difficult to work for, but really I think it's the aides who are at fault. Just yesterday the current one said she wasn't going to come back anymore. Just like that. No notice. What would we have done if Mommy hadn't been coming to me for Christmas?"

"You mentioned an agency?"

"Yes. It's supposed to save all the hassle of vetting the candidates but I think it would be easier to put an ad in the local newspaper ourselves. Cheaper too."

"And the name of the agency?" He was tempted to add, "in as few words as possible." At this rate he'd still be sitting there at six o'clock.

"Let me think. We used to use The Caring Company but they got taken over by... I forget the name."

"Lewisville Cares?" Rigby didn't want to put words in her mouth but there was a limit to his patience.

"No. I don't think so."

Damn.

"I'll have to ask Mommy."

"What about the name of the aide? The one who just resigned?"

"Again, I'll have to ask Mommy. I'd never seen her before. I think she's only been around for a month or two. Mommy said she liked her but I thought she was rude."

"It would be useful to have a quick chat with your—" Rigby bit back the word Mommy. "Mother."

"Is that really necessary? As I said I don't want her upset over this."

"A woman died and it could be your mother's car that killed her."

Marie looked stricken. "I hope you're not suggesting Mommy might have been driving it?"

"Of course not," Pearson said politely. "But your mother's the only one who's been here all the time. She might have heard or seen something important. And not realized."

Marie stood up. "I'll go and see if she's feeling up to having visitors."

"Five bucks," Rigby said as she left, "the answer's no."

Pearson merely rolled his eyes.

"We don't even know the old lady exists. Mommy could be a figment of Marie's imagination, a decoy to distract us from the person we should be looking at."

"Which is?"

"Her."

Pearson frowned. "Why would she call us and tell us about the car if she was the driver?"

"Exactly. That's what she wants us to think. A perfect cover. And if her fingerprints are on the car or the door to the garage, the one with the broken lock, what would that prove? You could argue it would be weirder if we didn't find the fingerprints."

Pearson squinted. "And Izzy fits into this how?"

Rigby drummed his fingers on the table top. "I haven't worked that out yet." He stopped drumming. "But I will." He smiled.

"It's just a question of joining the dots. And we're almost there."

He shut up as he heard voices in the hallway. A stooped white-haired woman inched her walker into the kitchen. Mommy did indeed exist.

Pearson smirked at Rigby.

The woman eased herself down into a chair opposite them and eyed them over, her gaze settling on Pearson. "Marie tells me you were one of my pupils."

Pearson nodded.

"You don't look familiar."

Rigby groaned inwardly. This was no time for a trip down memory lane.

The old lady's gaze shifted to him. "Now you, you do, but you're too young to have been one of my pupils. What did you say your name was?"

"Paul Rigby. Can we—"

"Of course, Joe Rigby. Your father, I guess. You look just like him." She smiled, ignoring Rigby's startled reaction. "You can't remember them all. There's so many over the years. But some of them stick with you. The ones who made a mark. Good or bad." She eyed Rigby again. "And Joe Rigby certainly sticks out."

Rigby gaped at her. She remembered his father from over thirty years ago? What had he done to be so memorable?

The old lady sniffed. "Quite a character if I remember rightly."

Rigby glanced over at Pearson who was struggling not to laugh. His father, a character? No way.

Mrs. Carmichael turned back to Pearson. "Chief of Police, eh? You did alright for yourself."

"Mommy," Marie interrupted. "I don't think the detectives are here to discuss the past."

Rigby struggled to push the revelation to the back of his mind. There'd be time for that later. After he'd cracked this puzzle.

"Marie said you'd had several aides recently. Could you give us their names?"

"It's been like a revolving door. So many. But I thought this one, I thought I'd finally found the right one. But Marie, she says she's gone too."

"And their names?" He didn't want to be rude but he wanted to keep Mrs. Carmichael on track.

She sighed. "I'm afraid my memory's not so good now."

He glared at her. She'd just remembered his father from over thirty years ago.

She must have read his expression. "Memory. It's a funny thing. I can remember things from the past fine but ask me about yesterday or last week and it's gone."

"Your latest aide. Let's start with her," Pearson said with more patience than Rigby could muster.

"Anna."

"And her last name?"

"Sorry, you'll have to ask the agency." She turned to Marie. "Or maybe you could fetch the file with invoices in. That would give us all the names."

Marie didn't move.

"It's in the bureau in the dining room. Run along and get it, dear."

As Marie left, Mrs. Carmichael smiled at them. "She's a good daughter. And I know she means well. But I'm not moving to Virginia. At my age! No sir. Come the new year, I'll be back here." She huffed. "Even if I have to take the bus." She pointed to the window. "Mind you, if that keeps up, we'll be spending Christmas here."

"If we have to travel by snow plow, we're getting back to Virginia tomorrow." Marie dropped a binder onto the table in front of Rigby.

He took that as a sign he could look inside. The invoice on the top was for November. It definitely had been a revolving door of aides. There were five names on the list, the last one an Anna Morales, who'd worked for two weeks. The others only lasted two or three days each. He glanced at Mrs. Carmichael. Wondered what it was about the seemingly sweet old lady that made it difficult to work for her.

He flipped to the next invoice. Stopped cold. There was only one name on the invoice. Isabelle Heaton. He flipped to the previous month. Isabelle again. And the previous month. And the one before that.

Isabelle was the lovely lady who'd left to move closer to her family? It didn't make sense. And Marie had said she'd never heard of Isabelle. How was that possible when she'd been looking after her mother? Was Marie in on this somehow?

He pushed the binder in front of Pearson. Raised his eyebrows.

Marie leaned across the table to see what he was looking at. Her mouth dropped open. "Izzy. I never thought when you asked. I only knew her as Izzy." She clasped a hand across her mouth. "It was Izzy's sister who was killed?" She gasped. "How awful."

"What's awful?" Mrs. Carmichael looked at each of them. "What are you talking about?"

Marie pleaded with them with her eyes. Mouthed "please don't tell her."

The doorbell rang. Rigby leaped up. "That will be Gina."

Chapter 74

"Seriously, Rigby, what are you trying to do to me?" Gina zipped up her white jumpsuit and pulled on a pair of gloves. "Two days until Christmas. I've got a mountain of presents to wrap, both sets of parents arrive tomorrow, and I've got three kids who are so excited I doubt they're going to sleep between now and Christmas morning. And did I mention the baking I still have to do?"

"You signed up for it."

"I know. What was I thinking?" She waved him away.

"You'll let me know as soon as you have anything?"

"No. I'm going to save it and give you it as a Christmas present."

"I've got an interview at six. With a likely suspect."

She snorted. "Christmas may be a time for miracles, Rigby, but that's not going to happen." She disappeared into the garage.

He hurried back inside, stomped the snow off his shoes and took a deep breath. They had the car. They had the license plate with Izzy's fingerprints on it. Izzy could be linked to both locations, albeit not recently at one. They'd also caught her in a potential lie about where she was that night. But what they still couldn't do was put her in the driver's seat when the car hit Gail. That was going to require a confession.

Back in the kitchen, the chief appeared to have avoided upsetting Mrs. Carmichael by talking tales of school.

"It's strange I don't remember you at all," she said as Pearson stood up, signaling he was ready to leave. "You must have been one of the quiet ones, the good ones. Sadly, they're the ones who make less of a lasting impression." She turned to Rigby. "Not like your father."

Pearson grinned and then turned to Marie. "Thanks for making the call. It's been a great help. You understand we'll have to follow up on the number you've given us to check where you were that night. For the record."

"This is my first time back since the summer. My husband will confirm I was at home in Virginia." She showed them out.

"What do you think?" Rigby asked as they brushed snow off his car.

"I think I need to call Molly and tell her I'm going to be even later than expected."

"You want in on the interview?" Harper would not appreciate being kicked off the case at this point.

"No. But I'd like to view it in real time. You're going to have to get her to confess or finger someone else. And that's not going to be easy, because for all we do have, what we don't have is motive. Why would Izzy want to kill her own sister?"

Chapter 75

"Izzy's lawyer's here. Izzy isn't." Harper didn't even give him a chance to take his coat off.

Rigby checked his watch. Spot on six. He went out to the lobby and asked Collins to check in with Weldon.

"Nobody's gone in or out." Weldon told them over the radio.

Damn. Had she snuck out the back?

"Can you see a yellow car parked two blocks down?"

"Hang on a minute." They heard the sound of Weldon getting out of his car.

Rigby bounced his fingers on the counter. He'd screwed up. He should have arrested her when he'd had the chance. But where could she have gone in this weather?

"Yes, it's here," Weldon said. "Covered in snow, but I see it."

So if she'd gone, she hadn't taken her car. And where the hell would she walk to in these conditions? There were no buses. Taxi?

"Call around the taxi companies," he told Collins. "See if any of them have picked up a young woman this afternoon."

"Where from?"

"Anywhere in town," he snapped.

Collins glared at him but did as he asked.

Damn. The woman in red. Could it have been Izzy? Had she fooled him? Guessed that he'd be watching her?

The lawyer stormed into the lobby. "What's going on? It's

past six. Where is everyone?"

"Your client hasn't shown up."

"I can't hang around forever. I've got a Christmas concert this evening."

As if he cared.

"Hold on," he heard Weldon say. "There's somebody going in now."

"In? What do they look like?"

"Hard to tell from this distance with the snow. But based on the heels on the boots, red boots by the way, I'd say it was definitely a woman."

A wave of relief swept over Rigby. At least he hadn't screwed up on that front. "Can you find out who she is?"

"Excuse me, Ma'am," Weldon shouted. Then there was the crackle of the radio, before Weldon spoke again, sounding slightly out of breath. "Says her name is Anna Morales, lives on the second floor."

Anna Morales? What the—

He shook his head. "Is she still there?"

"Yes."

"Tell her you need to speak to Izzy. Ask her if you can go up with her."

He heard muttering, a door open and close, footsteps on stairs. A rattle of keys in a lock and another door open. A female voice called, "Izzy," followed by a frantic, "Oh my God!"

"Weldon, what's happened?"

"We need an ambulance. Now." Weldon spluttered. "It looks like she's taken an overdose."

Before he'd finished speaking, Collins was giving the address to the ambulance service.

"Is she breathing?" Rigby asked.

"Is she breathing?" Weldon repeated. The female voice could be heard in the background. "Yes. Anna says she can feel a faint pulse. But she's out cold. Anna can't get her to respond. We need to get her to hospital."

"The ambulance is on its…" The familiar wail of the siren came over the air followed by heavy footsteps as Weldon presumably ran down to let them in.

"Should I follow them to the hospital?" Weldon asked.

Rigby glanced over at Pearson who'd been alerted by Harper to the problem. Pearson shook his head.

"No. I'll go to the hospital. You stay there." Rigby caught Harper's eye. "Harper will be with you in a few." Harper nodded her agreement.

He could hear Anna sobbing in the background. "Are you in the room where you found her?" When Weldon answered in the affirmative—Izzy was on the couch in the living room—Rigby told him to take Anna into the kitchen, make her a coffee or something stronger if he could find it. But not to touch anything in the living room. Then he walked away from the counter and let Collins finish up on the call.

He stood by the front door, looking out onto the common. A group of carol singers stood next to the Christmas tree. A few passersby had braved the weather to stop and listen. Pearson came over. Stood next to him but didn't speak.

Rigby exhaled hard. "I berated myself for not arresting her earlier because I thought she'd fled."

"You made the right decision. Based on the evidence you had."

"But if she dies."

"She's still alive."

"But if she dies..."

"You'll have to learn to live with the decision you made. Which was the best decision at the time. You can't hold yourself responsible for the decision she made."

Rigby turned his back on his reflection. Replayed in his mind the image of Izzy going into her apartment, appearing at the window. "I know, but it's the fact that I was probably sitting outside her apartment while she tried to take her own life."

Chapter 76

Rigby made it home for dinner after all. His first instinct had been to go to the hospital, but Pearson told him in no uncertain terms to stay away. There was nothing he could do while the doctors worked on Izzy and assuming she did survive, she wouldn't be in a fit state to be interviewed that evening. Better to wait until morning. And seeing he'd sent Harper over to the apartment, what was left for him to do?

Rigby agreed begrudgingly. The chief was right and he sensed Pearson wouldn't tolerate any objections. And by morning Gina might have some initial results from the Carmichaels' car to back up their case.

Becca's anger toward him thawed a little when he explained what had happened. She heated up one of the stews his mother had brought over earlier in the week and they managed to eat in peace while Lotte slept.

His phone rang as they cleared away the dishes. He was almost afraid to answer it, not sure he could deal with the news of another suicide connected to one of his cases. He sank down on the sofa as he heard the news, the tension that had built up inside escaping like air from a burst balloon. Izzy had survived.

Becca sat down beside him. Leaned her head against his shoulder. "Maybe she deserved to die."

Her words were so out of character they took him by surprise.

"If you're right. She killed Gail. Robbed Martin of his wife, those little kids of their mother, not to mention what she did to her own family. What kind of person does that?"

He didn't have an answer. "If she'd died, we would never have a chance to find out. At least now, we might get some answers." He hesitated. "Assuming we can get her to confess in the first place."

Becca pulled away from him. "Isn't the attempted suicide almost a confession in itself? She knows the police are onto her and can't face the rest of her family learning what she's done. Can you imagine how they'd feel? How they'd react? Parents often say they'd love their child whatever, but how do they do that if one child has robbed them of another? Maybe she came to the conclusion it was better they grieved her too rather than having to cope with her alive, knowing what she'd done."

"What we think she's done. We still can't prove it. Or whether she was acting alone. Maybe there was someone else involved."

Becca looked horrified. "What? Someone in the family?"

"Not necessarily. But it's possible. I thought about Martin. That maybe they were having an affair." Becca's horror turned to disgust. "But the way he's behaved toward her, the comments he's made. I don't see it."

"Could it be an act? Deliberate, so you'd dismiss the idea? Maybe the attempted suicide, that was all in the plan too. She was never meant to die."

"She came very close to succeeding by the sounds of it."

"Different people react in different ways. She could have taken a dose which she thought would be enough to make her attempt look genuine but wouldn't kill her and she miscalculated. After all, if her roommate hadn't returned when she did, it seems likely she would have died." Becca broke off. "Or could she have known when her roommate was due back and planned it accordingly?"

Rigby considered that. "You have a twisted mind, Miss Singer."

Becca pecked him on the cheek. "Comes from living with a detective."

"Only one problem, why would she think a suicide attempt

would stop us following up on leads?"

"Makes others more sympathetic toward her. You said you needed a confession to close the case. What if you don't get it?"

"She'll slip up somehow. And I'll be waiting."

Becca stood up, her expression suddenly furious. "Great. So you could be obsessing over this case forever."

"I'm not obsessing! I'm just trying to do my job." His temper flared. "And that reminds me. Did you have to pick Molly of all people to moan about me to?"

"I didn't do it deliberately. Molly asked me how I was doing." Becca shrugged. Her mouth twisted. "And I guess at that moment, I wasn't doing well. It just came out."

A loud wail came from the bedroom. Becca rolled her eyes and heaved a sigh.

"Here, let me get her," Rigby offered.

"No point," Becca said sharply, heading to the door. "She's due for a feed."

Chapter 77

The forecasts were wrong. More than a foot of snow fell on Lewisville overnight. By the time Rigby had dug the car out, his mood had gone from mildly disgruntled to downright furious. Fortunately, the snowplows had been out ahead of him and the drive to the station house was completed uneventfully.

He called the hospital. Got the usual run around because he wasn't family. He called Hannah instead, assuming she'd know how her sister was doing.

"Mom and Dad are beside themselves," she told him, after admitting she hadn't yet been to the hospital. "This coming so soon after Gail. What was she thinking?" She hesitated. "If she'd stopped to think for a moment what it would do to them. But thinking of others has never been Izzy's strong point."

Harsh words against someone who worked with sick and elderly people and had offered to give up their job to look after a deceased sister's children. But Hannah made up for them by saying she was about to call the hospital and she'd let him know how Izzy was doing.

Harper confirmed they'd found two empty containers of Tylenol and a half-empty bottle of wine in the living room, the latter presumably used to wash down the pills.

Anna had also told Harper how Izzy had been really upset when she arrived home the previous afternoon, saying that Martin's parents had turned him against her after all she'd done for him. It was Anna's day off and she had promised to spend the afternoon with a friend, but she'd told Izzy she'd be back by six and they would have their own little Christmas celebration that evening, with wine, chocolate and holiday movies. That would cheer her up. Izzy had agreed. Anna would never have gone out if she'd realized Izzy was suicidal.

"Is there no end to this woman's lies?" Rigby shook his head in disgust. "I was there when Martin told her to go. It didn't appear to have anything to do with his parents. More that she was smothering him, not giving him the space he needed." He fiddled with a pencil on his desk. "Of course, it could have been an act for my benefit if Martin's involved, but then why would Izzy be upset when she arrived home?"

"Keeping up the act? It's not just us they'd have to persuade that there wasn't anything going on between them yet."

"Nothing points to Martin. If he is involved, he's done a good job of hiding it."

"If he knows we're on to Izzy, it would put pressure on him. Might make him a little careless."

Rigby's phone buzzed. Hannah. She told him Izzy was awake but groggy and refusing to see visitors, even her parents.

Rigby cursed. And no doubt detectives, too. Would that include Martin as well? Hannah sounded confused at the question. She didn't know whether Martin would know about the suicide attempt, whether anyone had told him. If Gail had been there then… her voice petered out.

Rigby saw his chance. He told her not to worry. He had to go over and see Martin anyway. He'd give him the news.

The color drained from Martin's face, his mouth moving long before he managed to utter any words, the anger at seeing Rigby on his doorstep again forgotten. His eyes widened, horror stricken. "Was it what I said? Is that why she did it? I didn't… I didn't… I…"

He released the tight grip on the door jamb—he hadn't invited Rigby in—and raised his hands to his head. Martha ran into the hallway, still in pajamas, signs of breakfast around her mouth. At the sight of Rigby she clutched her father's left leg and hid her face.

"Not now, Martha. Please." He eased Martha away. Nudged her back toward the kitchen. "Go see Grandma."

Rigby stepped inside and shut the door, desperate to get out of the cold.

Martin made no protest. "How…" he swallowed hard. "How is she?"

"Alive." It came out harsher than Rigby intended. "That's about all I know."

"Her parents must be… Hannah too." He raked his fingers through his hair. Looked at Rigby beseechingly. "Do you think that's why she did it? I never meant… It was just getting too much, you know? It was as if she was… was trying to replace Gail." Tears filled his eyes. "Nobody could replace Gail," he said so softly Rigby knew it wasn't aimed at him.

"It was her decision." Rigby replayed Martin's words over in his mind. His heart sank. Damn, had the answer been in front of them all along?

"But did I drive her to it?"

Yes, you probably did, but not in the way you think. Rigby kept the thought to himself.

"No, you can't blame yourself for her actions, for her choices. You mustn't. You've got enough to deal with already. You can't add this burden. Your family need you to be strong."

Martin didn't look convinced. Should he tell him the truth? Why he shouldn't feel guilty? It was tempting. But the truth would only bring another greater layer of anguish for Martin. And the chief was right. Without ironclad proof it would be cruel to tell Martin a truth so devastating for the two families.

First, he had to get the truth out of Izzy.

Chapter 78

Gina's kids had wasted no time. Three snowmen of dubious shape sat on the lawn, guarding a multitude of snow angels. The creators were currently engaged in a snowball fight, shrieks filling the air. Seemingly what had started as an attempt to clear a path to the front door had been abandoned for more fun activities.

Rigby picked his way to the door, dodging misdirected snowballs, though from the kids' giggles he suspected their aim was true. Before he stepped onto the porch he scooped up a handful of snow, balled it, and tossed in their direction. It hit the youngest on the back. A loud wail went up, totally exaggerated. The front door flung open.

Rigby smiled sheepishly at Gina. "Sorry."

"He hit me!" his victim yelled. "It hurts."

Gina raised her eyebrows.

"I guess I might have thrown it a little hard."

Gina looked over to where the victim was trying to push snow down a sibling's back for mocking him. "No lasting damage done. What brings you here?"

"I thought I'd save you a call."

She gestured him inside. "Which call? The one where I tell you I've nothing to report?"

Rigby stopped dead. "Tell me you're kidding."

She grinned. "Yes, I am. But I would have appreciated a little more time to confirm my findings before I passed them on."

He told her about the suicide attempt. She shuddered. Led

him into a tiny office at the back of the house. There was only one chair so he remained standing. "What have you got for me?"

Gina gestured for him to go around to her side of the desk. She switched on two large monitors, one showing the photo Rigby had provided of the car, the other a photo she had taken of Mrs. Carmichael's car. If anything the latter looked a little dirtier, but the smudge across the school sticker was identical, as were the scratches Gina had pointed out. "It's the same car. I'd be willing to swear on it."

"You might have to." Rigby stared at the two photos. He'd be willing to swear on it too. The extra dirt could easily have been picked up during the journey from outside the Henderson house back to the garage.

Gina brought up a photo of the front of the car. "The headlight cracked but, unfortunately for us, didn't break otherwise we would have had glass fragments at the scene. But that with the dent, definitely indicates something bounced off it and given the location of the dent, it's unlikely to have been an animal."

"There was no blood or other matter that we could analyze?"

"No blood, no. The victim was wearing a thick coat, so you wouldn't necessarily expect to find any. And the head injury appears to have been caused when she hit the ground. Unfortunately, the snow mound she landed on was frozen solid underneath."

Damn.

"But I did find some hairs. Two to be precise, stuck to the hood near the dent. Two long blond hairs."

"And?" Rigby felt a surge of excitement. At last, something to tie the car to the accident.

"I've sent it to the lab for analysis. I think it's going to come back as a match to Gail but given the holidays, you could be waiting a long time for an official result."

He didn't care. If Gina thought it was Gail's he was willing to accept that for now. It was enough to confront Izzy with, see how she responded. And if the case went to court, they'd have the results by then.

"What about fingerprints? On the car or the garage door?"

Gina grinned. Rigby did too. Typical of Gina to save the best for last.

"There was nothing on the car but smudges, which is suspicious in itself, because you'd expect to find Mrs. Carmichael's prints at the very least."

Rigby's face fell.

"But there were some on the side door. Some relatively fresh, I'd say, compared to most of them. And the fresh ones are different. I'm running them through the system, haven't had any results back yet, but," she sighed, "knowing how impatient you are, I did a visual comparison between the newer prints and the ones we found on the back of the license plate."

She brought up two new images on her screens. Rigby leaned in for a closer look. "They look the same to me."

She laughed. Switched one of them out. "What about now?"

"The same?"

"You're right. They most likely are. But that first one wasn't."

Rigby frowned.

"That first one's mine, which is why we need the results from the system for a definitive answer. The differences can be miniscule. But look here." She showed him several instances where the two images were identical then brought the image of her prints up again to show that hers differed.

Rigby stepped back. "You're saying the prints on the side door are Izzy's?"

"I'm saying, I think that's what the system will tell us. We should have a result sometime today."

That was good enough to be going on with.

Chapter 79

Rigby laid it out to the chief. The tentative evidence, his theory of a motive. He wanted to arrest Izzy immediately, while she was in the hospital. Pearson listened without interruption then glanced across at Harper who Rigby had invited to join them.

"Still can't put her in the driver's seat," Harper said.

Pearson looked back at Rigby.

"She has to be an accessory at least. And if we push her on it, make her think she's going to take the fall for it all, I think she'll talk."

"And if she doesn't? If she "no comments" it all the way through?" Pearson asked.

"We'd still have enough evidence to get her as an accessory. That's going to take some explaining to her family. And Martin. Once they know she's involved, what does she have to gain by keeping the truth from them?"

"My concern is arresting her in hospital is going to bring the press down on her and the families in a big way. Attract more public attention than necessary at this stage. I think we wait until she leaves the hospital."

"What? And give her another chance to avoid justice?"

"You think she'll try again?"

"Or flee. Think about it. If I'm right, her grand plan has fallen apart and she's terrified of the consequences. The suicide attempt wasn't a ploy or a distraction. It was the only way she could see of getting out of the mess she'd made without having to face her family. Why else would she refuse to see them at the hospital?"

"If the hospital thinks she's still suicidal, they could hold her for seventy-two hours," Harper said.

"And how does that help us if they abide by her refusal to have any visitors?" he snapped. "We need to speak to her. With the warrant they can't deny us access."

Pearson exhaled loudly. "Okay, get the arrest warrant. But only on the accessory charges." As Rigby made to protest, he continued. "If we go for murder, this is going to be on the front page of every local paper, at the top of every local website, and if we don't pull it off there's going to be a huge stink. So let's keep this under the radar as far as we can."

"There's already a report about the suicide attempt in this morning's Chronicle, Sir," Harper said. At Pearson's dismayed reaction, she added, "Front page too."

Pearson glared at Rigby. "How the hell did that make a front-page story?"

"Hey, don't look at me…" Rigby began.

"It gave them a chance to dredge up the tragic hit-and-run as a possible cause for the attempt by the victim's sister. A family in grief. And—" Harper hesitated.

"Go on," Pearson urged.

"And still waiting for answers from the police."

Chapter 80

Sue Woodward met Rigby and Harper in the hospital lobby. She'd come at his request because he was sure her presence would be Izzy's first demand and he didn't want to waste any more time.

They rode up in the elevator together in a frosty silence after she gave him a curt "yes" when he asked her if she'd enjoyed her concert the previous evening. Izzy had been moved to a private room on the third floor where she was under constant supervision, which he discovered meant she was watched on a monitor by the nurse at the ward desk.

"I'm sorry," the nurse said. "Miss Heaton has specifically said no visitors."

"We're not visitors." Rigby produced his badge. "Detective Rigby. And this is Miss Heaton's lawyer."

The nurse got to her feet. "I still can't let you go in."

Rigby pulled out the warrant. "It's not a question of you letting us. We're here to arrest her."

The nurse looked dumbstruck. She'd obviously never had a patient arrested on her watch. She glanced up and down the corridor frantically and when she realized no one was coming to her rescue, she picked up the phone and paged a Dr. Williams.

The doctor's imperious "I'll deal with this, nurse," as if it were a minor nuisance to be dispensed with, made Rigby take an instant dislike to him. He prepared himself for battle, but the doctor simply glanced at the warrant and took Rigby straight to Izzy's room.

"I said no visitors," Izzy yelled at the doctor when she saw

Rigby enter the room behind him. "Get them out of here."

"I'm afraid I can't do that," the doctor said calmly, raising Rigby's estimation of him.

Izzy noticed the lawyer standing by the open door. "Make them go away. I don't want to talk to them. They can't make me talk."

"No," the lawyer agreed. "But they can arrest you. And if they want to ask you any questions they have to read you your rights first."

"I'm not answering any questions."

"Unfortunately," the lawyer said with a wry smile, "that doesn't mean they can't still ask them."

Izzy scowled. "What's the point if I'm not going to answer them?"

The lawyer turned to Rigby. "Can I have a moment with my client?"

A cup of disgusting vending machine coffee later the lawyer gestured for them to return. Rigby hoped it was worth the wait.

Izzy sat upright in bed, her hair pulled back from her face, similar to how it was in the photo at Lewisville Cares. Her eyes were red and puffy in sharp contrast to her wan complexion. He wondered whether it was a result of the treatment she'd had or whether she'd been crying. Was she relieved to be alive or angry she'd been saved? Not a question he could ask.

He watched her reaction as he formally arrested her, but she gave nothing away. Then he read her rights and eventually got her to say she understood them, but it was akin to getting blood from a stone. His hopes of getting anything useful out of her faded.

He started by asking her to confirm her whereabouts on the night of the accident, but got only a "no comment." He reminded her she'd told them she was home alone all evening, but got only an empty stare. Her lawyer queried the need for him to ask the question if he already knew the answer. He showed them a photo taken from the footage of the yellow car being driven away from Izzy's apartment, time stamped at eight thirty-seven. Pointed out it raised a discrepancy in what Izzy had originally told them. But maybe there was a simple explanation, one only Izzy could tell. She had no comment.

And so it went on. He could have been talking to a block of wood. She showed no emotion and he began to wonder whether the overdose had affected her mind.

It was only when he mentioned the fingerprints on the license plate that he saw a flicker in her eyes. As if she was weighing something up. He moved on, making a mental note to come back to it later.

He told her they'd found the car that hit Gail. And asked how her fingerprints came to be on the door to a garage of a house she no longer worked at. And how he was trying to understand how the license plate with her fingerprints on the back could end up on a car they'd found in the garage. He wanted her to see the case they were building against her, the futility of denying everything.

But she remained true to her word. By the end he was none the wiser.

"Why won't you see your family?" Harper asked. "They want to help you."

Izzy gave a little scoff, but to Rigby's amazement her eyes filled with tears. "Why won't you let them help you?" He decided to push it. "Could it be because you don't want to face them once the truth comes out? Can't look them in the eyes?"

"Detective!"

Rigby ignored the lawyer. "Because it's true, isn't it? Even if you only played a tiny part in Gail's accident—or should I say murder—you're hardly going to be welcome at the family dinner table."

"Detective! This interview is over, now."

Rivers of tears streamed down Izzy's face. She sobbed as if heartbroken. Which he reckoned she probably was. Not for her sister, but for the man she could never have. The life she could never have. The one she wanted so badly. A husband, kids, a home of her own. Everything that Gail had. Everything she thought she could have if Gail was out of the picture. But she'd made a big mistake. She'd mistaken Martin's tolerance of her presence for affection, deluded herself into thinking she could wheedle her way into his life and become so indispensable she'd ultimately take Gail's place. She'd been willing to kill to get what she wanted and never considered that hers was an unattainable dream. Or how many people she would hurt in the process.

He looked at her with no compassion. People committed murder for a multitude of reasons, none justifiable, but this was beyond his comprehension.

He made to leave. Told Izzy there'd be an officer outside her door until the doctors decided whether she should be held for further evaluation or released. If the former, she'd be moved to a secure unit in the hospital. If the latter, there was a cell waiting for her at the station house until she could go before the judge. He hoped she didn't have any plans for Christmas.

The last comment was unnecessary, unprofessional even, but he needed to let out some of the rage burning inside. Martin's reaction to the news of the suicide attempt stuck in his mind. The assumption of guilt where none existed, a natural instinct for a person who thought they might have hurt another, however inadvertently. Compared to this woman who was prepared to rip Martin's life apart in order to fashion it to her desires. And when caught, wouldn't admit it.

He wanted to shake her, slap her, worse. Harper's voice cut through his thoughts. He felt her arm on his as she nudged him toward the door.

"Are you okay?" she asked as he slumped into a plastic chair in the hallway. "For a moment, I thought I was going to end up arresting you." Her words were lighthearted but he could sense the underlying concern. "You looked as if you wanted to beat the truth out of her."

Rigby clenched his hands together to stop them shaking. He wasn't sure what had come over him. The case had taken everything out of him, affected him in a way he couldn't explain. He'd put his most important relationships on the line and he still hadn't brought the case to a satisfactory conclusion.

He pulled out his phone, showed Harper the photo of Lotte in her Christmas outfit. Then he showed her one of Becca with Lotte in her arms, a matching Santa hat on her head.

"Cute," Harper said, obviously bewildered by his timing.

He studied Becca's wide grin, the smile that didn't quite reach her eyes. "I was supposed to be in the photo, but I didn't make it back in time." He stood up. "I'm going home."

"But—"

"Please Harper, I just need to be with my family."

He walked away.

Chapter 81

Rigby shuffled in his chair and looked down at his knees until Nancy Tuccino coughed. He glanced up. "I walked off the job."

"So I hear."

Of course she'd heard. What did he expect? The station house would be buzzing with gossip. The chief himself had probably brought her up to date. But it wasn't at the chief's behest he was there. It was Becca's.

Becca had been taken by surprise when he'd walked in mid-morning the previous day. Even more so when he'd spilled out his thoughts, told her how he felt he was failing on every level. Disappointing the chief, her, Lotte, Martin, even his parents. He didn't expect to close all his cases, some just couldn't be proved to the level required to justify charges, but this case had affected him more than most. He'd allowed his personal feelings to run rampant until all that mattered was getting answers for Martin. Answers wouldn't bring Gail back, but they would hopefully allow Martin to move on. Maybe it was because he was now a father that another father's grief affected him so profoundly. Making him obsessed with getting justice even at the expense of his own relationships. But there was no excuse for refusing to admit what he was doing, to recognize the damage he was causing and do something about it before the relationship reached breaking point.

Becca looked baffled by his admission. Yes, it had been difficult since he went back to work. Yes, there'd been too many calls to say he was going to be late, but she'd known what she was getting into, the irregular hours, the last-minute cancelations. She understood the necessity but being stuck at home with a baby didn't make it easy. And when Lotte cried and wouldn't stop, she felt like a failure too. Nobody told you how tough it would be. She smiled. Added maybe because if it got out nobody would have kids. But seriously, she had no other outlet for her frustrations. Except him. But that didn't mean she loved him any less.

He didn't know what to say. So he'd taken her in his arms and held her tight. And they spent the rest of the day being nice to each other. He put his phone in a drawer so he wouldn't see the phone calls, text messages or emails that were sure to come in. Harper could close the case as well as he could. Possibly better.

Becca dressed Lotte in her Christmas outfit and they donned their Christmas sweaters and took multiple selfies until they had one they both approved of. When Lotte went to sleep after dinner, they put on Christmas music and wrapped a pile of presents for Lotte, knowing they'd be the ones to unwrap them in the morning. When their favorite holiday song came on they danced around the room, gazing into each other's eyes like star struck lovers.

Then he ruined it.

He got down on his knee and proposed.

Chapter 82

Nancy heard him out in silence. When he finally stopped talking, she grimaced. "Responding to a marriage proposal with 'you need to see your therapist' is pretty unusual."

Unusual? He'd been stunned. He'd knelt there like an idiot until Becca pulled him to his feet and explained.

About the times she'd been feeding Lotte in the night and heard him talking in his sleep—agitated, scared, occasionally terrified. If he woke with a start to find her watching him, he'd claim it was only a stupid dream. But she thought he was reliving the ordeal from his last case. The lack of sleep was beginning to show, adding to his grumpiness and forgetfulness. He needed to speak to someone.

She made no mention of whether if he did, she'd reconsider the proposal. But it didn't really leave him with a choice.

Nancy put down her pen. He'd loved to see her notes. Know what she really thought of him. "If you don't go back what will you do?"

He shrugged. "I'm sure there's lots of other jobs I could do."

"But what would you like to do?"

"Be a good father."

"That doesn't come with a salary, unfortunately." Her lips twitched. "And I don't really see you being content as a stay-at-home dad."

"Be careful what you say. I might be obliged to prove you wrong."

"The only proof I want is that you're fit for duty."

"So it's pointless me being here?"

"Is it? You know it is possible to be a good father and a good detective. Look at Pearson. Turner."

"Kendrick." He hesitated. "Oh, no, wait. That didn't turn out so well."

"What happened with Kendrick was unfortunate."

Rigby scoffed. "You can say that again."

"After his death I made myself available if anybody wanted to talk about it. You know how many I saw?" She didn't give him a chance to answer. "None."

"That's cops for you. We're not great talkers about our feelings."

"And yet given what you deal with, there's good reason why you should." She paused. "It's been a difficult year, Rigby. The chief's accident, Kendrick's death, and then your recent trauma. It all adds up and if you want to avoid ending up like Kendrick, you need to acknowledge it. It doesn't mean you're weak."

"Talking's not going to stop the nightmares."

"Admitting you're having them just might."

Rigby doubted it. He decided to change the subject. "Harper closed my case. The one I walked off. Ironic, isn't it? All that time I spent and no sooner had I handed it off to her than she gets a confession."

Chapter 83

Rigby had only found out about the confession that morning because he didn't look at his phone until then. All the calls, the texts, the emails—Harper had done everything but come and bang on his door to let him know so he could be in the room at the time. He felt aggrieved she hadn't.

He suspected Sue Woodward had a hand in the confession. Pointing out to Izzy that as soon as the news broke of her arrest, her family would be clamoring for the truth. How could she live without giving them that? Why, if someone else was involved, did Izzy want to bear the brunt of the blame?

Turned out there wasn't much blame to spread around. The only help Izzy had was from Scott Yates. She'd blackmailed him into replacing the stolen plate for her. Apparently, when they'd both worked at the hospital, she'd discovered he was stealing drugs. She threatened to go to the police if he didn't help her, but she never told him why she'd wanted the plate and Yates decided he was better off not knowing.

When Izzy had discovered it was unlikely she'd ever be able to have children she saw the collapse of her dream to have a life like her sisters. Initially she threw herself into the role of aunt, but after Suzie's birth Gail suffered from postpartum depression and Izzy stepped in to help, almost reveling in the idea that for once not everything was perfect for Gail. But jealousy was never far away. And the envy grew as she watched Gail and Martin interact with their kids.

It was so unfair. Gail always got what she wanted. She'd been the favorite child. Not that her parents would admit that, and Hannah didn't seem to care, but Izzy knew it to be true. She'd spent her childhood trying to emulate Gail, even taking up nursing because that's what her sister had done, but always felt she was living in Gail's shadow, never finding the happiness she felt she deserved. And that Gail took for granted.

She kept up her visits long after Gail had recovered, ignoring their tactful hints that she was outstaying her welcome. To her the girls were as close to her own as she was ever going to get. And over time as the envy festered, it turned to hate, and the idea grew.

They could be her daughters.

Martin had been grateful for her help during Gail's depression. In her mind he could be grateful again, so grateful that it would seem the natural solution to marry the sister of his dead wife. He'd been attracted to her once, but decided she was too young. Now the age difference was irrelevant. She was sure she could wheedle her way into his affections, especially if he saw how much the girls needed her.

She'd considered many options for getting rid of Gail and settled on the hit-and-run as being the one she was most likely able to distance herself from. She couldn't use her own car, of course, it was too easily identifiable, but she knew where there was a car sitting unused that would be perfect for the job. Put it back afterward and the likelihood of it being traced was minimal. All she had to do was wait for the right moment when Gail would be out alone, and Hannah's Christmas party created the ideal opportunity. As usual, she wasn't invited. For once, she didn't mind.

Her plan was all in place. She gave up working for Mrs. Carmichael, stealing the spare car key on her last day. Her plan was to leave it in the car when she returned it. She was a little concerned that if the car was discovered she might be interviewed by the police because she'd worked there but she reckoned the chances were slim and she'd be able to deny any knowledge. After all she would be the victim's loving sister!

She could have got away with it. Would have got away with it except she made one mistake. A mistake that was actually supposed to make it even more difficult for the police to track the vehicle.

The day before she planned to carry out the hit-and-run, she went to the Reed house as usual. Dale Jessup was there. She liked Dale. She'd met him on a previous visit and he'd given her a ride home when her car had refused to start. It was a white sedan not too dissimilar to Mrs. Carmichael's. Except his had a Florida plate. She saw a chance to cause a little more confusion if she was spotted on the roads. Would the police even bother following up on an out-of-state car?

When Dale said he needed to take a shower while she was there, she couldn't believe her luck. She had the plate off the car and in her trunk within minutes. She didn't want to get him into trouble though so she had to find a way of replacing it. That was where Scott came in. He owed her, big time. And he came through. Though he had a lot to say after the police turned up at the house asking about the car. She'd brushed off his concerns, told him there was nothing to worry about. Just to keep his mouth shut.

And he had. Even when the police turned up on his doorstep the first time, when he discovered exactly what Izzy had done. What choice did he have?

If Izzy hadn't changed the plate she wouldn't have ended up on the police radar. Or if she'd thought to wipe both sides of the plate before she gave it back to Scott.

One little mistake on her part, but it was down to Rigby's persistence that they'd got the confession, Harper told him.

He knew she was only humoring him.

Luck had been a factor too.

Chapter 84

Christmas morning arrived dark and early. Far too early thanks to Lotte. There were still several hours before they were due to go to his parents' house for lunch. Becca was sprawled on the sofa with Lotte at her breast. The floor was strewn with wrapping paper and boxes. They'd opened all the gifts under the tree, showing them to Lotte who looked totally unimpressed until Becca settled her in a new bouncy seat, rocked it gently and Lotte gave her first real smile. They'd spent the next half hour trying to make her smile again, camera at the ready. Lotte wasn't having it.

The doorbell rang. They looked at each other, puzzled. They weren't expecting anyone. Rigby eased himself up from the floor and went to the door. The whole Pearson family including Sarah's boyfriend stood on the step. They all wore silly holiday hats. Pearson, in particular, looked foolish. And by the expression on his face, he knew it.

Emily held out a small stuffed Christmas sack. "We come bearing gifts for Lotte."

Molly held out a bottle bag. "And one for the parents too. Merry Christmas."

He invited them in. Tried to remember whether there was an unopened bottle of scotch he could wrap up and give to them in return.

Becca insisted on making coffee while he and the Pearsons made small talk. The girls oohed and aahed over Lotte, taking turns to cuddle her. He got suspicious when Becca returned with a beautifully wrapped gift which she handed to Molly. Had Becca known they were coming?

The answer became clear when Pearson suggested they take their coffee into the kitchen. Rigby sighed. Christmas Day and the chief was still being the chief. Except, was he still his boss?

But to Rigby's surprise, Pearson didn't mention the case or how Harper had brought it to a satisfactory conclusion, or even ask whether Rigby had seen Nancy Tuccino yet. He merely said, "I'm not going to try and persuade you to change your mind. It's your decision."

Rigby eyed him suspiciously. "So what are we doing here?"

"I just want you to know that if you don't come back, you'll be missed. Sorely missed. Especially by me." He patted Rigby on the shoulder. "Merry Christmas."

Then he turned and walked back into the living room.

A Note to the Reader

Thank you for reading Long Shot, the fifth book in the Detective Rigby series. If you enjoyed the book and would like to be notified of new releases, subscriber-only special offers, and find out more about me and my books visit my website at MelParish.com to join my mailing list.

You can also get in touch with me on Facebook at facebook.com/MelParishAuthor or send an email to melparishbooks@gmail.com. I'd love to hear from you and I do reply personally.

Other Books

Detective Rigby Series
Silent Lies (prequel)
The Anniversary
Old Habits Die Hard
Under Suspicion
No Stone Unturned

Motives Series
Ulterior Motives
Motive for Revenge

Standalones
Trust No One

About the Author

Mel Parish grew up in Newcastle-upon-Tyne, England, but her thirst for travel means she has spent many years in London and Hong Kong and currently resides in New York.

Printed in Great Britain
by Amazon